NOW YOU

A Novel

SEE IT

ALLISON LYNN

A TOUCHSTONE BOOK
Published by Simon & Schuster

NEW YORK

LONDON

TORONTO

SYDNEY

TOUCHSTONE
Rockefeller Center
1230 Avenue of the Americas
New York, NY 10020

TOUCHSTONE and colophon are registered trademarks
of Simon & Schuster, Inc.

For information regarding special discounts for bulk purchases,
please contact Simon & Schuster Special Sales at 1-800-456-6798
or business@simonandschuster.com

DESIGNED BY ELINA D. NUDELMAN

Manufactured in the United States of America

10 9 8 7 6 5 4 3 2 1

Library of Congress Cataloging-in-Publication data is available.

ISBN 0-7432-5026-5

FOR MY FAMILY

ACKNOWLEDGMENTS

Sincere gratitude goes to Natalie Danford, Ruth Gallogly, Ellen Greenfield, and Moria Trachtenberg-Thielking, priceless readers and companions throughout the process; Chuck Wachtel for his early and unwavering faith; the NYU Creative Writing Program; the Pirate's Alley Faulkner Society, Julie Smith, and the Bronx Writer's Center for their support; Matt Pitt, boy reader; Leslie Hulse, Suzi Kwon, and Jean Tsai, for their translation and trekking help; and especially heartfelt thanks to Lane Zachary for tirelessly loving this book, Doris Cooper for her determination in making it happen, and to my parents.

NOW YOU
SEE IT

PART ONE
JULY 1968

David's father is sure it will rain. *Look up,* he tells David. *Those clouds will break soon.* The sky hangs low and dark; the clouds sit heavy over dunes which are so high that David cannot see over them. When he does look up, David is surrounded by sand and sea and this murky sky that his father is sure will break. Incredible, David thinks. Incredible that water can suddenly pour from nowhere.

David lowers his gaze and watches his father and brother toss their fishing lines into the surf. In the split second before the lines sink under the waves, the sun shines sharply off their lures. David says, *It looks like something you'd see in a kaleidoscope.* David's father explains, *The shine attracts the fish.* David is six, his brother Will is ten, and they are spending the month on Nantucket with their parents. The boys fish and swim and eat lobster twice a week, and David is immensely interested in lures that look like mirror toys.

His father casts into the water and mumbles as he reels the line in. *This lure won't do.* He wants the blue-and-white bullet-shaped plugs that are in his fishing chest at the house. While he continues to cast into the ocean, he asks David to walk back to the house for the plugs. David, used to fetching his father's fishing supplies and tennis balls, drags himself up the beach and onto the path that cuts through the dune. After a minute the ocean is behind him, hidden by the mountains of sand. He continues up the path and is surrounded by beach grass as tall as he is.

He thinks about the fish that his father promises they will catch, even though none has bit yet this afternoon. *They'll come out at dusk,* his father promised. *We've just gotten an early start.* Yesterday, on the motorboat, the fish bit all day. Using only cut squid and sea worms they caught scup and striped bass, and David's mother pulled in a bluefish that bent her rod completely against itself as she reeled it in. David continues along the path and thinks about the fish, about how his mother surprised them all, catching, with her first cast, the biggest fish of the day. David grins and then looks up at the path ahead of him, and when he takes a good look he sees that the house, atop a small hill, is farther away than it should be. And—*how can this be?* he thinks—the house is to his right instead of straight ahead, and he suddenly knows he is on the wrong trail. But there is only one trail, he is certain of this. He tries to gauge the distance to the house, usually just a short path-walk, now an incalculably far distance. *How? How come?* The house must be a mile away, he thinks, knowing only that a mile is a long way, too long to walk in time to get the plugs and return. Rising up the hill to his left he sees the paved road that stretches from town to the house. He knows he could walk to the road, this path must lead there, and then to the house. But the road is far away and small from where he stands in the reeds, and it will take hours to walk that roundabout route. What he knows then, is sure of, absolutely sure of, is that he may never get home. He is surrounded by the reeds and beach grass and is utterly lost when he sits in the sand and starts to cry.

He is so caught up in his sobs—he is alone, he can cry as loud as he wants—that for a moment he doesn't notice that his mother is there, laughing and holding him. David, she says, trying not to laugh now, *did you think you were lost?* She was on her way to the beach to check on her men when she heard David's wail. Look, she says, taking him by the hand and walking him ten steps back toward the ocean where the path he was on diverged from the main path. *You were only ten steps from where you should have been. You could have backtracked if you couldn't find the house, the beach is right here,* she says. And in a moment they are back on the beach. But David hadn't known that, didn't know you could backtrack. And there's his father, waiting for the plugs, listening to David's mother tell the story of how the boy got lost on the short walk back to the house, a walk they take every day to swim in the morning. *Oh David,* his mother and father are saying, and smiling. Will sits in the sand, waiting for the show to end so he can continue to fish.

Back at the house, David's mother gives him a cup of milk and a wool sweater to keep out the evening's approaching chill. When David is calm again, he and his mother walk together with the plugs back to the water and David is embarrassed, sees how silly he had been to think he was lost. Later, remembering this day, he will recall not the embarrassment, not his mother's good-natured laughter, but only the hard and true fright he felt, the very real terror in how easy it was to lose himself so close to home.

1996

"Come At Seven," the invitation read. Now it was eight, to the minute, on David's watch. *An hour late.* This was right, wasn't it, for a large dinner party? For a sit-down, you arrived on time, but for a buffet, one like this one, one whose hosts threw dinner parties as often as the taxi drivers' union threatened a strike, you wanted to show up just as the guests who'd arrived awkwardly on-time were bottoming out their first drinks. An hour late, David thought, as he watched the display above the elevator door. The red numerals lit up sequentially as their elevator reached the fourth floor, the fifth, and David steadied himself for the evening ahead. It was always the same. They complained beforehand ("Why on a Friday, when we've had such a drawn-out exhausting week already?"), then had a good time in the end. They'd done this before, David leaning against the cold mahogany panels of the elevator on its way up, his left hand curled around the waist-high stainless-steel railing, his wife absentmindedly looking in the mirror on the backside of the lift's door. Now, he caught her eye in that mirror.

"I think I'm having déjà vu," he said, already hearing the party's *Hey, heys* and *What's ups* and *Can I getcha a drinks* ringing in his ears.

"Again?" Jessica said. She laughed nervously, as if embarrassed by her own bad joke. She was tense, standing stiff and straight, and David figured her mind was ahead already, thinking about tomorrow morning. "Okay, come on," Jessica said. "Maybe there'll be some surprises this time, naked parlor games, male strippers, grain alcohol in the vodka tonics."

Now David laughed. And as the doors began to open, he saw Jessica steal one last glance at the mirror.

"It looks great," he said. It always looked great.

"What does?"

"Your hair."

And Jessica lowered her hand, which was half raised to tuck a stray wisp behind her ear. David lifted his own fingers and lightly touched the loose strand, the hairs soft and weightless. He knew that once she was inside, once they both had a drink and some food and spotted a few friends they hadn't seen since the last dinner, she'd relax and have a fine time. They both would.

"Ready or not," Jessica said as she slipped out of the elevator ahead of David.

"Ready." He followed her, straightening his jacket as he walked. *An hour late is perfect*: At thirty-four he'd been around long enough to know at least this much. He walked quickly down the corridor, catching up to Jessica just as she turned the knob and opened the door, and he entered the party directly behind her. An hour is exactly right, he thought, and a guy who knows this, knows these kinds of stupid but firm truths, that guy is okay. *That man will get his just desserts*. That man, David also knew, was a dime a dozen right now, right here, on this particular mahogany-lined and cocktail-embossed dinner-party circuit.

Inside the party, Billy Tornensen cornered David. "You going to the Municipal Arts Society benefit?" Billy asked, looking down into his drink and using one lanky finger to stir the ice. The surrounding cocktail chatter was already loud and sharp, bright tin barbs, like cacophonous urban wind chimes resonating just off key. "Welford and I were talking about getting you and Jess onto the committee," Billy said. Jessica had continued walking and was now ten steps further into the party. She looked over her shoulder at her husband and mimed pouring a drink. David nodded. Yes, he'd love a drink.

"When's the benefit?" David focused his attention past Billy, into the living room, trying to see who was here and where they were standing and what he was already missing.

"Three weeks. The committee's set for this season, but next is wide, wide open."

In the corner of the room, on an awkward piece of furniture—what do people call that? a couchette? a settee?—Debra Chambers sipped from a tall glass of wine. Her normally ruddy skin looked especially flushed. Interesting, David thought, watching Debra take a long, generous swig. Just last week, no, the week before, David had heard Debra was pregnant, expecting a little tyke with her new husband. But it seemed those rumors had it all wrong. Of course they did. David couldn't imagine the two, Debra with her high-pitched nervous chit-chat *(Oh, hi, um, hello, I, oh, um, how have you been? I mean, um, oh hell, what's that you're drinking?)* and Matthew, nothing more than a stock ticker with legs and a tie, rearing a child.

"Next season maybe," David said to Billy.

"It's not a lot of your time, a small chunk of cash, but it looks great."

David was pretty certain that "looks great" added up to a beautifully stacked heap of nothing in the end, but before he could politely respond, Jessica was standing at his side, handing him a highball poured full with rum and tonic and lime and a tall mound of ice. Billy lifted his own glass to Jessica in greeting. He kissed her on cheek and then excused himself.

Jessica leaned against the wall, seeming to gain strength from its stability.

"Smile," she said. David did smile. "When we have a kid to keep us home we won't have to do this any more." *When we have a kid.* The possibility was beginning to feel likely, tonight in particular. Tomorrow morning, at 10 A.M., they'd have the final interview with their adoption social worker.

David nodded to Jessica and shrugged his shoulders as if to ask, But what can you do? "Until then, at least we'll eat well," he said. Cate and Welford always fed their dinner party guests a full gourmet spread. "Let's peek in the kitchen." He motioned with his head to the door to their left. Even from the hallway he could see the kitchen's polished slate counters piled high with silver serving trays and etched crystal bowls lined up and ready to be filled.

"I already did. Cate's got a salmon in there."

"A whole salmon?"

"A whole salmon."

"Put *that* on the list," David said, referring to their running tally of things to be thankful for. "SALMON FREE-OF-CHARGE, Thanks to Cate." Jessica grinned and David put his arm around her waist, feeling her familiar curves in this familiar place, and they stood quietly for a moment as they waited—for, David figured, the next phase of their night to begin—when Jessica caught the eye of Sally Dickenson across the room. In one fluid motion Jessica waved, grabbed David's hand, and pulled him after her. David figured he could probably walk through this room in the dark, as if blind. He and Jessica had spent at least a dozen evenings in this very situation (maneuvering their way past the high-backed chairs and the low, elongated coffee table, careful not to knock against the table's cluster of small figurines—eerily gaunt dogs and cats and a stately braying horse) in this very location. David looked out the living room's expansive windows and noticed how, tonight, the lights in the building across Park Avenue were glowing especially bright, as if the neighbors were entertaining as well.

"Come on," Jessica said, lacing her fingers through David's and smiling at people as they walked. Before they reached Sally, she stopped.

"Is that Guy Beck's new girlfriend?" she looked at a couple to their left.

"Could be," David said. Next to Guy stood a petite brunette. "Doesn't seem his type." Until their recent break-up, Guy had spent five years with a lanky former runway model whose limbs reminded David of plastic pick-up sticks left too long near an open flame. She'd had the type of body that drove other women to eating disorders and made men—the kind of men accustomed to being with women whose ribs didn't show through their clothes—cringe and turn away. This new woman was *cute*, probably *chipper*, and definitely too perky to be a former model.

David recognized most of the faces around him. They were members of Cate and Welford's usual set. *Club kids*, Jessica called them, because they belonged to the Racquet Club and the University Club and the golf club, and they'd grown up vacationing at their clubs on islands off Florida or their exclusive holiday communities just a plane hop from North Carolina. Wherever they went, even if their purpose was to get away, they were members. They'd all shunned this lifestyle in college, worn Birkenstocks and Indian print tees, and tried to prove that they fit into a niche other than the one assigned to them. But when they moved back to the city they found that their old niche was the one they liked best, the only one that truly accepted and honored them, where they were instantly afforded membership privileges without having to endure earning them.

David enjoyed this crowd, appreciated its members, college friends and city friends of both his and Jessica's, friends who were smart and dynamic and involved and just happened to have recognizable names and the right genealogies. Jessica knew how to fit in—her mother had always made a fuss over manners and mannerisms—and David was amused by it all. He imagined that Welford lounged in a smoking jacket late at night after the guests were gone, and he pictured Cate serving canapés (or at least using the word *canapé*) even when they were dining alone. Call the whole thing staged, he thought, but it was no more or less contrived than his and Jessica's own thought-out attempts (his frayed khakis constantly paired with an expensive shirt and decent shoes, since he'd once had a girlfriend who claimed that *nice shoes and expensive sunglasses* could make up for any fashion blunder or persona tic) to look, in their timeless New England fashion, like you could be dapper simply by accident.

David and Jessica reached Sally at the far end of the room. "Hey, kids, it's a four-star night. We've got *salmon*." Sally smirked and knocked Jessica with her shoulder.

"We peeked already." Jessica kissed Sally and squeezed David's hand and laughed. "I'm starving *now*, though," Jessica said. "Where are those boys Cate usually has passing hors d'oeuvres?"

"I don't know, but I could definitely use a bite." Sally held up her hand in a *stay put* motion. "Don't move, I'm going to come back with a plate heaped full of whatever they're letting us eat until that salmon is dead and ready."

As Sally walked off toward the kitchen, Jessica moved closer to David to let a couple squeeze past her. The crowd was growing thick. In the corner of the room David spotted a huddle of Welford's single male work friends, already well on their way to minor drunkenness.

Jessica followed his gaze. "If Sally doesn't get back with the food, that'll be me in a few minutes."

David nodded. He said, "I think Cate skimped on the finger food and put her whole budget toward the fish." Jessica did look hungry, a bit pale. David reached into his glass and retrieved the tonic-soaked wedge of lime. "Here." He held out the fruit to Jessica. "This will ward off the scurvy, at least." She loved anything tart or sour and could eat a lemon whole, sectioned like an orange.

Jessica took the lime and playfully sucked the flesh from the rind. The tension—a tightness, a subtle sorrow she'd been carrying high on her shoulders since the day they started going through the adoption process—began to slip away from her slight frame. As Jessica relaxed into the party, into her old self, David thought, *She looks great*. She looked like the kind of woman whom some men, men who spoke like Billy Tornensen or Welford, would call *swell*. They'd say she was swell in a pointed, enthusiastic way meant to connote high praise. She was tall and slim and undeniably naturally cute, and smart and sharp. Tonight, as she relaxed, she even started to look young again.

Recently, when David was out at night—at parties, or drinking with people from work after they'd closed an issue of the magazine—sometimes he'd wonder about his own parents when they were his age, about how they'd spent their nights. They hadn't gone to haute dinner parties populated by people who left their kids home with the help, or who didn't have kids because they'd never sustained a relationship long enough to consider making copies of their keys, let alone producing progeny. His parents hadn't gone to Midtown dives with people from the office for late-night drinking. David remembered his folks hiring the occasional babysitter so they could sneak away for an hour of tennis. He recalled his father rushing his mother out of the house so they would have time for a quick early cocktail with friends who, too, wanted to get home before the children went to bed. That seemed right, even at the time. Even now.

Jessica dropped the lime rind into an ashtray, picked up her drink from the side table next to her, and took a sip. "You there?" she asked. She cradled her glass, now empty except for ice, with both hands and looked up at David. "You look like you're having a thought."

"Just the usual. Seems like it's going to be a late crowd tonight."

"Not me. I think I could fall asleep already."

"Come on, we always have fun once we finally get into the swing of things. It's Friday night." David caught a whiff of something strong, vinegar and lemon. Dinner would be served soon. "When Cate and Welford unveil the food, we'll feast." He looked at the buffet table, under the window, where the hosts usually lay out olives and cheese, but tonight it was empty.

"Don't you wonder why we still do this?" Jessica paused. Her gaze was to the ground now, her eyes on the intricate pattern of the carpet. Someone opened a window and a breeze briefly swept the room. "Is it just me? I feel—I feel like I've had it."

"Had what?" David's mind had wandered, to the food, to drink, now he came back. "You look great, I told you that." Hadn't they both *had it*, though? Didn't they have every right to be teetering at their wits' edge, until tomorrow was over, at least?

"No," she said, shaking her head and shaking off his response, answering, apologetically, "I know, thanks."

David looked down at his glass, as empty as Jessica's. "Want to grab a refill?"

She seemed to lighten, to take in some air. "Let's," she said. "Maybe we'll find some food and meet a few people we don't already know along the way." She looked up squarely at David and smiled briefly, leaning toward him, as if she was about to say something else, let him in on a joke, make a pronouncement, confess—*for what? Why so guilty?* David wondered—but then, instead, she simply took another sip from her empty glass, the ice cubes making a hollow sound as they slid against her teeth.

The morning after the dinner party, David could think of nothing but these trod-into-the-ground phrases: a moment of reckoning, the start of something new, the lull before the storm, the inhale, *the going-for-broke*. This morning was a situation made for clichés. It was the kind of time, he noted, when people said things like, "Honey, just be yourself." It was this fact: Any situation that called for the line "Just be yourself" was surely a situation in which *that*, "yourself," was a nearly impossible thing to be. It was a situation that called for a person to be *more* than himself, to go beyond his everyday humanity. To be better. To suck in and put out. To reach for the ring.

"Honey, just be yourself." David couldn't stop himself from saying it. *A break in the action*. A pregnant pause.

David and Jessica sat across from each other at their kitchen table with only a bowl of underripe pears and a half-eaten muffin between them. Bright morning light fell in through the two small windows over the stove, the sun hitting the table directly in front of David as if framing his morning. He picked up a pear and put it down again. Last night's dinner party had been a fine distraction (they'd come home late and sated, and fallen straight into bed), but today had come regardless and now they waited anxiously for the adoption social worker. They'd already met with him three times in his office—twice together and once, each, separately—and by now the social worker, Bradley Keeslar, knew all the details of their family histories, how they'd met and married, their views on education, and their struggle with the infertility treatments. Today, this home visit would be their final meeting. Was their home okay? David thought so. The only thing to do now was to wait and see if that was the outsider's consensus.

David picked at the muffin and ran his hands over the table's vintage 1950s Formica. When they'd found this apartment three years ago—one year into their marriage and exactly six months after their living in David's cramped, former bachelor pad had grown into a joke no longer funny—the simple fact that there was room for a kitchen table had been enough to win them over. These small signifiers (*eat-in* kitchen, *walk-in* closet, *garden* views) had come to differentiate between what might be just another Manhattan apartment and what had potential to be a home.

"This kitchen is a good omen," Jessica said at the time. So on having their offer on the apartment accepted, one of the first things they did was buy this table. "Put that on the list of things to celebrate!" Jessica said. ROOM FOR A KITCHEN TABLE. Right after DIDN'T GET MUGGED TODAY and DRANK EXPIRED MILK AND NOTHING HAPPENED. After they moved in, David had dreams about this table the way some men dreamt about leggy blondes they could never land in their waking life. The table reminded David of being a child at his grandparents' house, where he sucked down Nilla wafers and Mott's applesauce and other normally forbidden processed foods. In moments of optimism, David pictured a full brood of his own squeezed around this table, greedily devouring whatever foods parents spoiled their children with today, in an age when everything seemed forbidden and delicious at the same time.

David and Jessica had prepared for today's visit from the social worker. The apartment had been scrubbed clean by a service that sent three women who could speak no English, but were fluent in the principles of efficiency and arrived and left within forty-five minutes. David stowed all their sharp knives in locked drawers and Jessica hid her nail scissors in the bathroom vanity. After this prep work, David caught Jessica standing on their apartment's threshold, looking in as if through the lens of a camera: *This was their home at its best.* This was their home, a two-floor apartment that had been completely child-proofed and sanitized. Still, what it lacked—an emptiness they felt in the mornings when they woke up to a silent apartment and deep into the night when they were roused by nothing more urgent than the scream of a stranger's car alarm—was the child to justify their wariness and care.

And God, how they'd tried! Three rounds of in-vitro fertilization: the drugs, the egg retrieval, the embryo transfer. Countless tests that, in the end, came up with no baby and no discernible reason for their inability to conceive one. "Why do I even put these clothes on just to take them off?" Jessica commented one morning as she pulled on black slacks and a loose, crocheted sweater. "I may as well stock my closet with hospital gowns." Before they could stop it, Jessica's body turned from the figure they had both found beautiful into, first, a scrawny vessel for their hope, and then nothing more than a day-to-day reminder of how few chances they had left. She winced, flinched, when David rubbed up against her in bed. She claimed that the subtle irritations on her breasts—"Please, they feel worse than they look, believe me"—were a result of the gowns scratching her skin as she strained against the discomfort of the tests and the procedures. How much damage could a loose paper garment do to a woman's skin? David asked himself. He assumed, on the contrary, that the irritations were a side effect of one of the drugs—clear liquids he'd injected into her muscles every night for weeks on end, a pre-dinner shoot-'em-up cocktail that had become part of their evening routine. *How about a nice Perganol on the rocks, or, yes, straight up, perhaps?* Her skin wasn't only abraded and rough, it had turned dull and pale and for a time looked like the flesh of a woman in her forties rather than a girl who'd turned thirty-two just a few months ago. When David caught her examining her pallor in the bathroom mirror, she blamed her tired look and mental malaise on stress. Stress, David thought, was too hard a target, too hard to prove, difficult to picture, too textbook for a situation he was trying his best to believe was unique. He harbored his resentment against the drugs. The drugs were something he could focus on. He could look at a syringe in his mind's eye and feel the hate straight on.

After three failed in-vitro attempts their doctor didn't see much hope in continuing, and, financially, David and Jessica agreed that given the slim-to-nothing chance that a fourth try would work, they couldn't risk the exorbitant expense, topping out at $10,000 a cycle. Following their final round, Jessica and David had walked out of the doctor's office and did not touch or talk on the cab ride home or in their building's small foyer, where David fumbled with the lock—silently cursing himself, *imbecile, idiot*—or on the two flights of stairs up to their apartment, where David again fumbled with a lock, actually missing the keyhole the first time he advanced with the key, while Jessica waited impatiently next to him. With the second of the two bolts finally open, Jessica slid through the door. She walked slowly to the windows and closed the venetian blinds, blocking out the bright afternoon sun. As she faced the closed blinds—a column of light oak slabs that, when open, were appealingly austere, slicing their city-street view into perfectly manageable, parallel horizontal strips—David came up behind her and wrapped her body in his arms.

"I never believed those people," Jessica had said to herself, to the blinds in front of her.

"What people?" David loosened his grip on her waist. She

stumbled back, turned to look at David as if surprised he'd been listening.

"All those people who say our wounds are what make us interesting."

David had tried to fill the silence that followed. He wanted to make things better. "Come on," he said. He heard his voice come out angry and hard, when what he'd meant to project was exactly what he'd felt, a soft emptiness, a something not quite startling that he was sure could be remedied. He reached for what to say next, and for the careful tone in which to say it. It was Jessica, usually, who was so perfect at glossing over disappointment and making the slightly bad, or worse, seem somewhat fine. Now, this talent of hers faltered.

She spoke. "We've used up all our chances."

"We can still have a family. You know that. You know that," David said quietly, as Jessica looked on in muted disbelief.

And now, just months after that last hospital visit and that third failed implantation and the final hospital bill, a social worker would come to study their home. It should be simple. The guidebook they'd read—they'd picked up the guidebook on adoption to replace the guidebooks on infertility they had carefully boxed up and sent out with the garbage—said they had to meet legal guidelines requiring hot water and needed to have ample space and smoke detectors. David and Jessica had all this and more. The book said that getting this far was 99 percent of the battle. The book advised David and Jessica to relax.

Relaxing was something they'd discussed in-depth late one night after their first appointment with the infertility expert—a doctor who clearly noted that stress itself could hinder conception. "Maybe it's all the stress and the pressure, maybe that's our only problem," Jessica had said at the time, her voice thin and strained as she forced herself to sound hopeful.

Today, David almost actually *felt* hopeful. "Don't overdo it on your plans for the kid, act the part of the open-minded mom when Bradley's here," David said now, cradling a round pear in his palm.

"I am an open-minded mom. Don't you go talking about how much you prefer a boy."

"But I don't. I never said that." Had he? He couldn't remember even thinking it.

"But you do."

"My *folks* do. They only understand boy children. And do you know what they told me? Can you get this? That we should hope the agency comes through with a boy because, number one, then it won't have to wear hand-me-downs from Will and Annette's kid, and number two, the white male is the newest minority in the U.S. Did you get that? The white male is fighting for rights now, so according to my dad, the white male of our kid's generation is going to get all the special attention that blacks and women got in our generation."

"What special attention?"

They both laughed, the kind of easy laughs that had become rare. "Infertility is an all-encompassing roller coaster," the psychologist at the in-vitro clinic had said during their mandatory consult. "The ups and downs will affect your relationship and your job and your family." Now, this natural laughter felt good, sweet. Jessica laughed hard and the noise was almost soundless, a wheeze, a staccato breath of air that always made David stop his own guffawing for a moment simply to smile.

He was still grinning and she was wiping up the muffin crumbs when their door buzzed. "Come on up, third floor,"

David said into the intercom and noticed Jessica turn nervous, playing with her shirt collar, smoothing her hand over her hair, adjusting her belt, locking her knees. David knew what Jessica was thinking: that no matter how much you lived your life on the straight and narrow—putting the toilet seat down, keeping poison in locked cabinets, voting in local primaries, recycling metal and plastic separately, drinking white wine with fish, coveting no spouse but your own—when your judgment (*oh,* Bradley Keeslar said that he wasn't there to judge, was *not here to surreptitiously weed them out,* but he did have the authority to say *Yes,* to sign the final papers, and there was a power in this), when your judgment lay in the hands of one person who could find you unfit because you weren't warm enough or didn't seem to *care* enough or because never, in your whole life, had you really handled a child on your own for even an hour, when your judgment lay in the hands of one person, you were at risk. And together with that thought, David and Jessica stood picture still inside the doorway. When David heard the social worker's steps nearing their landing, he unbolted the door, cracked it a bit, and waited for him to appear.

Bradley Keeslar was dressed almost identically to David. He wore flat-front khakis, a blue checked shirt, green tie. A good Hermès fake, David noted, something to give the casual outfit a bit of weight. David was buoyed by the familiarity, by seeing someone who had clearly put as much thought into his outfit— make your clothes say *welcome,* say *like me,* say *be my friend*—as he had himself. Bradley extended his hand over the threshold and shook with Jessica and then David.

"Nice to see you again," he said.

"Oh, geez, come in, don't hang out there." Jessica ushered their guest out of the hallway. The hallway was unair-conditioned and probably bad for a child's health, especially an adopted child who felt the heat of just trying to fit in on a day to day basis, David thought. The apartment itself was cool. Even the walls— an ice blue in the foyer, a lemon yellow in the kitchen, and what Jessica called *off eggshell number 4* in the main living space— implied summer, coolness, comfort. Jessica and David showed Bradley around and what had been scared anticipation of his visit turned into pride in their things.

In the kitchen, David pointed out the cork bulletin board where their important numbers were listed (fire, police, poison control, in-laws, plumber, video store), and then put his hand on the small of Jessica's back. He watched himself play out all of the affectionate gestures that read *family man, loving husband* in the eyes of a social worker.

The three of them walked out of the kitchen and as they spoke—small talk, airy chitchat to fill the time while they crossed the threshold from one room to the next—David began to see the apartment through the eyes of an adoption agency employee. Man, David thought, we live in a palace. *Two floors of a brownstone.* Not literally a *brownstone:* the building was red brick and narrower than a classic brownstone. So their two floors were small, but two whole floors—two decent bedrooms and two full baths and an eat-in kitchen and a living room fit for parties—nonetheless. So *yes,* they did have a home to show off and be proud of, but as David and Jessica led Bradley through it all, they pointed out their things and displayed their pride with a studied sense of appreciation. Never boastful, always thankful.

"That's a beautiful rug," Bradley said, noticing the oversized Persian in the living room.

"Oh, yes." Jessica nodded toward the rug, a piece of carpet worth the equivalent of a social worker's yearly salary, at least. "Geez, we love it too. I mean, we would never have bought it for ourselves, but we happened to luck into it when David's mom and dad moved and couldn't find a place for it in their new house."

After the final in-vitro failed, Jessica confessed that she thought the infertility was their punishment for all that they *had*, what they had taken for granted. It was finally their time to be denied something. She said this in bed, after the light was off, when David was turned away. In the morning she didn't bring up punishment again.

Upstairs, David and Jessica walked Bradley through their own bedroom, spacious enough for a queen-sized bed, two dressers, a desk, and a year-old stack of books neither of them had found the time to crack open. The duvet on the bed was new, a crisp cream dotted with small French picnic scenes, like etchings, in blue. David's eye fell on the throw rug in front of his dresser—it was skewed and crooked, awkward, the only thing out of place. Today, even the small bottles of lotion and jars of cream on Jessica's dresser were neatly lined up. On their way out of the room David lagged behind and smoothed the rug flat with his foot.

Next, in the guest bedroom, David motioned to the near wall. "The baby's crib will go there," he said. He and Jessica had spent last Saturday drawing up mock blueprints of the room.

"And the changing table, I'd like to set that up under the window, for the garden view," Jessica said. Garden? It was nothing more than a concrete airshaft with a small wrought-iron bench and a smattering of potted plants and ivy, but the plants and ivy were lush and green, turning the space into a veritable downtown Eden.

Back downstairs, they sat in the living room and Bradley asked them about the surrounding community, whether they knew other couples with children in the neighborhood, whether they had looked into local nursery schools. He used terms like "child rearing tactics" and made a point to look the two in the eye, rarely glancing at the paper, the tip-sheet, in his lap.

In Bradley's office, on their first visit, both Jessica and David had been mesmerized by the wall full of children's pictures. Newborns and toddlers in various tough-to-hold poses.

"Are any of them yours?" Jessica had asked. David had been wondering the same thing. "Do you have children? The photos, they're all so adorable."

"Thanks," Bradley said. "I have two children." And when Jessica cocked her head and waited expectantly for more information, Bradley lifted up a framed photo from his desk and faced it toward David and Jessica for a brief moment. In the picture, Bradley and a woman—the children's mother, his wife—held two small boys, both toddlers, only a year or so apart in age. The boys looked like Bradley, the older one remarkably so. They were certainly his children. As if anticipating the next question Bradley added, with both authority and warmth, "I did not adopt my kids, but I have been working in adoption for a long time." As long as a young thirty-something could be working at anything, David figured.

Now, as David and Jessica sat next to each other on their living room couch and Bradley gently quizzed them about their views on fire safety and education, all David could picture was Bradley rearing his own children. David could imagine Bradley running home to those kids at night and falling onto his knees to thank whomever he prayed to that he'd been able to have children of his own the natural way, that he'd never have to suffer the infertility and adoption torture he watched his clients navigate from nine-to-five, week after week. Lucky me, Bradley must think. Lucky me.

Bradley leaned forward and uncrossed his legs. "When do you

think you'd talk to your child about adoption, and about his or her own adoption?" he asked.

"We'd be honest from the start," David said. *Lucky Bradley, lucky guy.* "No secrets here." This was the right answer, wasn't it? *When would we talk to our child about adoption?* David repeated the question to himself. Were they supposed to know this already, *now*, when there wasn't even a hypothetical dream of a kid in the works yet?

"We mean"—Jessica sat up in her seat—"as soon as the baby is old enough to wonder and understand. And is ready. Kids are smart and deserve honest answers." She sounded confident, sure of herself. David picked up on her cue.

"No reason to hide it," David interrupted. "We want the child to be proud of his past. Or her past. His or her past. You know."

Bradley smiled as if happy with the responses he was getting, as if there were no wrong answers here, and David liked him. Despite Bradley's own good fortune in the area of reproduction, David couldn't help but like his even-keel way of asking questions, of explaining procedures, of matching his shirt and tie, of looking a guy in the eye. All of this had made the whole unfortunate process bearable, if not completely pleasant. "I know you never planned to conceive your children across an oak desk," Bradley had said to them that first day in his office, "so I'll try to make the process as smooth as possible."

"Children do ask questions, don't forget that," Bradley said. "So how you talk to them and what you're going to say is something you should be thinking about early on."

"We've thought about it already," Jessica assured him.

Bradley looked at his lap for a second and scribbled a note on his papers. David strained to see if he was writing down quotes word for word. Then, having been able to read nothing of

Bradley's cramped handwriting from a distance, David regretted this attempt. I know what he's registering about me now, David thought: Must have cheated on written tests in grade school. Or: Nosy control freak. Perhaps: Insecurity about people judging him. At best: A keen interest in the activities of others.

"It's not easy, but you'll also want to be thinking about the birth parents. There'll likely be birth parents out there, and someday either they or your child may consider getting in touch."

Jessica looked at David and he saw her try to stifle a smile. Bradley had said *your* child, as if they'd already passed today's test and the adoption was a fait accompli. Bradley continued, "I've got some literature that I'll leave you on that. Take a look when you've got time to really give it a read." As the conversation wound down, he handed them a stack of photocopies and piled the rest of his papers back into the manila envelope he had drawn them out of. He shook David and Jessica's hands warmly and when he looked away for a moment, Jessica smiled, caught David's eye, hopeful. No looking back. The quiet after the rain.

"This may be the last time you hear from me before you're placed with a child, which could be months from now, or longer, but don't hesitate to ring me yourself if you have any concerns," Bradley said as he stood, preparing to leave. "Do you two have any other questions about the process now, before I leave? Anything occur to you since our last meeting?"

"Nothing, really," David said.

"With all the talking and reading we've done, we're experts ourselves already," Jessica said. "So if *you* have any questions about the process," she laughed, "don't hesitate to call *us*." With another round of handshakes and the first easy, genuine smiles of the day, David and Jessica walked Bradley to the door.

David reached for a beer from the refrigerator. Jessica followed, grabbed one as well, and, instinctively, David put out his hand to stop her. Immediately he corrected himself and withdrew. She'd been off alcohol for the full year while they were going through the in-vitro treatments. They'd decided to keep her off alcohol even when they were sure she wasn't pregnant—just in case. A few months in, however, David had tried to recall the prohibition.

"Maybe we're jinxing it, having you not drink as if you're already pregnant," he'd said.

"What's there to jinx?" she'd replied.

Now he and Jessica sat at the table where the day had started a few hours earlier, *that moment* and *this one* separated only by Bradley's visit. They drank their beers quickly, quietly. David thought of Debra Chambers sipping her wine at Cate and Welford's and of the small rush he'd felt, a sinister joy in discovering that Debra wasn't pregnant. He hated that he'd turned into the kind of guy who silently lobbed other people's misfortunes in the air, but he'd been the secondhand reveler, happy for so many other people, for too long. He and Jessica had been married for four years and trying to get pregnant for two of them. They had patiently waited in line and it was their turn.

"We'd make good parents," David said as if this were a new and unique thought.

"I hope that matters," Jessica said. "I can't stop thinking about how people who can have kids the natural way can have them whether their steps are shallow and whether they're willing to put a gate up." And whether they are child abusers, or whether they can afford any roof over their head, let alone sufficient space, David thought.

"I could be a good mom," Jessica said. "I'm a teacher, that counts. Bradley likes that."

"And I've got the savings plan at work, and the trust to boot," David said.

"And three totally lively grandparents," Jessica said.

"Your mom is no reference."

"That's not for you to say." Jessica looked at David sternly. She paused. "We live near two playgrounds. And, you know, we know how to play, we're still *fun*. Aren't we? How many parents can say *that*?"

David pushed his chair away from the kitchen table and reached out for Jessica, who was walking toward him. This kind of talk, indulging in the nuances of having their own child, discussing parenthood as if it might someday be *theirs*, was something they hadn't allowed themselves in at least a year. It was something they hadn't spoken about with such tangible possibility since their first realization that becoming parents wasn't going to be as easy as they'd always assumed.

Jessica lowered herself into David's lap, clutching her beer bottle with both hands.

"You're fun, you are completely fun," David said, his tone utterly serious, "and warm and all those other important things." This felt good, talking and laying it all on the table. He smirked briefly. "And you make a wicked peanut butter and jelly. And we make a wicked team."

"And," Jessica said, relaxing, allowing herself to sink into David's body, her voice tired and slow and sweet, "we want this kid so bad."

In a frenzy of baby-making, the first year when they were trying, David and Jessica had sex in the kitchen, the bedroom, and the bathroom all in one night. Or the couch, the floor, and the easy chair. So that when the child was old enough to understand desire and sex and where he came from, at that moment when other parents told their children that they'd been conceived in a Fiji hotel room or in a ski chalet in front of the fire or in a friend's walk-in closet during a party loud enough to muffle the noise, when their child was old enough to know, the answer would have to be, and they laughed about this at the time, "It could have been anywhere."

It had been dark for hours by the time Jessica returned from the gym that night. David lay sprawled on the bed, trying to concentrate on the page proofs in front of him. He'd brought home three freelancers' articles to line edit before work on Monday. "From Mount Elizabeth Station, it's easiest for a visitor to explore the surrounding Kimberley region by four-wheel drive, though you'll want to watch for wild dogs darting onto the truck tracks." He ran his fingers over the print and scanned the words, reading the same inane line over and over and over, trying to focus on anything but Bradley's visit. *Four-wheel drive*, he thought. *Elizabeth*, that would be a fine name for a girl, he thought. *Truck tracks* rather than a standard road. And what about *Kimberley*? Repeat a word, a sentence, enough times and the sounds lose all meaning. Kimberley *Elizabeth*. *Wild dogs* darting onto *tracks*. When Jessica entered the room, David looked up. He caught a quick glimpse of her breathing heavily in a sweaty jogbra and loose-fitting yoga pants before she walked into the bathroom and closed the door.

He heard something soft—the stretch of her clothes coming off?—and then the sound of the shower running, hard, high pressure, a concentrated stream. He could picture Jessica in the shower, her hair thrown forward and shoulders hunched as the spray beat on her back, and he thought about joining her. But then, he stayed put. For months now—or was it *a year,* could it be *a year already?*—emotional exhaustion had lain over their desire like a wet blanket. Under its weight, he wondered, why risk her turning him away? Why risk another episode of forced intimacy, another late night where they had sex just to prove that they *did* still do it? Relationships, sex drives, had their ups and downs, and he and Jessica had run into a demon of a rough spot, which they were surely about to clear.

When Jessica came out of the bathroom, she and David dressed for bed side by side and silently. With only the bedside lamp lit, David sat propped against a pillow and Jessica slid in next to him and lay her body flat under the covers, one arm resting on David's chest. She arched her neck to get a view of the TV he watched. On the local news channel, a female reporter— especially chipper tonight, as if the faux cheer of her voice might refute the deep, dark, movie-of-the-week nature of the crimes she was assigned to report—stood only a few blocks from David and Jessica's apartment. "Police have not released further details," the reporter said, referring to the rapist who had been stalking neighborhood women. "As in the previous instances, the perpetrator followed this victim home in the morning, just after midnight, and then he pushed her inside the foyer of her own apartment building." In all the instances, he then pushed himself onto the women right there in the entryways of their own homes, turning their former safe havens into the places they would forever fear most. This crime seemed so simple to David. *Talk about demons.* In a town so full of sick crazies and mental deviants, and with so many unlocked foyers and unguarded entryways, he was amazed that this kind of nauseating cruelty wasn't more common.

According to the TV report, police were investigating whether a similar crime in the neighborhood, a woman raped in her apartment by a man who'd climbed the fire escape, was related. David ran his hand through Jessica's hair.

"Change the channel," she said. "Could you change the channel? This reporter drives me nuts. She should be reading the weather, if anything, you know? Or—"

"—or covering dog shows," David finished her sentence, agreeing with her, and then flipped through the networks' evening news coverage.

"Oh, keep this," Jessica said when he landed on Channel 7's lead story for the night, a recap of the abduction of a student from a private school much like the one where Jessica taught. A male reporter's voice narrated over photos of the school and of the soccer coach who had kidnapped the girl and transported her upstate. There, for four days until the girl's mother tracked them down, the coach kept her locked in a manure shed behind his late parents' farmhouse. He had not raped her. Medical reports showed that other than the shallow bruises on her arms and ribs, she had not been harmed at all. The man didn't want to hurt her or abuse her or take advantage in any way, he just wanted to keep her.

"For what?" Jessica asked, her voice heavy with sleep.

"She was something he wanted to have," David said, having seen so many strange cases reported in the media, having edited and reported some of them himself, "and he thought he'd found a way."

David lay awake next to Jessica, who was fast asleep. David thought about when he was a child, the look on his mother's face when minor things went wrong. He remembered her expression in the split second that came just after she dropped and broke a glass—even a cheap glass, a juice glass from breakfast—but just before, a second later, she realized it didn't matter. *That single moment* before it registered *what* had broken (a cheap cup; it happened all the time), when her face only showed the recognition that something was gone. For a long time this, this image, to David, *that small shock* had been what sadness looked like. That *look* was David's earliest definition of *tragedy*.

Now as David thought about that shock on his mother's face in those almost hidden moments, he ran his hand over his sleeping wife's body, feeling the cool, sharp curve of her hip as she lay on her side. This morning, David and Jessica had taken a stranger through their home to prove they were worthy to raise a child. This woman who wanted more than anything (he could see it on her face, it was all she wanted, all) to bring her own child into this world, was being forced to prove her worth to raise someone else's. As Jessica shifted and rolled over, moving her sleeping shape slightly closer to him, David thought *This*, this was a tragedy. So where was its hero?

The next night David slept fitfully again, until just before sunrise when he jolted awake, noticed a space in the bed where Jessica should have been. The house was silent. David stood up slowly, as if afraid to rouse it. No noise seeped in through the windows. Outside, even the traffic seemed to doze. The clock read 6:04 A.M. Monday morning, the hours between yesterday and the week to come, Jessica had risen early. David walked to the door of the room, to the stairs, and made his way down. At the bottom, he looked around the corner, into the kitchen, and spotted Jessica.

"Hey," she whispered and looked up at David. She sat at the table, the Formica arrayed with a full party spread. A liter of sherry, a small bottle of cough syrup, a highball glass, a table-spoon. Her camisole hung limp over her shoulders as she slouched toward the goods. She smiled, sheepishly. "I felt sick, couldn't get back to sleep, I'll be fine."

"Do you think you should mix those?" David asked, standing across from her now.

Jessica raised her eyebrows. "Yes?" she let out a small, nervous laugh.

David walked to the cabinet and pulled down the whiskey and a bottle of cold medicine. "Without *these*, I mean." He lightly touched the top of her head as he passed, put the bottles on the table, then grabbed a tumbler for himself and he sat. "This is what I call a well-rounded dysfunctional morning diet." He poured himself a whiskey and sipped.

"I thought I heard the phone ring, it woke me," Jessica said.

"I didn't hear the phone."

"I'm sure it was just in a dream. This is going to make for a rough day of teaching."

"So don't go in."

Jessica eyed him sternly. She was insistent that as a teacher there was no such thing as calling in sick, the school expected its staff to be there regardless of physical condition, the students couldn't risk falling behind. But David remembered plenty of his own teachers, when he was a kid, taking a sick day here and there, or a personal day or an emergency emotional-breakdown vacation. He remembered plenty of substitutes (rumpled and knock-kneed and smelling of smoke) taking over his classes. His development seemed no more stunted as a result.

"Go in sloshed, the kids will think you're cool." In the dim morning light, David reached across the table for Jessica's cough syrup and took a swig. For solidarity, he figured. All of this to let her know he was here. "Lean over, I'll douse you in Nyquil." He made an exaggerated movement with the bottle.

Jessica grinned and shook her head. David took the table-spoon from her hand and laced his fingers through hers. She held his grip tightly. "Is it too early to start breakfast?" she asked. "I don't think I can fall back to sleep." She rose and looked through the cabinets. "Tell me again what goes with sherry? French toast, is that it?" She turned and caught David's eye, sly.

"Mmmm. Sherry with French toast, whiskey with raisin bran," David nodded. He stood and grabbed the bottles off the table. He tucked the alcohol back into the liquor cabinet, rinsed the glasses, and set them next to the sink to dry. Jessica removed the milk from the fridge. She opened the carton and wordlessly handed it to David to smell—the contents' due date rapidly approaching—before decanting it into a small pitcher and placing it on the table.

Travel Excursion's editors sat at a long, polished table and talked rapidly over each other with high pitched sentences. While David liked his job at the magazine, he truly hated these Monday morning meetings, all of his coworkers competing to get their ideas heard above the fray. And today, groggy from his 6 A.M. wake-up, David found the gathering even drearier than usual.

Two photo researchers leaned against the oak cabinet along the wall and whispered loudly to each other. "God, it's stuffy in here," one of them rasped. The air in the room was stale and heavy as if, over the weekend, it had been simmered and thick-ened and left to congeal. "We've already got art if we go with Malaysia instead," the design director said, his voice cutting the air with a stab. "We've got access to an exclusive Malaysia lay-out," he repeated. "What's the deal with Bali anyway?" The editors were debating whether to feature cheap trips to Bali on the cover.

Sitting at the far side of the table, David looked out the floor-to-ceiling windows. He was distracted by the thin smoke streaming from a chimney on the building directly across Sixth Avenue. Behind the smoke, the sky was crisp and clear. The sun was still at a sharp morning angle, giving off a bright white light. At this hour, twenty-nine floors below, pedestrians in light fall jackets and three-season suits would be rising out of the subways and onto the streets, walking quickly—as if running from the morning itself—into the buildings that spread like a hedge-maze through Midtown.

"No. No way can we risk Bali," said Eric Alvarado, the circulation director who sat next to David, shaking his head and leaning heavily on his elbows. "Everyone's doing Bali *now*. By the time we hit newsstands, Bali will feel old." His voice was gruff, loud. The editors were used to Eric's premature dismissal of nearly every idea they offered, but today he was probably right. Bali as a budget destination was already old news.

"We're not behind on Bali *yet*," said Curt Helprin, insistent. No one responded.

After a few moments, David spoke. "Maybe Bali deserves an inside story and Europe gets the cover." His tone was nonchalant, easy. He shrugged, actually thought this idea of his wasn't bad. As a rule, David didn't talk much at the meetings. He'd learned that silence was his asset. While the other editors kept their mouths going with every unfortunate idea that came to mind—"How about high-class urban bungee jumping?" "Caracas's Kosher delis?"—David kept quiet. His coworkers took this as a sign of deep thinking. So when he did speak, his words were taken seriously. And this idea, he thought, might be right. "Everyone else will be saving Europe for spring. We could do hot spas for the cool winter. And we could squeeze in a European ski fashion spread as well." Europe. *Spring.* He might be a father come spring. He could have a child. Where did people with children go on vacation? He could imagine taking a *ski* vacation with a newborn, that wasn't such a stretch. Ski resorts had nurseries right at the base of the mountain. He'd seen the painted wooden signs, cutouts of snowsuited teddy bears announcing ski-in ski-out childcare for two-planking parents.

"Advertisers love fashion spreads," David continued. He thought about travel, location, the ways that in one place, in this room, say, advertisers could be the weightiest concern in the world.

"Advertisers like the *right* fashion spreads," Eric Alvarado cut in.

"Speaking of hot spas," said Elliot Sunstein, the managing editor, wrapping up the discussion, "anyone coming to the retreat this weekend, you need to call the travel department to confirm your flights."

After the meeting, David dragged himself back to his office and began to flip through his e-mail. He looked up and found Curt Helprin sitting in the couch by the door, just waiting to be noticed. "You've got to get some tinted shades for your windows, the light in here is fierce," Curt said, shading his eyes.

"Not from where I'm sitting." David crossed his arms and smiled.

In Curt's presence, David often found himself slipping into the automatic banter that had passed for in-depth conversation when they were twenty-two-year-olds working as fact-checkers at *Time*. The friendship grew once they'd both landed new jobs at different publications and discovered they liked each other more than any of the other power-hungry, shameless, or just plain square young journalists they were encountering elsewhere. Ten years after they met, David had finally made his own name with a two-part investigative piece on the disappearance of an American businessman in Peru. The article won David raves, and a TV-movie-of-the-week option, prompting Curt to tell the guys launching *Travel Excursion*, "We should snag this guy, whatever it takes. He's good."

"I've been talking you up, man," Curt said when David first joined the magazine. "Do not disappoint." David had flinched under the weight of those expectations—all built on the success of his Peru pieces, which he saw as a fluke, a story he'd lucked into while down there honeymooning with Jessica—but he soon discovered that it didn't take much to *not disappoint*. And David was good at what he did. This desk work, editing, was remarkably easy for him.

"Lunch." Curt was talking, tapping his pencil against the arm of David's couch. "We've got options."

"We're having lunch?" David tried to focus on the meal, on the matter at hand. He knew he seemed distracted and thought about explaining it. Wasn't it about time to start telling friends that he and Jessica could be parents soon? David considered the simple way he might spill the idea to Curt: *Hey, man, Jessica and I are gonna adopt a kid.* He imagined the way Curt would respond: *Good for you, Dave-O. Can we discuss lunch?* Curt was both a dear friend and the last person who would understand. And there was something fine about that. Curt lived in the here-and-now, unlike so many other friends—and in-laws, and in-laws' neighbors—who thought it bizarrely appropriate to ask and question and nag. David watched Curt adjust his position in the club chair and straighten the cuffs of his shirt. For now, there

34   ALLISON LYNN

was a comfort in keeping his and Jessica's plans private. Disappointment had a way of tracking David and Jessica down, and David didn't want to tempt it.

"Serena and George," Curt said, "the flaks from Delmonico's"—who had been calling daily, hoping to get a mention in the January issue—"want us to stop by for lunch, but the catch is that they're going to join us and you won't believe how they talk." David knew how they talked. They'd been leaving chatty messages on his voicemail, full of run-ons and non sequiturs, as if they were speaking to a responsive person instead of a machine.

"We have another option?" David asked. Even when he was in his chattiest of moods, David did all he could to avoid meeting with smooth, swanky publicists and listening to their dizzying promo-babble. "Have you been to Pippi Suarez's all-you-can-eat techno lounge? No? Why, David! We're inking you onto the list ten minutes ago to-DAY!" Lah-di-dah-di-dah. A man could lose his balance running circles in these promoters' loopy sentences. And most of what these flaks had to offer—boondoggle club openings or neon travel accessories—weren't appropriate story topics for *Excursion* anyway. European spas in the winter, however—Elliot had liked this idea, thanked David for it after the meeting. Now, as a lingering aftereffect of that pat on the back, David felt light, as if newly anointed, cleansed, forgiven for sins he never knew he'd committed. Lunch with publicists would deflate this feeling.

"Option two," Curt continued. "Beer and soup dumplings around the corner. Good cheap grub, no flaks, and we don't talk *Excursion* at all."

"Option two," David said. "I'm in." They'd be getting enough business talk this weekend anyway, at the retreat. Franklin Bredrup, their publisher, was having all of the editors to Sun Valley for four days to discuss the results of recent focus groups and reader feedback studies. David enjoyed that kind of scientific talk—what the evidence meant, how to weigh the positive feedback against the negative, where all this indicated magazines were headed as a whole. Not that the retreat would be all work: Bredrup promised guided hikes, chairlift rides, a pig roast, and a constant flow of cocktails. This was exactly what David needed. A long plane flight away from here, a little work, a light dose of relaxation, and a schedule full of completely planned and totally optional events. Coming at the tail end of the social worker's home visit and the failed infertility treatment stress, a getaway without Jessica, without the sadness and strain that, David was sure, she would carry with her to some degree until they had that child, finally gave David something to look forward to.

August 1993

They can feel fall in the air. Even mingled with the sweat of the tourists who surround them and the sun beating on the overcrowded SoHo streets, reflecting off the metal-top tables displaying faux-silver rings and Day-Glo deco drawings, they can feel the idea of a breeze. That's enough to remind them that it is almost September, which will be David and Jessica's second full month in their new apartment. They sometimes forget that they are homeowners now. They can redo the floors if they want. They can tear down walls. They can shop all day in SoHo and if they see something they like, they don't have to wonder if it will work in the *next* apartment they live in. They own their home and they will stay put for some time to come.

Already today they have run through boutiques and crept through galleries. *"How can there be so much to sell but nothing I want to buy!"* Jessica says. They walk as quickly as the thick crowds on the streets will allow. Even the more obscure galleries are overrun with out-of-towners cramming their vacation into the last days of summer. As David and Jessica weave along the sidewalk, David holds onto Jessica, grabbing her hand, the strap of her shoulder bag, the barely there sleeve of her T-shirt.

They started the day looking for something, anything, to fill the new apartment. They have furniture, but none of the little touches to make the furniture look like it belongs, to remind David and Jessica that that they are more than temporary passers-through. They have plenty of room to house distractions. They have an oversized cocktail table, a turn-of-the-century French provincial they bought at a country antiques store less than an hour outside the city. The table looks surprisingly modern with its angular edges, and Jessica insisted they buy it and pay the outrageous delivery cost. *We'll have people over when we get bored of just being you and me,* she'd said, anticipating already what he knew she feared would happen sooner rather than later. Two people together forever? The idea sounds ultimately desirable and somehow wrong at the same time.

In the galleries they see mostly photographs. The new art trend, which they have read about in the art magazines they bought for their coffee table, is toward photos documenting the excesses of the last decade, a decadence nearly extinct now that the recession has set in. In the Ellen Stewart Gallery, Jessica admires oversized prints of Studio 54 in its heyday, of the underground transsexual scene of the early 1980s, of the basements where Wall Streeters blew cash on caviar that, since there was so much left over, they ended up feeding to their dogs and the whores they took home with them. *Too bad we missed out on all that,* Jessica says to David, who is thinking the opposite. *They were all so naïve, not seeing the way it would crash down,* David responds.

The shock of the crowds hits them as they exit the photo exhibit. Both look around to where they can go next, inside, away from all of the people. They select a restaurant with a big winding bar out front and soft soothing yellow lights and sponged walls. This is one of the pleasures they share: the unexpected luxury, the treat, the cheat, of drinking at a bar they don't know in the hours halfway between lunch and dinner. They face away from the windows that look out onto the street where the pedestrians throng on the narrow sidewalks and the cars slowly inch down the cobblestone streets. David and Jessica look around the nearly empty restaurant. Toward the back, two waiters share a late lunch. Their table is crammed with a random assortment of small plates containing, from what David can see, frisée salad, fried oysters, a vegetable terrine, mashed potatoes.

Are you hungry? David asks, admiring the way his wife doesn't mind sitting in an empty restaurant. She looks comfortable even, without feeling the need to make conversation. She drinks a shandy, her second. Today they have eaten only a crepe on the street for lunch. David can feel his second Mount Gay and tonic taking effect, interacting with the exhaustion of the day.

I don't know, I haven't thought about it, Jessica says, whether I'm hungry. I guess that means I'm not? Behind the bar, the bartender leans against a shelf filled with bottles and, expressionless, he keeps his eyes on the crowds outside. On the shelf, Amaretto stands next to an array of flavored vodkas, which stand next to an artichoke liqueur. David is hungry. The afternoon is already halfway over and they haven't even considered yet what they will do for dinner. Most nights evening arrives before they have thought about whether they are going to eat in or out and, by the time they do think about it, they are too hungry to decide and they simply grab a soup or salad or roast chicken from the gourmet café and take-out shop on the corner.

We could cook, Jessica says, draining the last drops of her shandy, a drink the same color as the neutral sponged walls of the restaurant. *We could window shop for food,* she says, implying that they head to the market, buy what looks good, and then figure out how to make a meal out of it.

They pay their bar bill and walk ten minutes until they hit Chinatown, where the crowds are still dense, but different. In place of the tourists, the streets are filled with shoppers handling kohlrabi and smelling ginger and arguing in clashing dialects about the price of a whole fish or a coconut or a block of tamarind. David and Jessica go into one of the markets; he follows her inside and is soon distracted by a display of rice sticks and bean threads, eight-foot-high shelves of soup stocks and noodles and soy bases.

David had two drinks at the bar. Three? He'd felt tipsy and woozy even before ordering that first Mount Gay. Tipsy with lack of sleep and the anxiety of his job, where an editorial hiring freeze means that a half-sized staff has been staying up late and doing all the work. He felt woozy with exhaustion and the restlessness that comes when sleep—

a good, wakeless night—is so far in the past, so far beyond reach, that he is sure he will never again have a night like that. He is spinning, clutching the shelves, trying to see over a stack of tea tins and spices in front of him, and suddenly, behind him, a woman forces him closer against the shelves as she tries to push a stroller by and speaks to him in a dialect he can't place in a language he does not know. He is surrounded by the shelves and the stroller and the smells, which are all so pleasant on their own or in the right combination bubbling on the stove, but here, all at once, are painful and putrid. He can't breathe. Jessica. He cannot see her. Jessica.

When did he last see her? He concentrates on forcing air into his lungs. He remembers her entering the market ahead of him. He can remember her walking in the doorway. He tries to remember what she is wearing. For a moment, concentrating with his eyes closed, he cannot even remember the length of her hair, what color shirt she has on, or what he himself is wearing, an outfit he picked out this morning as he and Jessica decided whether to walk or take a cab to SoHo.

He hears a man scream from the fish counter. A woman, not the one with the stroller, is squeezing in next to him to reach for a tin of green tea. In her other hand she clutches a bag of dried lime leaves, their acrid smell suddenly strong in the air as she inches closer to David. Jessica! Had he sent her home to preheat the oven? Had they decided what they were going to cook? Fish? Noodles? He tries to breathe deeply, moves into the main aisle where the crowds are worse, where he still can't spot Jessica, who always likes him to stay near in places like this, places where they might get separated by a crowd and have no way to locate each other and no familiar signposts to guide them. He's scanning the crowd, panning rapidly, moving his whole head as he looks into each corner of the crowded room of food.

And there's Jessica, smiling and talking to him and holding a ripe, firm mango, *To go with the coconut!* that he seems to be holding now. She is excited, cradles the mango against her body as if it were a pet, a small bunny that needed a home. And he grabs her hand and leads her away from the shelves, toward the checkout line, where there is space, where he can see Jessica—who, with her good-willed naïveté and inability to believe that the unknown could herald danger, he sometimes has to remind himself is not a child.

I thought you were gone, he says.

Where would I go? she asks. *Why?*

Nowhere. He pays for the groceries. *No reason,* he says, knowing he's merely a drunken fool who worries too much, who's lost his bearings because of the alcohol and lack of sleep. He puts a hand on Jessica's arm, notices how small it is at the wrist, like the bony leg of a songbird, and he turns his attention to the mango and the coconut and the rest of the bounty that together they will transform into dinner.

PART TWO

1996

"Is this what you want?" David's voice shook, caught on itself. He tried again, stronger. "Is this the kind of thing you want? What do other people give you? Straight-on headshots?" David sat on the floor of the guest bedroom, surrounded by the envelopes of pictures Jessica kept suggesting they put in albums. He reached his arm, with a photo, upward toward the detective. Detective Hallander and his younger partner had arrived a few hours earlier and now the older man, somewhere in his fifties, David guessed, looked at the picture. It had been taken at David's parents' house the previous Thanksgiving. "It's only a year old, not even."

The detective slipped the photo into his pocket. "Sure. This is fine, and if you have something closer in, that's great. One close-up, one full-body." He turned to leave the room. "I'll wait down-stairs. No rush."

David sat on the floor of the guestroom, their child-to-be's room, rummaging through the pictures. But there weren't many. After their honeymoon, they'd rarely taken out the camera. Even on vacations, they'd only taken a shot or two. David had been so certain that all this would never go away, would never change, would never age, that it hadn't occurred to him he'd need a memento. People who obsessively took pictures missed the real action, he'd figured, but now he regretted that theory.

David stretched his legs in front of him and continued flipping through the photos, closely examining these final pictures, searching for an image by which an anonymous John Doe might recognize his wife. "Put yourself in the shoes of a stranger when you look at the pictures," Hallander had advised him.

In the Thanksgiving photos Jessica's hair was loose around her shoulders. She was smiling, appeared to be at ease. In two of the pictures she was alone, in four she was with David, grabbing his hand or lightly touching his shoulder. She'd always been a master of faking a good time when the camera came out, but in these pictures her smile was real. In the photo David gave to the cop, Jessica, in her hiking clothes, sat on David's parents' front stoop, her elbows on her knees, head propped in her hands. In the second picture of her alone, the camera caught her almost in profile, her nose and forehead caving in on each other as she squinted into the sun.

In a picture taken during their move—David had insisted they take photos of their valuables in case the movers caused any damage—her hair was pulled into a severe ponytail. Her exposed neck looked long and delicate, like that of a dancer imitating a swan. Her features looked finer in this shot. She stifled a smirk and held up a Baccarat vase—a gift from her uncle for their wedding—at her own insistence after she joked that she, like the vase, was something that might be broken in the move, and what a shame if he didn't have evidence of her previous condition. David took a good look at the vase she held. They still had it, downstairs atop the kitchen cabinet. And the woman in the picture? Jessica? Where was she? What condition was she in? David concentrated on the picture, tried to remain firmly in the shoes of that stranger. David held the photo close to his face and scrutinized it. Was this delicate figure his wife, or was she the woman in the other picture, bulked up in fleece on her way to a Thanksgiving Day hike? Did the two women even resemble each other? He ran his fingers over the glossy finish of the photo.

Who was he fooling? He imagined the pictures on a bus kiosk, on the back of a milk carton, or plastered on a lamppost next to a flyer advertising a twenty-four-hour locksmith. Who's going to recognize a woman, any woman, with no more distinguishing features than anyone else from one milk-carton picture they glance at momentarily? It's all just an exercise, David thought as he went through the motions. But what could he do? Say no to the cops when there was a chance—"There's always a chance!" he could hear Jessica saying, her roll-with-the-punches perseverance—that someone, somewhere, would see Jessica's picture and know where to find her.

There's always a chance, David thought, just as likely a chance that she's going to walk in that door tonight. Who could say that wouldn't happen, who could out rule anything? He grabbed a photo of Jessica from the top of the pile and walked toward the stairs. On his way there, David made a point not to look into the master bedroom.

The bedroom was where he had *not* found Jessica when he returned from Sun Valley. *Steady*, he thought, as he walked past the bedroom door. *Easy now*. He lowered himself onto the stairs. *Whoa boy*. He acted the part of both the wrangler and the horse on a steep and rocky slope that, it turned out, was the only way from here to there.

In the kitchen, Detective Hallander sat at the table with Detective Gilchrest, the younger man who wore a denim shirt and wool pants that in no way identified him as a cop, or anything else. On the couch in the living room, an officer David hadn't noticed before filled out paperwork. These strangers in his apartment looked so clearly like they belonged—so clearly happier to be there, more at home, than David himself—that, for a moment, David thought, *I don't live here*. But then, all at once the cops looked up at David, pity and dread on their faces, and he knew this certainly was his life, what was left of it. *Easy now*. He reached the bottom of the stairs and faced the detectives. He could only guess what these men thought of him. They'd surely seen this before. But exactly like *this*?

This wasn't, he knew, how things were supposed to happen. The apartment looked like a place where nothing was awry. David thought a crime scene should sport signs of drama: luggage, still packed, in a heap inside the door where the husband dropped it on his return from his business trip. Dishes in the sink. Garbage overflowing. Windows thrown open. Muddy footprints marring the carpet under those windows.

But everything in the apartment was in place. David had returned from his trip on Sunday afternoon at three. He'd let himself into the apartment and when he didn't hear Jessica respond to the slam of the door he took his bag upstairs—noting that Jessica wasn't *there*, napping on the bed, as he'd assumed she'd be when she hadn't responded to his arrival downstairs— and unpacked carefully. He piled most of the bag's contents into the wicker laundry hamper and then hung his clean pants and folded his sweaters and returned them to the top of the closet. He flattened his empty duffel and slid it under the bed. He made the bed. What he noticed, then, was only the predictability of life. That no matter how many days he was away, he could always count on coming home to Jessica's unmade bed. Left on her own, order fell away. But add one other human to the mix and her fastidiousness returned.

Her running shoes were next to the bed and David noted that she wasn't at the gym. Or did she have two pairs? Did she have a separate pair for outdoor workouts? He had no reason to expect her to be home waiting for him on a clear fall afternoon. He shut and locked the bedroom's side window—had the weather been warmer while he was away?—and went downstairs to wait for her to return.

He watched CNN, drank a beer, read the Sunday newspaper that had been outside their door—Jessica too lazy even to bring it inside, he'd shaken his head—closed his eyes, and then, figuring that Jessica was maybe out having fun while he was sitting home simply waiting, he thought about who he could call to grab coffee or a drink, or to simply *go out*. And he thought: phone.

The blinking light indicated three new messages.

The first was from Sally Dickenson, calling the day before to let Jessica know where she and Marion would be meeting for a drink that night, Marion being newly divorced and *in need of girltime*. The next message—"Hi, just checking in, I'll see you tomorrow"—was from David, left after dinner but before drinks last night. The final message was again from Sally. She and Marion had waited for her at the bar, but it was midnight now and they were heading home, and, "I hope it's not my fault and I didn't leave you the wrong address before," she said and the messages ended. David saved the messages and saw Jessica's keys in their usual spot next to the phone. It wasn't like her to forget them, and now David waited for her to call. Without her keys she'd need to make sure he was at home. What David wouldn't allow himself to think, yet, was that it wasn't like Jessica to miss drinks or not to leave a note or to neglect to check the phone messages for more than twenty-four hours.

Not until after dark, long after dark as he was getting ready for bed, did David let himself think that something was wrong. Jessica had her own friends, her own life, she didn't have to be home when he got there. But hours later—wouldn't she have expected to eat dinner with him? She'd known he was getting home this afternoon. A less secure husband, David thought to himself, might wonder whether during his four days away his wife had met someone else. David laughed at the way he was turning his life into a miniseries plot. Then David thought seriously, had she met someone else earlier, maybe, and been sneaking around? When would she find the time?

He considered calling Sally Dickenson or Jessica's family or their friends. But *wait*. Had Jessica told him where she'd be tonight? He remembered the time he'd steamed up when she didn't arrive at his brother's birthday party until the festivities were ending. "David," she'd reminded him, "I told you I'd be in a training session and showing up late." Or the time he'd nearly missed a train to Connecticut because he was waiting for her on the platform. A minute before the train was scheduled to depart he ran on board and found her sitting in the head car.

"I was worried you weren't going to make it," she'd said, closing the magazine on her lap.

"You've been here? I was waiting on the platform," he said, skeptical and out of breath.

"You said to meet you in the front car," she said. And when he heard her say it, he heard himself saying it. To her, just that morning. So when midnight closed in and Jessica still wasn't home and hadn't checked the phone messages in more than twenty-four hours, he asked himself, Did she tell me where she'd be this weekend? He hesitated to call anyone to ask. He should know where his wife was. He should remember *this one thing* that she must have told him. But then, remembering the rapist in the neighborhood, remembering the girl abducted from a school just like Jessica's, he did pick up the phone.

And a day later, with Jessica still gone, the cops were here and family members were on their way.

"These are your important numbers?" the younger cop asked, looking at the list posted in the kitchen.

"Sure, most of them," David said. He was about to add, But I doubt the *video store* or *plumber* will be of much help, and then stopped himself. This wasn't a time to joke; the cops, serious guys from the looks of them, would hold a sense of humor against him.

"Could you put together a phone list of other people she knew, who might have seen her recently or might know anything that could help us?"

"Sure," David said again. "I'll do that."

The cops looked at each other and then in unison buttoned their jackets and gathered their things. On their way out, Detective Hallander asked David to swing by the precinct the following morning. Hallander asked, "For the initial report, any idea what she might be wearing?"

"I'll think about that," David said. "I didn't see her. I wasn't here."

David emptied her closet piece by piece. He'd already gone through her dresser. Five pairs of jeans—did she have six and was she wearing that sixth pair? He couldn't find her black cigarette pants, but he was sure she had a pair of navy leggings that weren't here either. And skirts—how many black skirts did she have? He found a knit shirtdress he'd never seen before. It didn't look new. Had she saved it since before they'd met? He found the cashmere sweater she'd worn to Cate and Welford's the weekend before. It still smelled of cigarette smoke. He came upon the traditional Peruvian garb she'd bought on their honeymoon. In the four years since, she'd never had occasion to wear it, which was unfortunate since if she'd been wearing it when she disappeared she'd be easy to describe: 5 foot 6, caramel colored hair, wearing a red and gold *manta* tied around her shoulders. You'd know her if you saw her.

Peru! And he thought, déjà vu. *Why hadn't he called*—from Sun Valley over the weekend, from Peru after the honeymoon—*earlier?* After their honeymoon David had sent Jessica home while he remained in Lima to research the missing American trekker. It was a good story. It was worth, he was certain, sending Jessica home alone. But after she was back home he had let days pass before making the time for a real, extended phone call to her. He chastised himself for it afterward: That was no way to treat a new wife. And now? Four years later? Again? In Sun Valley, shouldn't he have been thinking of her? All of the stresses he'd been so eager to escape were her stresses, too, and he'd gone to Sun Valley on Thursday night and not called until Saturday, when he'd left the phone message. *Idiot!* Could he have called earlier and hit upon some clue to where she now was? Who knew. He continued to sort through her clothes. The sorting felt somehow productive.

He found a button-down they'd bought while shopping together last month. On a shirt hanger he found the red sweater she never wore. It brought out the color in her pale skin and allowed her to stand out in a room, but she complained that it made her look like she was crying out for people to stare. He'd encouraged her to wear it. He liked having people's eyes drawn to her and now he set it aside.

David was sitting on the threshold of the nearly empty closet—Jessica's clothes piled on the floor outside the closet—when Will found him.

"David?" he called up the stairs. A moment later David heard his brother's feet on the steps. "I let myself in. It's just me."

"What?" David asked. He sensed the alarm in his own voice.

"I let myself in." Will came into the room, eyed David's perch amid the mounds of strewn clothing. "I still have a set of your keys." Will had picked up their mail and watered their plants when David and Jessica went skiing for a week in February.

"Spare keys," David said, pushing his way past Will and running downstairs. He found the spares, though, in the kitchen drawer where they were supposed to be.

"You okay?" Will asked. He had followed David into the kitchen. "Stupid question. Scratch that."

"I thought maybe Jessica had taken the spares on her way out, that's what happened, when she couldn't find her keys. That would mean I'm right. She's just stepped out, I forget where. She would have told me, I just wouldn't remember. I forget things. You know that."

"David, she didn't just step out. She was supposed to be at work today." Will spoke slowly, as if placating a child. David was disheveled, rumpled from hours of sorting through the closet, and could imagine the way he looked to an outsider right now. Like a certifiable lunatic to be treated with the utmost civility. Like a heroin addict three days into withdrawal in need of a talking down. Shit. But what the heck.

And Will did have a point. *Will always had a point*, David thought, wishing it weren't so. Jessica *was* supposed to be at work today, but she never showed. The school had called when she didn't arrive in the morning. *My God, what would it take for Jessica to miss work?* David was certain that her school's administration ("All these regulations!" Jessica lamented each time they instituted a new rule, a new warning for their staff) would take nothing but the most extreme excuse—a life-threatening disease or your own death perhaps—for an absence now, at the beginning of the school year. Before he could stop himself David almost made up an alibi for Jessica, but then he realized, if she hadn't shown up for work that meant she really was missing. She hadn't just moved to a motel around the corner to protest David's mistreating her in some way—a possibility the cops had alluded to. "She's not there?" David had asked the headmaster's secretary. "Have you seen her?" Then David called his own office and left a message for both the managing editor and for Curt: "I'll be out today, at least in the morning, family emergency." He figured that would answer all questions. If Jessica did show up, he could go in after lunch. But now it was afternoon and he had no more news than he'd had that morning. He and the cops had put together the fact that she'd been missing at least forty hours.

Will sat David at the Formica four-top. He opened the pantry cabinet and searched through the cans of tomatoes and boxes of cereal. David said, "In the freezer. There's ground coffee in the freezer."

Will opened the freezer and removed a small foil bag of grounds. He started measuring into the coffeemaker on the counter.

"Make a big pot," David said, not taking his eyes off the table-top. "Jessica's mom is on her way. She'll want a hot cup." She'll want her daughter, too, he thought, imagining himself a poor substitute. He pictured Jessica's joy at not having to withstand her mother's visit. For the first time all day he smiled. For the first time all day he thought the police might have been onto something when they asked if there was any reason she might have just walked out on her own. She knew that eventually her mother would have to come visit and harp on them. David was grinning and Will noticed.

"Amazing what the smell of coffee can do to you," Will said. David looked up. He had forgotten he wasn't alone.

* * *

Three days later and there remained nothing more to note than this: an open window; her keys left at home; no missing luggage; no missing valuables, for that matter; an unmade bed (*So lie in it*, thought David); four rapes in the neighborhood in the previous three months; missed drinks with Sally Dickenson and four days of missed work; a missed appointment to get her haircut; no phone calls to David; no phone calls to relatives or friends; no phone calls to the police. The haircut appointment had been noted in Jessica's appointment book that, as usual, she'd left open on her dresser. "I might have forgotten something, but all of her plans would be recorded right here," David told the cops during the two hours at the precinct when he'd talked and pleaded with them and behaved so desperately that right then and there—as they told him later—he'd been discounted as a suspect. Not that they didn't continue to grill him as if he *were* the likely perpetrator, prompting David's own parents, on hearing he was being interrogated, to rush to the station with their lawyer, who quickly stepped in to monitor the situation. Two interviews later—and with his alibi confirmed by the airline he'd flown to-and-from Sun Valley and by friends who swore that David was every bit the upstanding and authentically distraught husband he claimed to be—David was notified that he was officially off the suspect list and told (kindly, the cops seemed to think) that he'd only been on it in the first place *because you'd be surprised how many seemingly innocuous husbands have a hand in wrongdoing; that's usually how things turn out.*

"She wrote everything down in this book." David had handed over the leather-bound date book while the police questioned him. But what might she want to hide? The cops had alluded to her having a lover, to the possibility of suicide. "Nothing," David said. "She didn't keep secrets. We never fought. We were like one."

One what? he wondered.

On Wednesday, David had walked all of the nearby neighborhoods with photocopies of Jessica's picture, stopping into storefronts, leaning into cab windows, occasionally growing frantic and ducking into unoccupied doorways to catch his composure. "Did you see this woman?" he'd asked store clerks and strangers on the street, working to keep his panic under control. He wanted to sound professional, didn't want to scare away that one person who might know something. Don't be a lunatic, *follow procedure*, he told himself, not knowing what procedure was or who'd set it other than himself. Three blocks from home, the dry cleaner's assistant grabbed the photo, nodded, and smiled. "I know her," the man said, grinning as if he'd won the prize. David steadied himself, breathed deeply, hopefully, until the man continued, "She comes in during winter with big coats and sweaters to be cleaned." Of course, David thought. Of course she'd be seen in her own neighborhood, he thought as he walked directly home. Sally Dickenson had copies of the same photos, and she compulsively showed them around the neighborhood where she and Jessica were supposed to meet the night Jessica disappeared, but came up similarly empty. She apologized profusely to David, as if somehow she'd be willing to take part of the blame.

"It's not your fault," David heard himself tell her, secretly wishing it *were*, wishing there were someone to accuse, if only it could be that easy.

As it was, it all seemed impossibly difficult, the way nothing added up. Her keys, her wallet, were in the house. Even if she were only running to the store, to the gym, to get the mail downstairs, these are things she'd have taken with her. She'd need the keys to open the mailbox. She'd need them to get back in the door. So it appeared she'd been taken from inside their home (she wouldn't go out without her wallet, the keys, *she wouldn't*), but the cops had fingerprinted and come up with nothing. And David himself had examined the apartment, eyeing each square foot separately and carefully (the carpet, the walls, the stacks of magazines still in their perfect piles). And nothing seemed amiss. He was glad when the cops finally left, his anger against them—shouldn't they be out looking, investigating, rather than sitting on his couches poring over the same bland details of the apartment?—slowly growing. These are the men he was relying on to find his wife, and they seemed to be doing so little. But after canvassing the neighborhood himself and placing all the phone calls he could think of, and asking friends and family (including two lawyers and one former private investigator) to do the same, David too had run out of places to look.

On Thursday, Curt stopped by in the morning to make sure David was out of bed and to drop off coffee and a paper. David hadn't been *in* bed yet. He'd been sleeping on the couch. "Nothing's going on at the office," Curt said. "You ain't missing a thing, so don't rush back." On Friday, David's parents arrived at noon with lunch and stayed until early evening. That night Will stopped by again, as he had every day.

"David!" he said. David sat quietly at the Formica table, pulling a serrated knife across the surface, digging through the melon-colored plastic. He gripped the knife handle with both hands and, time and time again, thrust it with all his force into the far end of the table. Then he pulled the knife, and shreds of Formica, toward him.

"Didn't you always want to do this?" he asked Will, calmly.

"David."

"Did you wear that to work?" David asked, eyeing his brother's decade-old flannel shirt and his frayed jeans. Will was a renegade money manager. Will made all the money but David dressed the part. Will never wore a suit to work and often took afternoons off to rock climb, to scale boulders in Central Park. "Do your clients respect you?" David spoke snidely to his brother, condescending in a way he never had before. He had never questioned Will aloud. He questioned him silently, all the time, when Will did his own thing—like dressing inappropriately, on purpose, for work or for family parties or dinner with a client. David got up from the table and retrieved another knife from the drawer, a smaller steak knife, and handed it to Will, who was ignoring David's snide questions. "Work on that corner, will you?" David said, motioning to the far side of the table. "It's like linoleum, you know? Like when the basement floor started coming up when we were kids and Mom tried to super-glue it back down." David tore at the Formica and thought, *Jessica will kill me when she sees what I've done*, as if the destruction he was generating right now would draw her back to their home. Anger, he thought, was a novel approach. He'd tried everything else. He'd even lamented that he wasn't religious or spiritual in any discernible way, since, he figured, praying to God for Jessica's return would surely be easier than this. Than tearing up his surroundings. Than watching the walls for some image of her to appear. Than waiting.

"You can't sit here all night and tear up the furniture," Will said, sounding characteristically sure of himself, of this theory.

"Jessica's mom spent most of the afternoon here. Pretending to keep me company and wait for Jessica's call. Really, though, she was looking for clues. I'm sure. She snuck around upstairs and then sat here at the table, doing all she could not to ask what she wanted to know. I could see her dying to ask me, 'What did you do, David?' "

Elaine had stopped by alone. Jessica's father, Jack, had passed away seven years ago, not long before Jessica met David, from an especially short and harsh bout with cancer. From the stories Jessica told, David envisioned Jack as a sturdy, sane presence in her life. It seemed that Jessica had been closer to him than she was to her mother. Overbearing and protective, Elaine had a way of seeming annoyingly present even when she was in another state. But Jessica rarely talked of Jack, and only spoke of Elaine when the woman provoked her, or happened to show up on their doorstep.

"What? What does Elaine think you did?" Will pulled his chair close to the table and sounded genuinely intrigued.

"I don't know. I don't know what she thinks I did, but she's been waiting for something to accuse me of since the day I started dating her daughter. Maybe she thinks I didn't pamper her enough so the girl ran. Maybe I'm as bad a guardian as *she* was, so the girl ran. Maybe I bought the wrong toilet paper, maybe I wore a bad tie. Maybe I finally got fed up with the way her daughter slipped wheat germ into my cereal—" David's voice stopped as his eye fell on Will, who suddenly looked like the helpless one, trying to keep up with David's tirade, with David's attempts to keep talking around the situation in order to avoid looking at it directly. "I can only imagine what she was thinking," David said. "The way she was looking at me, like I'm the enemy. I was just waiting for her to ask so I could get my two cents in."

"Come *on*. For whatever it means, Jessica's mom even called me today," Will said. "I don't know where she got the number. She asked if I thought she should stop by Jessica's school, if there was someone there who could help. I told her the cops were on that. She's run out of things to do, David. She's just looking for distractions from the truth."

For a moment, before David or Will understood what Will had said, they were silent. A neighbor's radio, playing a talk station, drifted down the airshaft from above and came in, muted, through the kitchen window. David kept prying at the table. He clutched the knife tight and thought, How's this for a distraction. Will held his knife also, but sat motionless, slumped in his chair. Then David stopped mauling the four-top.

"What truth?"

"Sorry."

"The truth that she's gone?" David asked. "That some psycho's ripped her heart out? Probably raped her first, maybe he's a game player, fantasizer, made her dress up like dinner before he devoured her? Or buried her alive, but burned off her finger pads first so we'll never be able to identify her? Left her a spade, so if by some miracle she doesn't suffocate down there in the earth she can try to dig herself out? Or maybe he just shot her and left her for dead somewhere we'll never find her. Or left her somewhere where we will find her tomorrow, or the day after, or the day after that?" David spoke these scenarios quickly, running through a rote list of horrors he'd seen on TV and in the movies, horrors he could allow himself to visualize since they weren't real, they were Hollywood. Horrors so cliché they might act as a buffer between David and his reality. But as these worst-case scenarios came out of his own mouth, for the first time he saw that now, today, they might be real fact. Slowly, he continued. "What else? What else is the truth? I don't know. As far as I know, as yet we have no truth." His words seemed to crack straight down their fragile center.

"That's not what I meant. Take a breath, why don't you? The

only truth is that right now, and for the last five days, Jessica is not home. That's it," Will said.

David did take a breath, and then started in again, a bit calmer. "Hallander says that missing persons who aren't found in the first seventy-two hours aren't usually found at all. 'But don't give up hope!' he says. His own personal Hallmark greeting. Hallander Greetings, there's a money maker. Get a client to invest in that, Will."

Hallander also said that if Jessica hadn't been abducted, if she'd left to be with a lover or because of a lover's spat with David, if that was the case, Hallander said, "She'll be back, or she'll phone at least, in no time." But, David argued, they hadn't fought or argued or had a spat. "Sometimes the guy's the last one to find out," said Hallander, sounding suddenly like a cheap eighties TV cop drama. "Let's hope so," he added, as if this would be a good thing, Jessica having a lover, or harboring some secret anger against David, or having a fight with David that in his—his what? stupidity? blindness? self-absorption? undiagnosed attention deficit?—he hadn't even noticed.

"Hallander says there's no sign of anything suspicious," Will said. "I went by the precinct again on my way over here. He says nothing's turned up to indicate bad news. Which means there's no reason to give up hope." *Shit*, David thought. David hadn't been by the precinct himself since his questioning. *Didn't he look like a suspect* now? But he hated the place, the plastic tiled floors, the stale police station air, the dark dreary rooms where husbands were accused of their own wives' abductions. He hated the way the place turned the vague emotional truth of his wife's disappearance into a cold, generic crime to be processed.

Will, seeming suddenly to remember why he'd stopped by, held up the bag of take-out Chinese. "I guess you won't be eating at the table," he said. He stood, walked over to the counter, and began to unpack the food. "Maybe you should get out. Like tomorrow. I'll stop by in the afternoon and we could grab a quick dinner. Or just walk around the block." The idea of walking out the door seemed like an adventure David embarked upon frequently long ago, but no longer had the stomach for. The greater world had completely faded from his vision. "Have you even been outside since your interview at the precinct? You can't just sit here. You need to get outside."

"What for? What's out there?" David widened his eyes. "I think I know what I need."

"David, maybe it's like a watched pot," Will shot back, sharp and insistent, with knee-jerk condescension. "All this vigilance of yours. Maybe if you get out, just walk around. Have a coffee at the coffee shop instead of in your living room. Maybe if you get up and breathe she'll come home. Or maybe she won't, but you don't know that."

David looked up. His voice cold now, stiff as the twisted Formica, he said, "You know what? I'll be fine. Why don't you go home to Annette? She's going to forget she's married if you keep loafing around here with your poor invalid brother." Will didn't say anything. Annette hadn't stopped by since Jessica's disappearance, hadn't even called to wish David premature condolences. Will hadn't mentioned her name. David was reminded of how, immediately after David and Jessica started having their infertility problems, Will and Annette stopped bringing their daughter, Ginny, by to see them. Stopped bringing pictures, so that on her first birthday—when Will had no choice but to invite them to the family party—David and Jessica had been shocked to find that Ginny was no longer a newborn. Now, the same way they had tried to keep the baby out of David and Jessica's life, to use omission as a guard against pain, jealousy, divisiveness, now Will—who could never say enough about his frightfully earnest wife—made sure never to mention Annette at all. As if he and David were in this together. But we're not, thought David. Acting as his brother's partner in pain-and-recovery was not Will's bag.

David did get out. He was ashamed of his outburst in front of his brother. In one evening he'd spoiled three decades of perfect veneer and quiet front. David hadn't known how to act, couldn't locate the emotional or behavioral template he was supposed to follow. David felt like a member of the original cast of the kind of experimental play he found tiresome. Improvisational and directed by the writer. And acted by the director. How does a man behave when subjected to *this*? As David packed away the leftovers of the Chinese food Will had brought, he asked himself how Jessica would act in this situation. But he knew Jessica wouldn't be in this situation. He wouldn't allow himself to be taken from her.

He wouldn't.

Thinking about this, David went to sleep early. He closed his eyes and dozed for a time, but he'd been sleeping for most of the past five days and he woke at 1 A.M., buzzing on too much sleep and caffeine and MSG. He was still dressed in the sweater and khakis he'd worn all day. He'd again gone to sleep on the couch—a long square piece that, if he bent his knees to a 45-degree angle (telling himself that this cramped position was okay, good for the back, in fact, convincing himself that he'd read this somewhere), he fit on just fine. He'd argued against getting the 100 percent down cushions that Jessica had wanted. He'd talked her into settling for feathers around a foam core, and David was glad of the foam's firmness now. Falling asleep on the couch that first night she was gone he'd noted that, except for the length, the couch was more comfortable than the bed. But tonight at 1 A.M. he was awake and alert. He walked a circle around the perimeter of the living room before buttoning on his jacket, grabbing his keys, and heading for the door. Only when he was about to leave did he think about where he was going. For a beer, he figured, not certain of this. And, leaving the apartment behind, he walked down the two flights of stairs to the street.

On the street, club-hoppers made their way out for the night wearing combos of modern minimalism and vintage Pucci and hand-me-down leisure coats. Homeless men in the same ratty leisure coats lay pushed into the crack where the sidewalk met the buildings, sleeping off the day that they'd slept through as well. Blue suits on their way home from late-closing deals pulled up in office cars, dark sedans, or, if the office was pushing the less expensive car services, a mahogany hatchback. David saw an arm-in-arm couple in pajamas, walking their two large dogs—waist high and beefy as dairy cows. The dogs seemed familiar to David, then he realized it wasn't the dogs he recognized, but the man and the woman. A model whose haircut had been all the rage a year earlier and a TV actor known for his permanent Cheshire cat grin. The couple disappeared around the corner. Then three boys caught his eye.

The boys were in their late teens, dressed in the latest hip-hop grunge uniform. One of them had a Kangol beret shoved hard onto his head as if afraid it—either his head or the hat—might try to run free. The one with pale white skin wore his hair in dreads just past his shoulders. All three leaned against a car.

"Emmanuel's was thirst last night," said the one in dreads. "He's the shit."

"Yeah? Wait it out," said the Kangol hat boy, his voice hoarse and harsh, confident enough to be heard far down the block. The third boy stayed silent, took a drag on his cigarette.

David sat four doors away, on the stoop of a brownstone, and watched them. These boys could do whatever they wanted tonight without feeling the consequences tomorrow. When had David's life taken on weight, turned into a cycle of cause and effect? The quiet kid in the middle took a small joint out of his Gore-Tex anorak. Will was right: Outside was a fascinating place to be.

"Don't go wrecking nothing," the quiet one spoke.

They didn't seem to notice David, who pretended to tie his shoelaces, pretended to rebutton his jacket, pretended to worry over time, to fixate on his fingernails, as if waiting for someone. The boy in the hat pushed away from the car and started walking east, toward Seventh Avenue. The other two followed. David waited until they were almost at the corner and began to tail them. He could no longer hear their voices, but now he tried on their steps, their walk, the ease with which they carried a purposeful amble. As if they had chosen this way to present themselves, this characterization of their selves for the night. David lost himself in their gait, heard small bits of their banter. On Seventh Avenue the boy in the anorak put the joint back in his pocket. The Kangol kid drummed on every mailbox and trashcan they passed. To a chunky woman in thigh-high boots across the street he yelled, "Yo Yo Ma Ma Ma!" and when she didn't turn, his friends joined in, "Hey, you pretty shoe girl, be my baby baby." The boys were slowing down, David was almost on top of them, was almost one of them, when they turned a corner. And almost at once the three spun a 180 and faced David.

"Hey, man, what you big eyes dippin' at?"

"See something you like?"

"Want it, want it?"

David stood still, stunned.

The boy closest to David dropped his pants to his knees. "It ain't for sale. Get a good look, 'cause it ain't gonna be yours. Find someone else to stalk on." He zipped back up and the three turned and walked away. David stood suspended, frozen in place.

"He's wack, man," one of the others said, and they were gone.

With his eyes to the ground and his focus on the night's sounds (sporadic horns and then sudden silence), David walked nine blocks and found himself across the street from the precinct building. He watched the night cops come and go, looking for faces he recognized from his own visit to the building the day after Jessica's disappearance, when he'd stopped by, in a daze, for questioning. Now he gave himself a point for every familiar face, and when his score reached three he walked around the corner and slunk to the ground, hidden in the nearby brownstone's shadow. He lay his body flat on the hard concrete.

This is what it feels like to be missing, he thought as sleep came on, feeling good. The night was cold and comforting all at once. David faced the street and rested his head on his outstretched right arm. Occasionally he opened his eyes to see the shoes he heard approaching. The people wearing the shoes took no notice of David. He lay still against the concrete. This is what it feels like to be missing, he thought again. He didn't think about the other ways to be missing—to be dead, hacked to pieces, raped—because he wasn't ready to feel that. And he delayed thoughts of tomorrow, when he would have to step back into his life.

MARCH 1990

The doors and windows are all shut but drafts seep in around the sills and the old, ill-fitting glass panes. *What's a houseparty without a small disaster?* someone utters while David huddles over the fire with Billy Tornensen, stoking the flames to get them to burn bigger. Who would have thought losing heat in March would be such a catastrophe? It is often warm in March, but this year January's cold has returned for a final round—and has chosen this particular weekend for its command performance.

The house itself, chalet-style and built in the sixties, is small and compact enough to hold in the fire's heat, if David and Billy can keep the flames lit. By the fireplace, modular couches form a semicircle around a low table, which holds three nearly empty bottles of wine. In the hour since most of these weekend guests have arrived—running in from their warm cars to an unexpectedly cold house—they have all been drinking steadily.

The caretaker will get the oil tank fixed by morning, if we can only keep warm through the night! says Caroline Maas, whose family owns the cabin and who has invited these dozen friends up for the weekend. David doesn't know Caroline, or most of her friends. David's been brought along by Billy Tornensen, Caroline's cousin, who didn't want to drive alone or be stuck with one of Caroline's pals for the whole ride. *Come along, why don't you?* he'd said. David didn't have plans for the weekend in the city, so he accepted.

Once the fire is burning strong, David straightens up and turns around to face the room. The wine looks good, and now there's a large block of cheddar and a box of crackers on the table, too. Outside, the scene is bleak. The trees are bare and black, their limbs weighed down with the last ice of the season. The wind howls obscenely as it whips against these trees. Four girls cram into the love seat closest to the fire—*Body heat!* one of them exclaims—their bodies mostly hidden under a large down comforter. On the couch opposite them sits a thin woman, attractive, definitely attractive, with her knees to her chest, looking cozy inside a cashmere turtleneck and clutching a goblet of red wine in her hands. Her eyes are on the fire. David sits next to her.

It's cold, you know? David can think of nothing else to say, his small-talk skills seem to have frozen along with the rest of his body. *And I usually like the cold weather, I'm a New England boy.* He's holding his own now.

You need some of this. She reaches out her glass to David, offering him a sip. Her voice is soft, a bit curious, somewhat hesitant. She is sizing him up, he thinks.

David takes the glass and she immediately gets up from the couch, leaving him. What has he done to drive her away already? He looks good, he thinks. Across the room, a short, athletic woman who can't be much older than twenty complains that even the wine is too cold, it being *red and all, best enjoyed at room temperature.* Next to her, her boyfriend rolls his eyes as if, perhaps, this comment is the last straw.

But what happened to the woman whose wine David is holding? He cranes his neck and spots her walking back toward the living room from the kitchen. She passes by a guy David was introduced to when he first arrived—a banker, tall and sturdy and professionally gregarious—who is now filling a row of tumblers with ice and measuring out the whiskey, a top-shelf Southern, that he's brought as a house gift. The woman laughs at something he says and waves away his offer of a strong mixed drink.

Better? she asks as she sits down next to David again, now holding a new goblet, which she fills from the bottles on the table. She sips from this second glass while David finishes the first.

Much, he says. *Though I may have to move on to whiskey if this cold keeps up.*

Mmmm, she says. For a while, neither of them speaks, as if waiting. *I'm Jessica.*

David nods. There is silence again. She's watching him. Oh! *Oh, I'm David. The uninvited guest. I tagged along with Billy Tornensen.* He'd assumed she knew this, he being the only stranger in the room.

Now the woman smiles and leans a bit closer. Despite the cold, or maybe because of it, her pale skin is flushed warm and red. She appears immune to the harsh weather, even though, given the look of her bony wrists and all-over lithe frame, she can't have much of a fat layer to keep her warm. Even through her heavy sweater he can see she has lean, elegant shoulders. He can imagine stretching his arm around them, cupping one of her shoulders as he sits next to her. She drags a hand through her long, fine hair, pulling it away from her face.

What's a houseparty without an uninvited guest? she says. *You'll be called on to provide the unexpected mayhem, you know. Not that we haven't had enough for the night. We turned onto three wrong side roads—three! All my fault—on the way here.* She laughs, an airy, enthusiastic laugh. *Only to arrive to an ice-cold cabin.* Then, as if the thought has just occurred to her, *Billy dragged you along so he wouldn't have to suffer one of us in the car. Right? The cad! He's so predictable.*

David can't tell if she's serious or sarcastic, but his hunch is to take what she says at face value. *Tough crowd. I'm hoping Billy dragged me along because he thought I'd have an okay time, though he'd be thrilled to hear his cad act is working.*

Oh, geez, I'm kidding. Caroline said Billy was bringing someone new and fun. Jessica looks hard at David's face, as if searching for something familiar. *You know Billy from school, yes? I used to share an apartment on the East Side, on Seventy-third, with Heather Rubin, so I know I've heard about you, but I don't think we've met.*

Oh? He likes this. He knew Heather in college, runs into her on occasion in the city.

Just that you exist, she says. *I think.*

Her place in the seventies? I think I almost came to a party there two years ago. He remembers the invitation, a photocopy on card stock with their neighborhood's skyline penned in at the bottom. He can't remember why he didn't go.

If you'd come, maybe we'd be old friends by now. She shrugs. *It was a fun party. I'd say maybe there'll be more, but my new solo apartment's a shoebox. My mother is horrified. I'm supposed to be settled in a duplex by now—with a man and a savings plan—having babies and all, according to her schedule.* She pauses, sips. *A duplex! Who can find one of those these days?*

So's mine—the apartment, a shoebox. David is glad he isn't a woman, with parent pressures to deal with, though Jessica seems to have a healthy sense of humor about it—unlike most of the other women, all so eager to please, whom David runs into on the weekends and occasionally hooks up with, futilely hoping, each time, that his first impression of her, of that specific her, is wrong. *I like to think of it as less—*

Less furniture to buy! She finishes his thought for him. *It's the only positive thing about small apartments. I've got nothing. A bed and a dresser and a few great rugs. I could flee on a moment's notice with all my belongings on my back—if it came to that.* She laughs.

Exactly how bad is your credit? David jokes. *How fast are you going to have to flee?* He's about to make a crack about Billy, who very publicly lost half his savings and his job with the market crash two years earlier—and has managed to recover it all *and then some* since—but suddenly David looks up. From behind the couch Billy has dropped a wool blanket over him and Jessica. *Keep warm through the night, kids,* Billy says, catching David's eye, nodding his head toward Jessica and grinning in approval.

Jessica spreads the blanket over her lower body. David inches closer to her and picks up the corner of the blanket closest to him, pulling it over his own legs. She continues to drink her wine, taking small, slow sips. Houseparties are a good thing, David thinks. Jessica reaches over and clinks David's glass with her own. A toast—*to what?* To more of this, he figures, thinking, already, that after this weekend, assuming he can provide the right kind of mayhem and that they all survive the bitter cold, this is a woman he might be seeing again. He rarely meets a woman who doesn't, in the first five minutes, do something to truly turn him off. Is he too picky? He doesn't think so, he's just been waiting for someone—someone appealing, alluring in the natural, unstudied way this woman is—who doesn't make it all, from the start, so difficult. David's never been one for contention or contrivance or complication. Maybe it can be this easy, he thinks. If he'd met her two years ago, would they be together now? Or would they have been introduced at that party and never spoken since?

But he's ahead of himself. Right now he's simply looking for someone to keep him warm for the weekend, and—if the weekend goes well and he phones her and she phones him back—for the rest of this season, and the next maybe as well. Outside, a car pulls up, the caretaker's truck, and a small cheer erupts from the girls in the room. Then Jessica laughs at something Caroline has called out to her from the kitchen. And David—warm now, either from the fire or the blanket or the wine or the woman next to him, a woman who is giddy herself and whose figure, slender and squirming to stay warm under the blanket, is suddenly giving him a rise—reaches for a bottle of wine and refills her glass, and his.

1996

The apartment was turning into a dump.

It was 10 P.M. and the only light came from the streetlamps below, shining in horizontally through the slats of the window blinds. David thought he should close the blinds and shut out the street. He should turn on the lamp next to him. He should read the newspaper, he should call a friend (but *who?*). David watched the sky through the blinds and knew that in some set number of hours the sun would rise and people would again fill the streets. David thought about this lesson he'd learned: Even if your wife was sliced out of your life with the precision of an Exacto knife, even if in response to her disappearance you chose to do nothing with your days but sit on your couch and wait, time did not stop. Nor did it slow. Days were passing by barely noticed, like local stations seen through the window of a speeding express train. Days? David had stopped marking time by hours and days, and he was now crossing off, in his head, entire weeks at a time.

And now, nearly a month after he'd last seen Jessica, this is what David could not stop imagining: Jessica, that last day, the day before she disappeared. He tried to get a visual of *the moment before*. Like any other morning, most likely. The day surely began with Jessica slowly rising from bed. The sound of the shower. Or—it was a Saturday, a lazy day—perhaps a pause before she turned on the shower as she considered *not* showering and pondered simply crawling back into bed for another half-hour of sleep. The bed would be empty. David was in Sun Valley. She decides to shower. Stepping one foot first into the tub just as the steam begins to rise. In front of her, the steam; below her, the bathmat one of her feet still rests on. Next to her, the porcelain sink that she grips for balance. Behind her, the door which links the bathroom to the bedroom, a door that is closed to keep the warm air contained. Two points define a line. Three points define a plane. What do four points make?

David tried to get a visual of Jessica that last morning and all he got was a solid sense of the space within the boundaries defined by the steam, the bathmat, the sink, the door.

David began to take solace in things that had a tangible presence. He knew this was facile, predictable, *given his situation*, and he liked that. He'd walk circles around the apartment and touched lamps, power cords, the wall, ballpoint pens, picture frames, the afternoon mail, the coffeemaker, the coffee table, books. The stand the TV rested on. Doors. Doorknobs. He'd grip the handle on the refrigerator and note the way his fingers circled the metal. He'd try to picture the way Jessica had gripped things. With a firm touch? He couldn't remember. She'd always had a firm handshake, something he liked. When David tired of touching things he would sit directly in the center of the couch, in front of the TV, and watch cop shows, fictional police dramas. He looked for the flaw to the logic, ways the storyline slipped up, ways in which the inevitable ending (Aha! The landlord did it! *Again*.) was perhaps wrong. Ways in which, even after the credits had rolled and the small-screen perp was in jail, David could conceive of another conclusion. He watched carefully for evidence that the smug screenwriters had unwittingly convicted the wrong guy, leaving the real villain still out there, never to be caught. Pompous Hollywood scribes, he thought, *so convinced there's an ending for every story*.

David spent an entire day sitting on the floor facing the living room windows, his back against the couch, watching the light from outside rise then fall, casting sharp shadows, his own anger slowly building as the sun moved across the sky until it finally dimmed and disappeared. David's lack of any real routine had become a new routine. He tried to remember Jessica's routine, on a Saturday. Where had she been going when she was taken? What had she been doing? He pictured the shower again. Was that where she'd been? He pictured her on the sidewalk, a dark car pulling up in full daylight and three thugs dressed in leather stuffing her into the trunk, the bystanders along Bedford Street assuming it was all a joke, or not a joke, but *not something they were willing to risk their lives for*, and turning the other way. Or that famous neighborhood rapist, shoving his way into the apartment, fighting his way toward Jessica.

And he continued to think about this: The moments that, *after the fact*, didn't add up. Things left in the house even though she had disappeared. Her keys. Her wallet, her credit cards. She couldn't have gone out with nothing she owned. Even the credit card she'd applied to on her own, in her own name (she'd insisted on being the sole signer, something David assumed, at the time, was a girl thing, *female independence*, staking her claim) was still here, and, according to the card company, had not been used since long before the day Jessica went missing.

But if she had been taken from their home, wouldn't there be signs of a struggle? David remembered coming home to their empty house after his retreat in Sun Valley. Nothing was out of place, save for the bedsheets, thrown off in the pattern Jessica made when rising each morning. Nothing had been touched. David phoned the cops again to drive this point home, how strange that everything was in place, but they only repeated to him that they *already knew this*. Still, wouldn't there be strange fingerprints? How come they hadn't found any in their search? Shouldn't there have been unidentified strands of hair? If she were taken in the kitchen while preparing lunch, there would have been dishes out, maybe glasses broken. Instead, nothing about the scene was suspect.

It came down to this: It seemed she hadn't been taken from the street, from the outside. And it seemed that she hadn't been taken from their home. And *this was the thought* David had now, like a nagging pain not quite strong enough to merit medical attention: It was as if Jessica had been airlifted out of their life. Of his life. What if she had *just walked out*? Because that is how, as he looked back at the scene from some distance, it appeared.

Ridiculous. Taking nothing with her? Why? What would cause a woman to leave? Could a person survive in the modern world without credit cards? Without her ID? Jessica liked her things, these *things* (she'd spent the better part of her thirty-two years picking them out, trying them on, spending entire months deciding on the apartment's wall colors alone), why leave them? *How?* Like stepping off an airplane on your first skydive, perhaps.

What does it take to enter the freefall, to convince yourself to *actually step out* of the plane. And why step out anyway? What's so bad about this plane? David wondered.

David remembered the night at Cate and Welford's, their last dinner party before Jessica disappeared. The ways sometimes, at a party, Jessica would seem far off, in a daze. He always made excuses (too much alcohol, too pretentious a crowd, bad sushi) and considered the ways anyone might drift for a moment when conversation lagged. But maybe there was more. Maybe it was he who'd been drifting, not picking up the clues. "I feel like I've had it," she'd said. Had *what*? David had assumed she'd read *his* thoughts—was alluding to what he'd been thinking about, the days, coming soon, they hoped, when they would spend their nights at home with a baby and not feel obligated to attend every little gala that came their way.

But maybe this wasn't what she'd meant. Maybe she'd been having a separate thought, one of her own.

What if he'd let her continue, what if he hadn't been so anxious to sweep her discontent under the dinner party table? *What if he'd been patient enough to let her finish her own thought for once?*

He remembered the other times she'd said things that didn't fit and he'd let them slip by. He pictured her at the top of the Tipón ruins in Peru during their honeymoon. *Peru.* She'd looked out over the view of the Huatanay Valley, where towns virtually disappeared into the cracks between the mountains. She'd stood at the top of the ruins, high above the valley, her toes inches from the ledge. "A girl could just step right off if she wanted," she'd said. What had they been talking about, what was the conversation preceding her comment? He couldn't recall. But he could hear her voice now. "A girl could just step right off if she wanted."

David continued to examine the other possibilities, all of which, anyone could tell, were more likely and less delusional. Someone in the house. Someone outside the house. *Someone taking her.* This wasn't a country like Peru, like other Third World destinations, like the Wild West in the 1800s, where people disappeared all the time. He went through her address book again, looking for names of people she might have called if she forgot her keys (*Can I come over, I've locked myself out!*), but he'd already called these friends, most of them twice. He looked for names that were unfamiliar to him, but found none. He searched for signs that anyone, anyone had invaded their home. There were no signs. There was simply the total and complete absence of Jessica, her departure having been quiet, having disturbed nothing but the implied order that once dominated and served as a comfort in David's life.

Weeks crossed off at a time meant that a month after she disappeared, David was spending entire days like this, watching the walls and the TV and the scenarios he replayed in his own mind. Walking softly as he waited for his life to right itself. The phone stayed silent. No one called. It's not like when there's been a death in the family and the phone doesn't stop ringing. It's not like when there's a nameable illness and the neighbors drop by in rapid succession. There are no stock consolations or sympathy cards for the unknown.

So no one called, as if by not calling David they were leaving Jessica an opportunity to reappear. Those who did have words to offer—Will, Jessica's mother, David's mom and dad, the police—didn't call either. They simply stopped by. As if calling first might give David time to get away.

On a Wednesday afternoon, just after an unannounced visit from his parents (his mother crying softly and his father pacing silently, as if working to solve an intricate mental puzzle), David did try to get away. Enough, he thought.

He put on a shetland sweater and corduroys, laced up his hiking boots, rented a car, and drove over the Triborough Bridge toward New England. He was on his way to Vermont, where—even now, at the start of leaf season—he knew he could find a vacant room in an inn or motel, or a space at a campground where he could spend a few nights. He craved a place where no one knew his story, where he didn't see other people's pity in every friendly gesture. Worse than the pity he saw on people's faces were the faces without pity. *How bad can these people's lives be that they don't stoop to feel sorry for me?* He craved being one of them, too caught up in their own credit troubles or last night's bad date or yesterday's mediocre dinner—*The pears were underripe!*—to notice that they were supposed to be lavishing their sorrow quota on David.

It was cold outside, and crisp, just the kind of weather to hit a man in the face and wake him out of a stupor, David figured. Off the Triborough he sped through Westchester and headed north toward the Connecticut border. Then, just before the exit for Larchmont, David turned the car around. He didn't want to spend three days, or even two, surrounded by maple trees and high-spirited leaf watchers and pumpkin pickers. He didn't need to go to Vermont. He could sit at home and not answer the phone, not answer the door, hide in the closet if Will let himself in, and have the same effect, David realized as he paid the same tolls he had moments before driving in the opposite direction.

Why leave? What good would that do? Regardless of where he was, David couldn't for a moment forget about the empty space beside him, the person not there to brush against him in bed, not reading the paper next to him on the living room couch, not on the phone in the kitchen talking up the telemarketers who called early in the evening. One night, hearing the phone ring at 6 p.m. and knowing that, as usual, it was the phone company or a cable outfitter or the bank with a new and irresistible offer, David screamed toward the kitchen, "Tell them we don't want it!" imagining Jessica there, chatting politely into the phone. "Can you call back later?" she'd said once, David overhearing. What had they been offering that warranted another conversation? he'd wondered, but forgotten to ask. Who had it been? Now, though, Jessica wasn't in the kitchen. When the phone continued to ring David reached for the receiver next to the couch and raised it off the cradle, then immediately replaced it on its perch. The phone rang again, and David again waited to make sure Jessica wasn't going to pick it up, and again he picked up the receiver and immediately replaced it. In the afternoons, when David couldn't finish his lunch, he'd push the plate across the table as if there might be someone, a wife, who wanted a taste. In the mornings, when David woke up, he lifted his head from the pillow and looked at the blank space next to him. It was in that space that he could almost see the outline of Jessica's shape, the transparent nothingness that followed him everywhere.

Curt finally called (just as David's negotiated unpaid leave of absence from the office was ending, a leave he'd been granted easily, the late fall being slow at the magazine) and suggested, gently, without his usual note of jaded sarcasm, that David might get a kick out of returning to work, that if he was sick of playing lone-star-at-home and happened to want to come back, everyone would make it easy on him. David didn't react as he thought he would. He'd assumed that when this call came he'd politely decline, he'd possibly resign. What kind of solace would the office offer? Instead, David looked at the emptiness beside him and shrugged. *Should I go?* When the nothingness gave no answer in return, didn't even sway, declined to glance his way or give any sign whatsoever, David said, okay. "Okay, I think I'll come back to the office."

PERU 1992

The plane flies over the Andes low and close, and Jessica pulls David near to her. She tugs on his shirt until his face is to the window beside her, where he can get a full view. He doesn't know what he expected to see, but this isn't it. This is beyond expectation. He's seen mountains before (the Rockies, the Sierra Nevadas, the White Mountains, the Green Mountains, Tahoe) but never like this. These ridges, viewed from so close above, rise and fall with the sharp undulations of mud in motion. Suddenly, plate tectonics makes sense. He can see how the earth's layers crashed against each other and buckled. David imagines he can hear the crack of the layers moving, grinding. The tops of the ridges are white with snow that seeps in fine lines, like running rivers, down the crevices that mark the mountains' hard, brown surfaces. Through the plane's window David can see these mountains and nothing else. Then, without warning, everything is white. As the plane descends, the entire view disappears behind an even, dense fog. Slowly, shapes begin to appear again and David makes out the outline of Lima below. The city fights to assert its existence through the thick smog.

"There it is," David says softly into Jessica's ear.

The city comes into view more clearly and, at first, they can see only the dusky shantytowns that crowd the outskirts. Makeshift shacks of cinderblocks and discarded wood, with ill-fitting tin roofs and unfinished second stories. A moment later they see Lima's center city itself where, in the distance, Plaza San Martin's fountains sit dry and, nearby, 1960s high-rises jockey for attention against austere cathedrals and seventeenth-century churches. The streets are crammed with cars that hardly move. The random, congested, barely moving pattern of the traffic reminds David of New York on a day when the visit of a dignitary—the president or the pope—threatens the usual attempts at order.

Below the airplane, the Rimac River runs into Lima. Its water is low and brown and thick, seeping, lethargically, like pus from a wound. David remembers what the books they read said: "Peru is a land of contradictions." Lima hugs the river, but faces a near-constant water shortage. The Rimac is polluted by refuse from the surrounding *pueblos jovenes*, the shantytowns—the land that spreads out around the river and Lima is all desert.

The airplane descends sharply into the valley until it is completely below the smog and approaching the runway. Jessica and David sit up straight in their seats and instinctively reach for each other's hands, holding tight, and then tighter (David shifting his fingers so that his wife's ring doesn't cut into his own flesh) as the plane hits hard against the ground—bumping twice before finding its footing—and begins to slow to a smooth stop.

In Lima, before dinner, David and Jessica explore their hotel's neighborhood. The sky remains a thick haze and the buildings come in hues that span no further than the natural shades of dirt and concrete and glass. The streets are empty. David and Jessica follow their map to the craft market and it is here that Lima's brighter colors and people—merchants hoping to make some small change from the travelers who see this destination on their tourist maps—finally come alive. David and Jessica walk past stands filled with alpaca knits in blues and greens, pottery painted in earth-tinged primaries, finely ground spices in bright rust and ochre. Carts of vegetables boast a dozen varieties of potatoes in yellows and pinks, and, nearby, crates are piled high with cherimoyas, apples, and mangoes.

"*Que es eso?*" Jessica asks a saleswoman. Jessica holds up a split-open fruit, its orange flesh spilling out juice.

"*Lucema. Una lucema,*" the woman says, then turns away and continues stacking apples.

"Hold it up. Hold up the *lucema,*" David tells Jessica. He takes out the camera, takes a few steps backward, and snaps her picture. He continues looking through the camera for a moment, after Jessica has looked away. It is this Jessica, the one who isn't posing and composing herself, isn't aware she's being taken in, that David wants to capture. He snaps a second photo of Jessica, now half-turned away and watching a man weigh potatoes. She is taken by surprise. She jolts and turns at the sound of the shutter.

"*Stop,* please," she turns to David and laughs nervously. "Come on, save the film for later in the week when we're showered and tan." She puts the *lucema* back on the cart where she found it.

Compared to the locals, though, Jessica looks clean and fresh. While the fruit and the vegetables and the plants for sale all boast bright colors and shiny textures, the people are dry and dusty. David focuses his camera again and takes a picture of the man with the potatoes, his white jersey yellow with age, and his hat—woven of threads that were once, it seems, bright reds and blues—bleached from the Andean sun. He and the others who man these carts appear to be refugees from the rural north and south where violence—the randomly expressed rage of the Sendero Luminoso, the Shining Path—continues to reign. This land can support more than fifty thousand plant species and eleven hundred types of butterflies, but the people flee for their lives. David watches the dusty men and women and, as he eyes their wares, bountiful and cheap, he is awed by the contradictions, the juxtapositions, the beauty versus the beauty destroyed.

"Why did we decide to spend two nights *here*?" Jessica asks after the first full day of their honeymoon.

Jessica is tired, as is David, and Lima is no place to relax. Their hotel is in Lima's Miraflores district, the upscale shopping suburb where Euro nightclubs and shiny hotels and casinos induce Lima's elite to forget about the surrounding poverty. The water supply, even here, though, is scarce, and upon checking into the hotel David and Jessica had been warned not to flush toilet paper but to put it in the receptacles. The paper will clog the pipes, they were told, since the water pressure is not high enough to carry it through.

When planning their itinerary, David had purposely scheduled this extra day in Lima. He'd thought it would be a shame to be in Peru and not fully explore the capital city itself. But they'd seen all they'd need to. In the morning they'd traveled downtown and toured the Plaza de Armas—teeming with people even midday—and Plaza Major, and they'd seen the Government Palace and the paintings of Ignacio Merino. They'd compared the carved mahogany balconies on the old structures surrounding the plazas to the glass facades of the low, square office towers in the banking district just two blocks away.

Now, after lunch, they are back at the Hotel Aristo and sit at the small bar and drink beers. Tomorrow they will fly to Cuzco, where the real honeymoon is set to begin.

"The palace was interesting, don't you think?" David says, doing his best to make up for the fact that they didn't hop a flight to Cuzco this afternoon. They are here for the night, the room is paid for, and it is too late, now, to leave today. So what else can he say?

And, truly, the palace had been interesting. The security outside: police troops armed with automatic rifles, staring out suspiciously from behind the gates. Beyond them, the palace, a sprawling structure painted an artificial cake-icing yellow, appeared innocuous and asleep.

David sips from his bottle of Cusqueña. He hadn't believed what everyone said, that Lima is a wasteland. But those people were right, David should have taken their word.

Behind Jessica, David sees the hotel's chief of security walk by. He wears a buttoned-up navy flannel suit, the pants tucked into knee-high boots, a beret. Over his shoulder hangs a semiautomatic. He appears as if he's stepped out of a 1970s thriller set in Central America, more out of place than actually threatening as he strides through the lobby. David can't imagine any kind of intrigue going down at the Aristo, a hotel that is smaller than most of the other luxury hotels in Miraflores, and one of the few without a casino. It looks like an upscale resort inn, nestled welcomingly in the city. Still, no matter how comfortable the Aristo is, David thinks, *Jessica has a point*. There is no reason for them to still be here. They should be hiking by now, climbing rocks, birdwatching.

"I didn't know it would be like this," Jessica says, as if unwilling to let the topic go.

The sun is beginning to set and the bar, lit by an overhead skylight, grows darker. Jessica's face falls into shadow. David considers reaching out to touch her, thinks about how beautiful, in this half-shade, she looks.

Jessica shakes her head, "I'm sorry. I'm always grumpy at the start of vacations. Until I get into the swing of things. But I do wish we weren't here." David understands. In the two years they've been together, David and Jessica have gone on ski trips and beach vacations and spent long weekends in London, visiting friends, but have taken no major foreign travels to places where they don't already prescribe to the local customs and don't already speak the language. This is new to them as a couple. Some people need time to adjust, David tells himself.

"If we weren't here, if we'd left Lima today, we'd be wondering what we missed. It's not so bad," David says. "It's your honeymoon. Who cares where you are? We're together, you know? The hiking will seem great after this."

Jessica nods and smiles, and David touches her shoulder. She picks up her drink with one hand and reaches over with her other, grabbing onto the waistband of David's pants. She starts to pull him toward the lobby. "Come sit on the couch," she says.

He squeezes her shoulder, but doesn't follow. "Save me a seat, I'll get us fresh drinks."

"Perfect," Jessica lets her hand linger on his waist and then walks across the lobby to a wooden couch, an ornate, heavy Spanish antique. A bellboy walks past her and through the staff door behind the bar. The bar and lobby are empty, save for Jessica and David and the bartender, who has begun to light candles, short square stumps of white wax that glow dimly. While David waits for the bartender to open the two new beers, he asks for his take on the local nightlife.

"If you go to Disco Amadeus, I think you will enjoy it," the bartender says. "Lots of Lima kids, but also very many Americans. Bring your passport. It is for members only, but they like Americans. With a passport you will get in."

David thanks him and the bartender continues, "Unless you want to go to a *peña*, want to hear the folk music. Andeans hang out there. It is not the same, unless you would like that."

"I don't know, maybe," David responds.

What would Jessica want? Across the lobby she sits forward on the couch and looks at David. Their eyes catch. David can imagine her saying, *We don't have to hit the clubs just because they're there, you know?* He thinks she will want to relax, to get the night over with. They're booked to leave Lima on an early plane tomorrow. This sounds right. David thinks perhaps they should just grab a quick dinner, get their stomachs conditioned to the food. At the moment, two days after the wedding, David is still full of champagne and salmon and cake, still wondering at all those people who claim to be too busy at their own weddings to eat. "The food's the thing," a giddy Jessica had said to David as they ate platefuls at their own reception.

"Jessica," David says, a little too loud. She sits up straighter. He mimes eating and shrugs his shoulders. He takes the two new beers from the bartender, walks across the lobby, and sits next to her on the couch. "Maybe just an authentic dinner tonight and a good night's sleep while we have a chance?" he says.

"I'd like that," Jessica nods. Then, "No, no. Don't you think we should get out? We're here after all. Yes? It could be fun." And while David wonders at her change in demeanor, in enthusiasm (does she really want to go out or is she trying to be amenable, to get this honeymoon back on track?) she continues, raising her eyebrows and lowering her voice, "Or we can, you know, crawl into that bed *now*, instead?" She takes his hand in hers and tilts her head to the side, coy, sarcastically coy, flirting with her own husband and waiting for a response.

"I'd like that," David laces his fingers in hers and pulls her up off the couch. "I'd really like that," he says. In the elevator he pulls her to him and they kiss and everything is fine, falling into place again, *honeymoon back on track*, he thinks, and she reaches her hand up his shirt, laying her palm flat and warm against his skin. He pulls his face from hers for just a moment. "See?" he says, and her mouth, just inches from his, is in a smile, eager for more action. "It doesn't matter where we are."

During their second day in the mountains, when their swing through Lima is nothing more than a jet-lagged memory, they take a side trip. They leave the car in Oropesa, just a short drive from their hotel in Cuzco. Oropesa looks like all the other towns they have driven through: simply a collection of finished and half-finished cinder-block huts—many windowless, some painted exuberant shades of lavender or mint green, all of their roofs connected by an elaborate network of TV antennas and electrical wire—clustered close to the road. David and Jessica park on the edge of town, in front of a walled-in soccer field, its walls stenciled with political slogans and advertisements for Pepsi and Inca Kola. David hoists their day-pack onto his back and they set off on foot for the ruins.

"There is no reason to go to Tipón without a guide, you want a guide," the desk clerk at their hotel had said. Tipón is not one of the commonly visited ruins, she explained, and they would learn more with a guide. "You will want to hear about the history, and what to look for in the rocks," she said. "Or maybe you want to go to the Pisac ruins. There are tours every day. All the time." But David and Jessica wanted to get away, by themselves.

From town, the walk to Tipón is straight uphill, and in the high altitude David and Jessica stop every few minutes to catch their breath. Each time they stop, David turns around and looks behind them to see how small the village appears below, how far they have come. Beside them, the trail is lined with a sparse smattering of eucalyptus trees whose leaves hang limp like large copper charms off a girl's bracelet. Through the trees, David can see the bottom of the trail, the distance they have already traveled.

Jessica's breathing is heavier than David's. She bends toward the ground, her loose hair dusting the dirt, and then, after only a moment, she reaches for his hand and pulls him up the trail again. David's head begins to ache. He can feel the thinness of the air. After an hour, they reach the lower ruins of Tipón. David is the one lagging now. Jessica gets there first and is waiting.

"Oh, man," he says, staring straight ahead of him. "Explain this to me."

The land in front of them is elaborately terraced, flat stone plateaus giving shape to the earth. Long trapezoids of rock wedged next to each other, building an oversized staircase that leads upward.

"I wish I could. Do you have the book?" Jessica asks.

David reaches into his bag for the small guidebook they'd picked up outside the car rental shop and offers Jessica his bottle of water at the same time. She takes a long drink. "I thought," he says, "there would be more people up here. But it is so nice and quiet."

On the way up they passed only one group of trekkers, French speakers, going the opposite direction. Now David and Jessica walk along the terracing. David reads aloud a paragraph explaining that the terracing had ostensibly been created to increase the crop yield but, in truth, now stands more as a symbol of the Incan power, of their ancient domination. At the center of the ruins flows a spring.

Jessica runs her fingers along the crack where one rock meets another. "Can you believe how long this has been here, these two rocks pressed together?"

She hops awkwardly up to the next level of stone, climbing the staircase until she reaches the top. The sky above is clear and open. After an hour of hiking through loose brush and eucalyptus trees, this is their reward.

They follow a sign and walk uphill again, for another twenty minutes, to the upper ruins. Here, they find themselves surrounded by ancient stone dwellings, the remnants of a storehouse. These guys were serious architects, David thinks while examining the building's intricate construction, blocks stacked in perfect form at perfect angles—and what was once the local bath. Below, a small town—the traditional cinder-block structures with rolling Spanish roofs. The roofs' perfect lines of rolling clay mimic the uniform rows of tilled crops in the patchwork of fields that they butt up against. As a result, the buildings, looked at from above, seem themselves to be square plots of crops flat against the earth, part of the patchwork. Row after row, the entire small village seems camouflaged as farmland, seems to disappear into the landscape. And far to the south— *Look!* David turns Jessica's head—to the south they can see clear over the Huatanay Valley. Vast, open, and still. The sky is so transparent and the air so thin that David thinks he could reach out and touch the view.

Jessica's breathing turns quiet now. She stands unmoving, looking over the valley, so quiet that she appears afraid to move, afraid this view might run away, make a break for it.

"It looks so unreal," David says.

"Which way are we looking?" Jessica asks softly. "Which direction is that?"

"It's south," David says, amazed that even here, with the sun and the landscape as her guide, she has no sense of direction. "We'll make a human compass of you yet."

"It's so undisturbed." She's speaking slowly, her words quietly slipping out under her breath. She inches nearer to the edge of the mountain, as if aching to get closer to the view. "It looks like a tableau you could walk right into! This is where—did you see it in the book?—not here, but places like here, you know, the mountaintops where the Incas built cities, this is where they'd sacrifice a woman. That's what the book says. And look how easy it would be! To throw a girl off a mountain, you know? Right here." She pauses, David listens for her breath, now a subtle in and out. She says, as if talking to herself, to the mountains themselves, "Right here," she says, "a girl could step right off if she wanted, could just throw her fate into nature's hands."

David is about to make a joke. *Yeah, but you're no virgin, especially this week!* comes to mind. Or, *we've got sacrifices scheduled into the itinerary for tomorrow, don't jump the gun!* But he sees that Jessica isn't in a joking mood. *Don't jump the gun!* But he keeps quiet. She looks over the view as if looking into the weighty eyes of Incan history itself, her gaze intensely focused and far off. She stands still for a moment longer until, grinning, as if suddenly nudged back into the here and now, she grabs the backpack from David and then lowers herself onto a rock and begins to unpack their lunch.

Jessica rolls her driver's side window halfway down, then a second later inches it up again, fighting to keep the car cool inside while forcing the road's dust to stay out. She is behind the wheel. She loves to be in control of cars, but lets David navigate. "You're the one who's good with maps, you're the one with a sense of direction!" she'd said just this morning when they set off from Cuzco, handing him the road map and letting him guide her onto the road to Oropesa. And Jessica is a fine driver, overly cautious if anything, so David enjoys ceding the wheel to her. He prefers to sit back and watch. Here, though, he can barely see anything through the dust kicked up by their Toyota Corolla, the only new-model car available at the Cuzco rental agency. There is little to see on the short ride back to Cuzco, anyway. Jessica drives slowly and keeps her eyes sharp on the road because the car has no side mirrors: Too easy to steal, the rental agent explained.

Jessica concentrates and hunches close to the windshield. The Peruvian drivers speed and swerve. They lean on their horns to warn the dogs and pigs and small children who wander in the road. The action in this country is all in the street.

She and David are too tired to speak. David looks into his own lap and keeps thinking about how the Incas crafted their buildings, laying the stones in mathematical patterns created to withstand even the strongest of earthquakes, creating a perfect symmetry, achieving what modern architects only manage with protractors and contractors and interior designers and backing from private investors.

"David!" Jessica gasps and brings the Corolla to a quick stop, briefly throwing David toward the dashboard and waking him alert. Outside her window, two police officers approach the car. The officers' dusty Land Cruiser blocks the road ahead.

"What is this?" she speaks to David under her breath while lowering her window.

"I don't know. A drug check? Maybe we were speeding. No, you couldn't have been. Must be something routine. Maybe we just need a car wash. Maybe it's the missing mirrors," David says. He can't stop himself from talking, from filling the space between now and the time, only seconds from now, when the officers will be beside the Corolla.

The shorter officer bends to the level of Jessica's window and speaks quickly in words neither David nor Jessica can understand. The other officer walks around to David's side of the car and stands tall next to the passenger side door. His waist is level with David's window and David sees the full arsenal—pistol, machine gun, baton—that hangs from the man. At Jessica's side, the first officer continues to rattle off a list of demands.

"*No entiendo,*" Jessica keeps repeating. And "*Soy americano,*" and then, three times, "*hable despacio por favor.*"

"What?" David insists to Jessica. "What's he saying?"

"I told him to speak slowly," she says quietly, firmly. "I don't think he's making any sense," she insists. The man continues to speak. "Something about the car, wanting the car," Jessica says.

Back at the rental agency, the saleswoman laughs. "I forgot to tell you that," she says. "But since you are back with the car, too, you must have learned on your own."

Apparently, the local officials have had some luck scaring tourists into selling their rental cars for next to nothing. They've found that speaking nonsense Spanish works wonders when it comes to confusing the gringos.

"The *policia*, they can be scary, *si*? But worth the scare to see the ruins at Tipón, do you not think? If you have trouble, you give the police a few *sol*. The police here, they are not very expensive, they do not expect much," the saleswoman says to David and Jessica.

David has his arm around Jessica, who seems amazingly calm. After Jessica had told the police, in stilted Spanish, that the car was not hers, after they saw they would get nowhere with her, they left without an explanation. The saleswoman hands them their receipt.

"They will not shoot you for the car. They do not shoot Americans for the car," she says.

At dinner that night, over heaped plates of white rice and yellow potatoes and trout, Jessica is almost giddy about the adventure of their day, and David tries to play along, but has to force himself to speak and converse and look into her eyes. He is feeling shy, even around Jessica, perhaps at the fact that their survival of the scrape—well, the car's survival, and their return with it intact—had nothing to do with him and everything to do with his wife, who kept her cool while he shook and yammered at her from the passenger seat.

As they finish their cocktails, the hotel's concierge sits down to chat. He speaks with David while Jessica, still full of energy and adrenaline, wanders the lobby and looks closely at the local weavings that decorate the walls. Noise comes in from the street, the voices of young children running in circles, hoping to bump into a foreigner willing to shell out a few *sol* for their "Postcards! Postcards! Postcards for sale, *un sol! Por favor!*" David tells the concierge all about the day at Tipón and briefly describes their run-in on the way home.

The concierge nods. *"Este es el pais de les maravillas,"* he says to David. It is a saying that, all over the country, locals repeat to their children, to travelers, to the merchants they see every day. First, David understands only the literal translation: This is the land of marvels. Later he will understand its colloquial meaning, the message these locals intended to relay with each repetition: Anything can happen here.

1996/1997

After months of brooding alone at home, David was happy to be back at work. He welcomed the ringing of the phone. He didn't tire of hearing the faux, faceless voices of the nagging publicists and the wannabe writers. He used to hate this. He remembered that much. But now? It was all part of his new-found appreciation for routine, his mundane perseverance, his refusal to break. There was a safety in this.

"Even if you are just going through the motions, you're doing great. You look great, we're all with you, man," said Curt, who was slouched in a club chair in David's office. David had been back at work for a month and a half. Jessica had been gone twice that long.

David said nothing. He looked out his corner windows and tried to think of a time when he hadn't been just going through the motions.

"I mean," David finally responded, still not looking at Curt, "you know, I've got to at least show up to grab the paycheck."

"Sure," Curt forced himself out of the deep chair and grabbed the page layouts he had brought in to discuss with David. "Six forty-five at the elevator bank," he said, heading out of David's office. Then, over his shoulder, "If you're not there, I'll know you've had second thoughts. No pressure."

For the fourth time in as many weeks Curt had offered to bring David to a party, to help him reenter the social scene. Curt believed in getting on with things. "David," he'd said, "you've got the work thing down now. You've got to exercise the other side of your life. You can't die too."

David wondered, *too*? Have we named this thing death? And he felt a comfort in that. Death from the beginning he'd been able to accept. An ax murder, a rape-strangulation, a slashing-mutilation. These things he could mourn. Being left—*for what?*—Jessica having slipped away, that was the possibility he couldn't mourn, couldn't fathom. So now, in an effort to avoid another night at home when Will might stop by and when the police would not call, he said yes. His attendance at a party would give all the other revelers something to talk about. It was his little bit of charity this holiday season. This is the way people did things: they reemerged and caused others to stare and then, after some time, everyone might forget that this person—this pathetic guy—was a victim to be pitied.

"What's a nice ex-wife like you doing in a place like this?" David asked Nadine, hoping he sounded funny, sounded at ease, sounded like he actually might be having an okay time. Nadine was Curt's onetime spouse—and the first and only person David had found the nerve to approach at the party. The gala was a high-energy affair in a rented SoHo gallery, strung with cheap Christmas lights and crammed full of finance guys and model wannabes and fringe characters like Nadine. As Curt's ex-wife, Nadine was a mere caricature of a person, someone who had become the butt of their office jokes, as in, "Will anyone want to read a profile of alternative plastic surgery in Tangiers? Yeah, Curt's ex-wife would take a look." Only because she was so smart and sassy and beautiful and had such a perfect, effortless body, were they allowed to demean her so freely. Impressed with his line, determined to continue his attempt to let loose, if only for a moment, David started to repeat himself. "So how'd a girl like you end up—"

"I got it the first time," said Nadine, barely grinning. "I'm still allowed out of the house. Divorce doesn't kill a woman. Just the opposite, in the best cases."

David smiled. Nadine looked good. In the four years since her split from Curt, David had only seen her occasionally, always at large gatherings like this one.

"You seem surprisingly chipper for a guy who, from what I've heard, hasn't seen the light of day in quite a while," Nadine continued. "So what's a nice boy like you doing in this rattrap?"

"I'm just taking Curt's advice," David said. In the cab to the gallery, Curt had suggested that the "New David" appear at the party. "The new David is just like the old David," Curt said, "except that the new David at least pretends to be having fun." The old David, David thought, wouldn't be having this inane cab-ride conversation. The old David, David thought, had a wife. He looked around the party, an uninspiring crowd pretending to *have fun*, and wondered if this was how people without home lifes spent their nights. David almost had a home life once—a wife, the right furniture, the tangible idea of a child within reach—he and Jessica having made it *this close* to being a real family, sealing the deal, leaving all this behind.

"Not the advice he gave me, or is that why you came over here to chat?" Nadine asked.

"He gave you advice?" David worked hard just to keep up his end of the conversation. It had been a long time since he'd flown solo at a party. Maneuvering a social crowd as a single man? Approaching a bartender and ordering only one drink? He'd practically forgotten how.

"His role as my personal how-to manual didn't stop when we signed the papers, unfortunately. He told me that you could probably use some company right now. He thinks we would be compatible."

"Compatible?"

"With our clothes off."

"He'd want you to do that?" David suddenly felt the urge to refill his still full eggnog, to check out the buffet, never to talk to Curt again. He scanned the room and spotted Curt by the door, acting every bit the gentleman as he helped a tall redhead shed her coat.

"He's into sharing. Was before, too, which was part of our problem, our incompatibility, I guess you could call it." Nadine shrugged and looked at David for a reaction.

David knew all about the women Curt had been with recently. He frequently threw the women's names into conversation and hung them each on a defining detail. Cathay who wore the impossible garter belt, Toni whose midwestern accent always ruined the mood, Elizabeth who appraised estates for Christie's, Heather who claimed Curt was only her second lover. There were more, and for the first time David wondered if Curt had had them all at once. If they were in twos, David couldn't imagine how they would have been paired. Stella who always craved shellfish and Karen who chirped when she climaxed? Lauren who brought her own props and Mary with a fondness for toys? Share?

"He doesn't talk to me about that stuff," said David.

"Whatever," responded Nadine. "He talks about that stuff with everyone. Even his mother, when they talk. I just didn't want you to be surprised to hear that Curt is looking out for your best interests."

The first thing David noted when he entered Nadine's apartment was the fact that it was only half full. She was still living in the loft she'd shared with Curt until he moved uptown to a modish one-bedroom and took all their furniture—mostly bad

1940s reproductions—with him. David shifted on what was left, a felt-covered ottoman, while Nadine hung their coats and poured two glasses of port. "Curt tried to take the rolling bar set with him," she said, opening the set's lower cabinet to return the port to its resting place, "but I won out after explaining that he couldn't keep a bottle of alcohol around long enough to need a place to store it."

"Sure," said David, scanning the walls, expecting to see a left-over photo of Curt keeping an eye on the evening. Instead, David was faced with two huge abstract oil paintings of what looked like large rust-colored eggs.

"Oh, God," Nadine said. "The egg paintings. Cate Manahan's sister did them and I needed something for the walls to match the carpet," a kilim in colors just off the adobe-tinted norm, David noticed, "and she offered these. She needs a place to store them since her studio's been co-opted by the gallery next door. And she figures eventually they'll grow on me and I'll slip her a check and own them."

"They're great." David searched for a flattering word to describe them but came up empty.

"They're a monstrosity. I'd rather have wallpaper than those things."

"Good wallpaper," joked David.

"Good wallpaper, that's something I'd like to see." And she slipped away from the living area, toward the bathroom. David closed his eyes and sipped the port. Nadine had brought him here—hailed the cab, paid for the cab, rung for the elevator, sat him on the ottoman. He suddenly liked being taken care of, liked being able to turn his mind off. He didn't want to be drinking the port—he'd had enough alcohol for the night—but he liked being told what to do and wasn't ready to fight it yet. He heard Nadine walk back toward him, but kept his eyes shut.

"Open up, kid." And when he did, she stood naked in front of him. He looked only at her face, above him, and the glass of port she held on level with her mouth. "It's late already. I figured I'd get the ball rolling."

"Right," he said, feeling the night slip even further out of his grasp. "That's kind."

She pulled a footstool next to the ottoman and sat down, extending her bare legs. She took David's near-empty glass from his hand and placed it beside him. She grabbed his hand and put it on her thigh. "I figured you wouldn't want much conversation to set the mood, all those jolly attempts to work up to this or whatever. The last thing you need now is a lot of awkward talk." She shifted her legs against each other in a makeshift scissors kick meant to propel the night forward.

This had seemed like a good idea as the party wound down. Curt had been flirting with a young waif at the buffet but took a moment out to encourage David to *at least be nice* to Nadine, to let her try to help him. "Don't be stupid about things," is what Curt said. And David thought then, looking across the room at Nadine, who only wanted to help, that this, moving on, was one of the twelve steps to dealing with his reality. And Nadine wouldn't be a threat. She wouldn't even expect a phone call in the morning. He'd see her at the next social event and Curt would make some joke about how using the transitive property they'd all slept together and Nadine would make some stock complaint about threesomes being trite, and they'd all forget about it. Going home with Nadine had seemed like the right thing—he had to start moving forward, at some point, in some way—even though David hadn't been the least bit aroused by the thought.

Now, looking at Nadine's legs, David was unable to notice anything but the veins at the top of her thigh where her leg met her hip. Where she should have been milky and white and sexy she was marred by blue bloodlines just under her skin. His eyes moved to her knees, which were flat and smooth where Jessica's would be dry in this winter weather. Jessica's knees would jut out from her thin legs, the dry skin above her knee caps asserting itself. Nadine's hand was on David's thigh, rubbing the wide-wale corduroy of his pants one way and then the other, as if it were his skin she were arousing. He smiled at her and made a sound—a false imitation of pleasure, a forced half-moan half-hum that he had never heard from himself before. As the noise lingered in the air, he took his hand from her skin, picked up his port glass, and stood. You can't do the twelve steps out of order, he thought, making up the rules as he went along. It might be dangerous, he might maim himself. He looked down at Nadine, who was so anxious to be with a man who, all night, had done nothing more sensual than not resist.

"I think I should refill now," he smiled, "while I still can."

"I'll get things ready," she said and quietly shuffled into the bedroom. David walked across the living room, past the rolling bar set, and out the door. He took the elevator down. Only when he had reached the outside door, and had begun to open it, did he realize he was still holding the port glass. It was crystal, probably part of the set she and Curt had registered for when they got married. *I could steal it*, David thought. But, realizing that it wouldn't match his own set, and that stealing a bar glass hadn't been a thrill since he was sixteen, and that he'd had his chance at rebellion once tonight and failed, David took the elevator back to Nadine's apartment and left the glass outside her door. He set it neatly to the left of the doorway so she wouldn't unknowingly crush it on her way out the next morning. He then took the elevator back downstairs and walked the fifteen dark blocks to his own home. Twice he crossed the street to avoid groups of kids who reminded him of the three he had followed that night during the week of Jessica's disappearance. Then he scolded himself: Look at me. Hipster street kids couldn't care less about one more scared old guy in a tie.

"Elliot's been searching for you," Kaitlin told David as they passed in the hall. David had just arrived at work, an hour late. The holiday season was finally over and the office was back in full swing, but that had no effect on David's purposeful tardiness. He had discovered one of the prime benefits of his extended, vague bereavement: No one outside his immediate family was willing to reprimand him for minor misdeeds. Sure, eventually his petulance would wear thin and grate on those around him (*So fire me*, he thought, considerably worse things had happened), but for now he made it a habit to show up at work whenever his mood dictated. He figured most people wasted time *on* the job. They squandered chunks of the day doing the crossword, calling long-distance friends, color-sorting their paper clips. David preferred to waste that time at home, doing all he could to delay getting out of bed—over the holidays he'd given up the couch and was again sleeping in the bed he'd shared with Jessica—and tossing himself into another day.

Before heading to Elliot's office, David stopped at his own desk and flipped through the message slips that had been left for him by Samantha, the assistant he shared with Curt. Elliot had called twice in the past half-hour. Also: one publicist, one freelance writer they'd sent to Portugal to report on cooking schools, and one call from Bradley Keeslar. The social worker had called the week before, also. That had been the first word from him since just prior to Jessica's disappearance, more than four months ago, when he'd completed David and Jessica's homestudy. Last week Bradley had left his message on David's home machine (the outgoing greeting now mentioned neither David's nor Jessica's names, only the phone number, "You've reached—" and the perfectly innocuous "Feel free to leave a message after the tone"). Bradley said, simply, "Hi, David, Hi, Jessica. Hope the new year's treating you well. Nothing to report on your case, but want to touch base in person. Call me at the office. Thanks." David hadn't called back. Everything in his life seemed to be a *case* these days, and explaining the big one, Jessica's disappearance, to Bradley, whom he hardly knew, reeked of irrelevancy.

David hung his coat and scarf in his office and then dropped a stack of papers on Samantha's desk in the hallway. She sat up and adjusted the straps of her jumper. Cute, David thought. Samantha, never one to miss an expensive flash-in-the-pan trend, was dressing as a schoolgirl again—which was certainly better than her recent flirtation with a style David could only think of as nouveau hooker.

He continued down the hall to Elliot Sunstein's office. Elliot sat back in his chair, his legs propped up on his desk while he watched the TV across the room. The Weather Channel was highlighting hurricanes. After David had been standing in the doorway a minute, Elliot looked up and swung his legs back under his desk.

"David, hello, come in."

David lowered himself into a chair and waited while Elliot searched through a short pile of papers. He found what he was looking for: a one-page photocopy that he briefly scanned, as if reminding himself of its contents, and then handed over the desk to David. "Maybe it's just South American hooey, but if it's real, I thought you'd want to look into it," Elliot said.

It was a newspaper article, and David recognized the typeface. It was from the *Lima Times*, Peru's English-language weekly. AMERICAN TREKKER SIGHTED ON ISLA DEL SOL.

The article was short. A mainlander had announced plans to build a resort—complete with tennis courts, parasailing, and frozen drinks served poolside (*poolside!* the article repeated)—on Isla del Sol. The article read,

Islanders have protested from the sides of the street, pelting tourists with large stones. No tourists have been seriously injured, but at the height of the protests on Sunday, the tour boats deviated from schedule and debarked the island at midday, at the requests of the fleeing tourists. Since then, the number of visitors has been severely diminished, save for the small number of Lima and La Paz journalists who arrived to investigate the unrest.

While the situation has grown quiet, locals continue to threaten violence and line the streets when the boats dock. Among the crowd on the dock on Tuesday, one journalist believes he spotted an American business leader and outdoorsman who disappeared in this country more than four years ago, Derek Mark Jhensen, wearing a disguise of traditional Andean attire. Jhensen, founder of the troubled U.S. consulting firm EnvirCor, has not been seen since 1992.

The American was gone, however, by the time the journalist, Jaime Arguedas, a border affairs correspondent for *La Republica*, could get close enough to question him. "I reported Jhensen's disappearance for my paper, it was only a few years ago, and recognized his face immediately. Despite his new beard, something he did not have in the photographs circulated at the time he disappeared, he still has a very recognizable face, a very American face despite his Peruvian costume. He moved quickly, I was hoping to speak to him."

Derek Mark Jhensen. David's eyes rested on that name. Jhensen was the businessman whose disappearance David had covered while on honeymoon with Jessica. There'd been a few random false sightings of the man in the years since but, from what the authorities could discern, he hadn't, truly, been heard from or seen. He might as well be dead. He might very well be dead. Or on Isla del Sol? What would Jhensen be doing on Isla del Sol? The journalist, Jaime Arguedas—his name was unfamiliar to David. He'd covered the disappearance for *La Republica*? Barely, David thought, or I'd know him. The Peruvian press had hardly paid any attention to the story of the missing American back when it happened. David remembered the aftereffects, at least in Peru (and the States, he thought), of a person disappearing: for a time there was intense interest, investigation. Then, once it became clear that there would be no easy answer, the interest dwindled until—in almost no time—it seemed no one even remembered that the person who had disappeared existed.

David read the article a second time, but couldn't focus. He looked up. Elliot was watching the TV again, apparently riveted by the way hurricanes ravaged tropical areas. David looked back to the paper in his lap. It seemed so wrong. Jhensen wouldn't be on Isla del Sol. Only an asshole journalist looking to make up headlines for the heck of it would claim Jhensen had been there. Isla del Sol was a tiny float of land in Lake Titicaca's Bolivian waters, covered from coast to coast on foot by dozens of tourists daily. Every morning the ferry shipped sightseers to the port and every night the same ferry shipped them back to the mainland again. A haven for tourists. This was not where Jhensen would want to be.

"I know Jhensen," David said to Elliot, who, on hearing David's voice, picked up the TV remote and shut the set off. "I followed his tracks down there. I know where he likes to go. He wouldn't be on Isla del Sol." Shit, David realized as he heard himself talk about the trekker, the missing trekker, *if David couldn't locate his own wife*, not even a cold trace of her, *who was he to assume he'd know where a total stranger would be?* He thought of Jessica. As if she and Jhensen had fallen into the same carefully set trap.

"Okay," said Elliot, doing a paltry job of hiding his disappointment. "I assumed it was probably nothing but South American tabloid crap. Still, it had potential to be interesting. For you at least."

David could imagine what Elliot was thinking: If Jhensen got back in the press then David's name would be back in the press, and that's a lot of free publicity for *Travel Excursion*. After David's first articles on Jhensen came out, David was interviewed by most of the major news outlets. The story had been picked up by regional papers and all the news magazines—it's not every day that a well-known businessman (one whose tangles over illegal waste had landed him at the center of a Department of Justice investigation) disappears on an adventure vacation. And it's not every day that a journalist like David happens to already be on the scene to gather the exotic details. The story had made David's name, and now it could help garner *Excursion* a bit of publicity, which would be fine. The magazine, still being new and all, could use the extra push. But there was no chance, David was certain, that this *Lima Times* story was actually true. And even if it were? What was David supposed to do about it? Head down south to rescue the guy? He had barely thought about Jhensen since the articles were published—since he'd gotten his whopping paycheck, and then that bonus, embarrassingly generous, for the TV-film rights.

Following Jhensen wasn't David's bag anymore. These days David was simply an overpaid New York editor with a penchant for doing nothing and a clear lack of skill when it came to finding people.

"Yeah, it's just South American tabloid bullshit," David replied, mimicking Elliot. "Like there's not enough real news for Peru's journalists to cover right now?" David shook his head. A month earlier the Japanese ambassador's residence in Lima had been seized by members of Peru's MRTA, the underground Marxist movement. The MRTA had one demand: that the Peruvian government set free their political prisoners currently caged in the country's deadly, inhumane prisons. Waiting for this demand to be met, fourteen MRTA members continued to hold seventy-two hostages inside the residence in Lima's San Isidro district, an area David knew well. He'd been following the story in the press, looking for glimpses of the city he'd visited with Jessica. "Those Lima journalists should be feasting at the moment, and they're a hungry bunch."

Elliot nodded and took the article back from David. He laid it on the side of his desk.

David spoke again. "Anything else?"

"That's it," Elliot said. "The January issue looks great. Even Patricia"—Elliot's wife and an art designer for one of the women's glossies—"found time to read it front to back."

"I take no credit, I'm just one of the workers." David smiled and stood up to leave. Elliot turned the TV back on, raised the volume slightly. A crew was rebuilding a house blown down in Antigua. "How's your week look?" David asked, speaking up over the TV's noise.

"Slow. Want to schedule lunch? I've got the end of the week free, we could catch up."

David liked these kinds of exchanges, the nailing down of everyday details. Elliot scheduling lunches. Bradley Keeslar unknowingly calling to simply touch base. David liked these reminders of the way things kept moving at their steady pace whether or not he was paying attention. "Absolutely."

David began to walk out of the room, then turned back toward Elliot, who was filing the Peru article in one of his desk drawers. "You and Patricia ever talk about having kids?"

"What?" Elliot looked up, as if he hadn't quite heard David.

"Nothing," David said. And then, halfway out the door, "I'll ring you about lunch."

Back in his office, David opened his atlas and turned to Peru. Using a permanent black marker he inked over all the places he was sure Jhensen would avoid. He knew Jhensen at least this well, he'd followed his trail, talked with the people Jhensen had talked with. Ridden the same roads. David made dark lines on the map and colored in the spaces between them. When David was finished, and all the places the hiker would not be were shaded in dark silhouette, the places he might be *at that very moment* jumped off the page. Next David flipped to Bolivia, where he was certain the trekker might venture as well. Using a yellow highlighter he colored in all of the places that he, David, might seek refuge if he were Derek Mark Jhensen, a man thousands of miles from home with no attachments to cling to and no bridges left to burn.

Peru 1992

The café in Puerto Maldonado looks out on the only busy avenue in town, and David and Jessica sit at a table right in front. Today, a week and a half into their honeymoon, the two are finally comfortable with the altitude, completely awake and alert—no longer taking small naps in the middle of the day or having to spur each other on to keep up with their itinerary. The ache in their heads is gone. Even in Puerto Maldonado's famously oppressive humidity David and Jessica look fresh, crisp. Over plates of ceviche and strong cups of local coffee, they watch the lunchtime traffic. They are finally taking a day to relax.

On the street, women carrying bundles pull carts behind them. Their dress falls into two categories: traditional garb of heavy prairie skirts and wool sweaters with *mantas*, swaths of woven fabric, wound around their bodies; or the completely European style of dress David grew accustomed to seeing in Lima, women in knee-length skirts and polyester blouses. There are men on the street as well, in soccer jerseys and sweatpants or ill-fitting sweater vests or the occasional too-small sportsjacket covered in dust.

"Bloomingdale's and Pier 1." Jessica motions to a man wearing pleated pants and a light windbreaker in a style left over from the early 1980s. She is teasing David, coaxing him to play their game from up north, labeling the people on the street in terms of where they'd likely shop.

She leans forward and waits for David to pick up her challenge. He turns back to the crowd, where he spies a fellow tourist. An easy target. David points and says, "J. Peterman and Eastern Mountain Sports?"

"That's an easy one." Jessica shakes her head and forks a pile of fish and onion dripping in lime juice into her mouth.

The Peruvians' skin, in various shades of brown and beige, is smooth and healthy looking despite the amount of time they have spent in the sun—though one thing David has learned in Peru is that the sun does, truly, age people. A guide in the jungle David had assumed was close to his own age was, it turns out, only twenty years old. The woman who served them their breakfast in Cuzco, who looked wonderful for a forty-year-old David thought, was, in fact, only thirty-two. The waitress had been shocked to find out Jessica was twenty-eight. "But you look like my child!" she'd said. "You look like you are still in school!" Jessica had been thrilled. All it took to look young, they'd discovered, was to come to a country that aged its people.

On the street today, the sharp light shines white off the dark hair of the Peruvians who rush across the square, lending a glare to the small plaza as a whole. Beside the plaza, this café is filled with travelers leaning over maps and planning their trip into the jungle or taking a break on their way out. This is the way station. This is what the traveler craves, no? David thinks. The line between two worlds, waiting to be crossed.

David catches Jessica looking at her reflection in her water glass. She is lost in the picture of herself for a moment before looking away and raising her hand. The waitress, dressed in the kind of black skirt and white shirt that waitresses wear all over the world, spots Jessica's signal and starts to walk over.

"*Por favor*," Jessica says, motioning for the check. David isn't ready to leave yet. Jessica has a way of always preparing to go before he is ready—her actions aren't malicious, she simply gets ahead of herself, as if there's somewhere else she is supposed to be.

"*Una momento*," the waitress says as she passes by.

David is about to tell Jessica to slow down and relax—to

remind her that they are in no rush, that there is no one with a reservation waiting for their table—when he hears her gasp.

"Oh, David!" Jessica reaches across the table and grabs his hand and his attention. "Look! That's the cutest thing!" A child is approaching their table from the square. The girl is two and a half feet tall and perfectly round, teetering as she walks, an experiment in balance. Her short braids stick nearly straight out from her head. She drags a homemade kite by its tail. *"Hola!"* Jessica says to her in the high-pitched voice women use when a child is in the room. *"Hola, bebe."*

"Oh, David," she says, mock pleading, leaning toward her new husband. "Can we take one home, please?"

David laughs. "Yeah, well, we may be taking one home already."

Jessica sits up, takes a quick breath. "My God, you're right." She laughs as well. Nervously? David wonders.

They'd decided to play Russian roulette with their fertility during the honeymoon. She'd felt bloated in the month before their wedding and had gone off the pill, thinking maybe it would help. Then, feeling wild, they'd together decided to go protection-free while in Peru. "Ooooh, danger," David had joked. Life's predictable enough, they'd figured. Their wedding itself had been by-the-book. Why not see if fate wanted to throw a twist their way. A twist? The first night of the honeymoon, in Lima, Jessica had said, "Here goes, the wheel's spinning," as he slipped inside her, and they hadn't discussed the subject since. Still, since then Jessica has been positively giddy in bed.

The child on the street has almost reached Jessica when the girl's mother runs toward her and scoops her up from behind, close in front of David and Jessica's table. The woman mutters an apology in Spanish and disappears into the crowd with the child.

"She was pretty darn cute," David says.

"You're such a sucker for young females." Jessica bites her lip, an expression David has come to interpret as meaning: *I feel lucky. This is good. Let this moment last.* We're living the dream, David thinks to himself, not knowing what this means—embarrassed to be thinking in movie clichés. Jessica grows quiet, intent as she flips through the travel book in her lap. David pays the check.

Walking back to their hotel, David is half a pace behind Jessica and runs his hand lightly through her hair. The moist air is like therapy to her tresses, which today lay thick and smooth and shiny. David likes this. He lets his hand fall to her shoulder. He still loves her shoulders. He spins her toward him, looking her in the eye before leaning down and kissing her. Over her shoulder he sees a scooter rental shop one block down Gonzalez Prada.

"This way," he says. "I want to see about renting mopeds for tomorrow morning."

"Oh, definitely," says Jessica, letting him guide her down the street.

Off the main drag, Puerto Maldonado is not a tourist town. After spending so much time in Cuzco and the rain forest—where the local residents walked around with their palms held out for American dollars, as if cash might drop from the sky—this glimpse of a real street pleases David.

But it turns out that David and Jessica aren't the only tourists on this street. Another couple is already at the scooter shop, handling two of the bikes, rusty black numbers that look barely able to support the weight of a human, let alone a motor and a gas tank. David and Jessica instinctively walk faster as they near the shop, as if fearful that this couple might nab the only scooters in decent enough shape to handle a trip around town.

When they reach the shop, David opens his mouth to talk, but then hears the man speaking Spanish to the boy renting the scooters. Jessica leans in to listen. "Not enough *what*?" Jessica asks, butting in.

"Fuel," says the man, turning to Jessica. "One of the scooters was essentially empty. I had to leave my wife with it and come back into town for gas, and now I'm explaining that I shouldn't have to pay for the spare fuel since, you know, it shouldn't have been empty in the first place. Simply a matter of principle." The man shrugs and smiles, showing all the wrinkles in his tanned face. His tall, thin stance is imposing, but up close these wrinkles betray his true age. He must be nearly twice as old as David and Jessica, must be sixty or so. "Explaining as best I can," the man says. "My wife's the language expert, but doesn't agree this is worth arguing. She's sitting it out." He nods toward her, perched on a crate nearby. "Strong woman, has her own principles! Can't blame her."

"Your Spanish sounds fine," David says. "I can only—"

"The only foreign language David has mastered is pig latin!" Jessica interrupts.

"As long as he's fluent," the man says, introducing himself and his wife, who has wandered over now, as "Perry and May Cohn, happy to meet you." May explains that this is their third trip to Peru, but their first to the jungle region. "You can never really get a full hold on this country. You'll see. We'll be coming as long as we're still walking."

David prices the mopeds and tells the boy they'll be back the next day. Then he and Jessica, with the Cohns, walk back toward the main strip and recount their experiences in Cuzco.

"My God," Jessica says, "you have to hear how they tried to take our car!"

Perry nods. "We've heard it before. You're fine?" He sees David and Jessica nod and continues, "And did you see the patrols between Urubamba and Ollantaytambo? That's where the troops run their most aggressive tourist interference."

"They were there too," David said. "But just patrolling, it seemed. Not stopping cars. Remember?" he says to Jessica. "It looked like they were doing training exercises?"

"Just a part of the local scenery." Perry's voice is warm, he sounds thrilled to hear that David and Jessica have met the cops and been subjected to the local law enforcement tricks. "All part of a Peruvian holiday. What else have you seen?"

While Jessica and Perry and May walk steadily on, David stops at a large open window—impossible to close really, since it is nothing more than a hole in the rough clay wall—which allows him to see clearly into a small private living room. Six men sit in metal chairs around a small TV, suspended halfway up the wall on a tin shelf. Save for the chairs and the TV and a poster advertising Spanish cigarettes, the room is empty. Everyone in Peru has a TV, it is how people connect. Newspapers are nearly impossible to find, but all over the country, in the jungle and high in the Andes, David and Jessica have spotted TV satellite dishes in the most unlikely backyards.

The men inside the room wear work clothes. Their neutral-colored shirts and pants are stained with what looks like oil. No, David thinks, it must be mud, earth, and David figures out who these men are even before Perry leans in beside him, looks, and says, close to David's ear, "Gold panners. Indians hoping to get rich from the meager dust that's to be found here."

David nods, but he isn't listening. He's looking at the TV. The face on the screen looks oddly familiar, like an actor he's maybe seen playing a bit part on late-night TV, or a guy he'd sat next to at a tennis match some time ago. The face is from a still photo, blown up to fit the screen, and shows a man in his mid-forties, two or three day's growth on his face, dark hair, lots of color in his cheeks, as if he's been exercising. The edges of a parka, a ski parka from the looks of it, are visible around his shoulders, and a colorful hand-knit hat is pulled tight onto his head. Put him in a pair of glacier glasses, David thinks, and he looks ready to tackle Everest.

"That guy looks familiar," David says aloud, softly, as if to himself.

"Looks kind of like you," says May, who has approached. "I mean, in winter, and ten years from now. Not *like* you, but, in that way, clean-cut and active and American. That type." The Cohns are from Canada. "He's definitely got that United States look, that merchandized sportsman look. Manicured trekker fashion, I suppose you could phrase it. Not unlike you," she says to David.

For a moment the three of them are silent—Jessica remains further down the street, looking in the window of a small hardware store—as they listen to the TV. David can understand nothing of the Spanish that the newscaster speaks. Even without understanding the words, the voice carries David along. He's intrigued by the rhythm. It sounds almost syncopated, like a high school jazz band's rendition of Spanish.

"The newscaster isn't a native Spanish speaker. He's Quechua, a local," says May, who is, it turns out, a linguist specializing in South American languages. "Hear the way his voice lingers on the vowels? You hear that a lot in this region, when people aren't speaking Quechua itself."

Now the odd rhythms make sense to David, but the face,

reduced suddenly to a small square tile in the corner of the screen, remains unexplained. "Who's the guy?" he asks.

May listens to the broadcast, holding up her hand to silence her husband, who has begun to speak. "He *is* American!" says May, self-congratulatory. Then, "He's an outdoorsman, from the West, down here mountaineering, maybe? I didn't catch it. He was supposed to be back in the States already, but never returned, so now officials are trying to trace when he was last heard from or seen. He's been known not to call from long trips. It seems he takes lots of long trips, so his friends and family weren't worried. But now, he hasn't returned and hasn't picked up his mail in Lima, where he left a post office address, in two months." May looks from the TV to David and then back to the TV.

From down the street, Jessica watches, curious, but she doesn't join them. David waves her over but she simply shrugs her shoulders and looks back into the hardware store, examining the goods.

"See, May?" Perry thrusts his hands in the pockets of his shorts and faces her squarely. "That guy on TV, he probably tried forging new routes in the wrong remote areas, and that's it for him. Score one for the Shining Path." David's thoughts are still with the trekker's face, that photo. David could swear he's seen that face before. He can almost place it, as if with *one more clue* he'd be able to pull the man's entire annotated life history out from the underused files at the back of his brain.

"The newscaster didn't say," May says. "You never know down here. Should make for some interesting follow-ups. Peruvian TV news is rarely so interesting. Or so international."

"May's always trying to blaze uncharted trails," Perry tells David. "I'm her voice of caution." David tries to bring the trekker's face back to his mind, to place a name with it, to locate its familiarity, but he can't quite get there.

The news has moved on to soccer scores, but before continuing to walk, David and the couple peer in the window for a moment longer. Turn the camera on us, David thinks. What would we look like? He imagines the window as the TV screen and the three of them, two older Canadians and an American journalist on honeymoon, their heads outlined against the dirt of the street behind them. What would the Quechua say about this?

Like Jessica and David, Perry and May are staying at the Cabana Quinta. When they reach the hotel's lobby the two couples stand awkwardly for a moment, until Perry reaches out his hand to shake David's. "Nice meeting you two. We're right upstairs if you need tips on where to go. There isn't much of Peru we haven't seen, at least not much that you'd want to see."

"Or maybe dinner, since—"

Perry cuts May off. "Sweets, they're on honeymoon," he says. Then, to David and Jessica, "But if you decide you'd like company, we'll be here another two days. May has research to complete."

"We're here through tomorrow—"

Now Jessica interrupts David. "We'll definitely track you down. You've been so helpful already." She smiles warmly, looking happy to be with David, happy to be meeting other travelers, genuinely thrilled to have received such enthusiastic approval from two older people she's just barely met. David looks at her smile and thinks, We do look fantastically *right*, here, honeymooning, side by side. He tries to imagine him and Jessica later, at Perry and May's age, how right they will look then. But he can't see it. He's surely pictured this before, hasn't he? They've never talked about the future in any diagram-it-out, what's-the-plan kind of way—there's been no need. They want the same things, don't they? Doesn't everyone? He can't remember. *It's the altitude*, he tells himself, his brain is working at half-speed. After the older couple walks away, Jessica turns to David.

"You there?" she asks. "You look like you're having a thought."

He turns to Jessica, thinks of what to say, what to share. "The altitude," he says. "I can't get over how thin the air is."

"But not *here*. We're lower down again." She looks confused. "You okay?"

"Fine, no, I'm fine. I was just thinking about it, I like it here," he says.

She pulls David toward her and whispers, "Perry and May, isn't that exactly what you'd expect two hip older Canadians to be named? So perfect it hurts."

"You bet," David says, smiling, leading Jessica to the winding staircase on the left side of the lobby. As the two reach the landing, where the stairs curve beneath a rustic stone wall and continue up to the third floor, for a moment there is no one in sight, no one who can see them. He is lucky to have Jessica, he reminds himself, to have this plan for the rest of his life, laid out before him here, in his wife. They don't need to *talk* about their future, they have implicitly bought into it, invested in its bounty.

David thinks about the American outdoorsman—a familiar face, David is sure he knows him, has seen him before, *he knows this man*—a man who's future is unknown, who is completely alone right now, in the mountains perhaps, frying up a guinea pig for dinner, or dead, his body unfound, a solitary corpse buried in the jungle or left to decompose in the sewer system beneath Lima. But David has chosen to be safe from these solo fates. He looks at his wife, hidden with him beneath the stairs, looking every bit perfect, and he steps closer to her, remarking to himself, as their arms brush against each other with every step, how it feels, for this second, to be so completely a twosome.

1997

"**W**hy the *fuck* didn't you *call* me," David screamed into the phone to Detective Hallander. Not used to hearing himself yell, David jumped back from his own voice and its urgency. This situation certainly warranted the extreme high note. The new week was starting off badly. Elliot was out of town and suddenly the magazine was falling to pieces—layouts sized wrong, copyedits lost in the system—and David had thought that making time to read the paper would give him a decent mid-morning break. Instead, this. "Is there a fucking reason, Detective, you thought I did not need to be informed. Is there? Or isn't there?"

David stood over his desk with the Metro section spread in front of him. The front page had been devoid of any real news—except the nondevelopment that there was nothing new in the hostage situation in Peru. Seventy-two hostages still inside the Japanese ambassador's residence. Savvy captors, David thought, able to keep so many top-level government officials, supposedly the sharpest political defense minds in the country, from finding a way out. Either a testament to the brilliance of these revolutionaries, or to the stupidity of Peru's top officials.

David flipped to the second section, where the lead article—stretching straight across three top columns—detailed the latest rape in his neighborhood. This time, though, the crime went beyond rape. The victim was dead. The other details matched those of some of the earlier attacks. The criminal came in through a fire-escape window, wore a condom, nearly suffocated, or in this case did suffocate, the victim. It was the first crime by this perp since Jessica's disappearance.

"We have no reason to believe," Hallander spoke slowly, his voice infuriating in its control, "that this is in any way related to your wife's disappearance."

"You don't know that," said David. "Did you maybe think the guy was so freaked out by whatever he did to my wife—say murder, say maybe his first actual killing—that that's why he stayed quiet for nineteen weeks? You never thought of that, did you? Never crossed your mind, did it? You don't know."

David dropped a load of work on Samantha's desk and took a cab to the scene of the rape-murder. The small prewar building sat next to a café where he and Jessica often came for brunch on weekend mornings. In warm weather they would wait in line for an outdoor table and, once seated, analyze the pedestrians who passed, guess at their home furnishings. Jessica would put down her spoon, piled high with oats and berries, to eye a man in a Burberry's cashmere scarf and stovepipe pants. "Eames chairs, Knoll couch," she'd say. Out of the corner of his eye David might examine a woman in a forest green cardigan and Mary Janes. "Framed prints from the Met, Ralph Lauren duvet from the outlet."

Now David stood outside the building where yesterday's crime took place and looked into the café's windows. For a brief second, while his gaze was fixed on the scene inside, through the glass he thought he saw Jessica. She knew I would come here, that I'd chase the criminal! he thought. He held still, not wanting to spoil the possibility, until, almost immediately, he saw how wrong he was. The person who sat at the window table, long caramel hair in a braid, was a man. The person he'd mistaken for Jessica was a guy.

The only other people on the street were a few weekday stragglers on their way to an early lunch. Midwinter was always gray, bleak, the sky a constant nondescript shade of slate. Today, even the neon in nearby store windows looked somehow washed out, barely cutting through the persistent, raw dreariness. David, in a faded navy parka and charcoal wool pants, blended in as he crossed his arms over his chest to ward off the wind. He'd expected a crowd outside the crime scene. He'd been on a *crime scene* before, in Lima, outside a club late one night, and there'd been police barricades and ambulances and a small crowd and a stifling heaviness in the air. But at this scene, today, other than a couple of beat cops entering and leaving the building and one reporter who left just as David arrived, there was no movement. Should he head inside? David wondered. He knew from the newspaper article that the victim's apartment was on the third floor. What would he ask, what did he want to see? A young woman—twenty-four or twenty-five years old, David guessed—approached the building's front door and slipped a key in the lock. David followed her into the foyer where she retrieved her mail from its box.

"Do you have a sec?" he said and she turned, stepped back sharply. "Do you live here?"

She stood stiff, facing David.

"Were you here when the rape took place? Were you at home?" he asked.

"You mean, last night?" She nervously looked down at her mail, what appeared to be a few catalogs and credit card statements. She quickly looked up at David as if studying the details of his face.

"Yes, last night. You hear anything? Maybe you saw someone strange maybe loitering outside?"

"Are you a cop?" Her breath was fast and loud. She slipped her key into the foyer's inner door behind her.

"No."

"I didn't think so."

"Did you notice anything? Did you know the girl? I need to know." David paused. "I'm investigating."

"Talk to the cops. I wouldn't know—" She turned the key and

cracked open the door behind her, just wide enough to slip her body through. And when David tried to follow her through the doorway, hoping to get a glimpse of the crime scene upstairs, the now scared girl pushed the door closed in front of him and warned, "We aren't supposed to let people we don't know come inside behind us. Please." After the door closed David got a final look at her face, challenging him from beyond the glass panes, cold, scared behind its tough front. My God, David thought. My God, he realized how easy it must be for a woman to feel vulnerable when her home has proven, less than twenty-four hours earlier, easily pervious to the outside. My God, he thought. That could have been Jessica. That could have been the look on Jessica's face in the final moments before someone, perhaps the very someone who stood in this foyer less than twenty-four hours ago, crashed into her own safe haven. Is that what she felt? He tried to picture Jessica's face with *any* expression but came up blank. Oh, God, he thought, *fuck*. And after waiting another moment between the outer door and the locked inner door, David quickly let himself back out onto the street.

David was shaking, chastising himself. He'd terrified a woman who was probably dead scared already. He was still standing there, trying to steady his shakes, a minute later when Detective Gilchrest, Hallander's younger, corduroy-clad partner, came out of the building's door. Gilchrest looked at David as if only half-surprised to see him there.

"You accosted a resident on her way in?"

"Accosted? I wouldn't say that. I asked if she had any info on the rape. I'd call it a simple inquiry. I asked some questions, thought she might know something, might have been here," David said.

"Look," Gilchrest said, "understand that the females in this building are skittish right about now. Okay? That girl was ready to finger you for this rape. If there was a sketch artist with us she'd probably be describing you right now. Don't—" he paused, "don't do this to yourself."

"I asked her a couple of questions, that's it." David imagined how, had there been a sketch artist, the scene would have followed. What would the daily tabloids have labeled him? The Preppy Prowler? The Gray Flannel Rapist? Would the artist capture his inner discontent or would the picture merely show a subtle sense of malaise? *Fuck*, David thought, remembering the day he was questioned in the precinct about Jessica. The last thing he needed was to be suspected of another crime. And why not suspect him? David figured. On the TV cop dramas he'd grown so accustomed to watching, it was always the least likely guy—the one with the best tailor and the most classic haircut—who was found with the murder weapon in his laundry pile.

"I thought maybe I'd get a look at the crime scene, that maybe it could tell me something about my wife," said David. The cops had gotten nowhere on the case.

An older couple walked out of the café next door and waited near the entrance—the woman drawing her hands into the sleeves of her coat for warmth. The man read a posted notice in the café's window, an off-Broadway play flyer boasting raves and four-star reviews from underground weeklies. A moment later, a young couple came out and joined them and together the four walked on. Then, five girls, lanky teens with slouched, stooped postures, came around the corner talking loudly over one another, fighting to get words in. The girls entered the restaurant and the street was quiet again. A cab slowed, as if to dispatch a fare, and then drove on. Gilchrest lit a cigarette and then held the pack out to David, who shook his head No thanks.

"I'll take you up to the crime scene," Gilchrest said, "if that's what you really want, and if it means you won't show up unannounced again." He put the cigarettes and lighter back into his coat pocket. "But to be honest, there's nothing to see. It really only looks like someone's apartment that's been way messed up in the bedroom, mattress half pulled from the bed. The body's been taken away."

"I figured," David said, though he hadn't actually thought it through that far. He pictured the girl who'd gone inside, scared. "I used to worry about Jessica getting lost in shopping malls, you know that? Like her sense of direction, or self-sufficiency, was below the shopping mall threshold."

"That's in the report, I think. A police file is better than a diary, it's all there. I have a kid who's five and she gets lost in the video store, we have to keep her on a leash. When she wants to be funny she barks, like she's our pet." Gilchrest waved to a uniformed cop on his way out of the building. "We're all feeling for you. The case is still very open, don't doubt us on that one."

David nodded. What was he supposed to do? How could he say, *Sure thing, righto, thanks, keep doing that job of yours*, when clearly doing their job was accomplishing nothing?

"So you want to come up to the scene?" Gilchrest asked. "I can't see that anything positive will come out of your seeing this mess. Except that you won't recognize a thing in common with your own apartment, when it was a crime scene. You might as well save yourself climbing the stairs."

What are a few flights of stairs, David thought, calculating the number of flights—six? eight?—he went up and down every day coming to and from his own third-floor home. "This rape has nothing to do with Jessica," David said, telling Gilchrest and convincing himself at the same time.

"It's really not related," Gilchrest said back to him. "It's like, there's a lot of crazies around the city, not just one, you know?

It's not like they even know each other. There's no Ambassador's Club for loonies. It's just one random crazy after another with nothing to link them except the city limits."

"So I don't need to come up," David said. "There's nothing for me to gain from coming up."

"That's probably the right decision. And, look, don't come back. Don't pull this again, spooking tenants is heavy stuff, this is your last break," Gilchrest slapped David lightly on the back. "Be well, okay? You look good. It's all a matter of moving on. I see this stuff all the time, and tomorrow I start my day all over. You know?"

D avid woke often at night, usually only a few hours after he'd fallen asleep, sometimes with a bad dream, always with a start, and often aroused. He'd awake with a world-class erection and he'd think of Jessica, *A-Number-One* she'd have rated his hard-on in a whisper and with a laugh, and he'd find himself wishing she were there, her body taut against his, as worked up as his was. David woke up hot, wanting, and these thoughts of Jessica, of her absence—these thoughts took hold of his desire and twisted it, killed it on impact, turned his need sour while deeming it sharply insignificant. He'd try to think back to when he last got off, last let himself feel that release.

The longer he went, he'd thought he'd crave sex more. When he and Jessica suffered their worst dry spell, right after they'd given up on conceiving a baby the natural way, he'd found himself jerking off with the frequency of a thirteen-year-old who'd just discovered the power of his own erection, every bathroom fair game: David had been both embarrassed and impressed with his youthful desire, his enthusiasm. So now, he'd thought he'd be driven crazy with desire for nothing in particular, but instead, he was almost never aroused. He felt his machinery grow rusty, wanted to put it back into use, to know he still had it in him, to feel that moment of *let-go*—expected, anticipated, and still somehow a surprise every time—that moment when time took a much needed break. I could go to a strip club, he thought. I could go to a gay bar just to try something new. I could go to a high-priced call girl. *Shit, I could fuck a Forty-second Street whore and no one would fault me for it.* Except Jessica, he thought. Maybe Jessica wouldn't see the justification. But damn, David bet she would. People had needs and he had carte blanche, given his situation. Weren't people under trauma supposed to have wayward cravings, to indulge in aberrant behavior, no explanation necessary? Still, David lost his desire. He didn't even have it in him to be appropriately aberrant.

One night when he woke with—*yes, yes*—a desire that felt real this time, an ache that demanded attention and was not going away, he rose from bed and crept downstairs in the dark. He turned on the TV, found a suitable skin flick, two women who, in fact, looked like real females and not facsimiles, and a man who wasn't unattractive and didn't make too much noise, the women as interested in each other as they were in the man, and David tried to focus on the scene, to be in it, to get off, *to want it* (this was supposed to be a turn-on, close-ups and odd camera angles and all, he knew this), but instead he found himself imagining Jessica walking in right then and there, seeing how far he'd fallen. He closed his eyes and tried to override the image of Jessica with thoughts of Nadine, of the new interns at work (but they weren't all that hot, they were simply young, too young, and fresh and sweet), of an especially experimental college girlfriend he hadn't seen in ten years, someone whose face occasionally came to David even when Jessica had been there, under him and naked, but it was still Jessica's face he saw now when his eyes were closed—and he shut the TV off and watched, instead, his own arousal as it faded and slipped away.

Finally David returned Bradley Keeslar's calls. Jessica's disappearance had been kept out of the papers. With no body and no sign of violence or of any crime at all, the media hadn't been interested anyway. "Put that on the list of things to celebrate!" David could hear Jessica say.

At first, David had wondered if getting some coverage might help—getting Jessica's face out there—but the detectives assured him that what they'd done (sending Jessica's photo out to merchants in the Tri-State area—dry cleaners, pharmacies, delis, garbage men, banks—and to FBI bureaus and police precincts nationwide) was more helpful and didn't lead to the kind of false reports which were inevitably phoned in after news stories ran.

So the newspapers had stayed away and, as a result, five months after Jessica's disappearance Bradley still didn't know what had happened and each time he left a message to "David and Jessica" it tore David up until he finally returned the social worker's calls.

"There's been a change to our status," David said over the phone, carefully picking the words he thought Bradley himself might use. David recalled everything he liked about Bradley. His soothing presence. His ease with tough situations ("I know you never planned to conceive your children across an oak desk," he'd said). The way everything seemed to make sense when it came out of Bradley's mouth. The way he'd given David and Jessica hope. The way, with his clothes and his demeanor and his perfect little sons, David felt, when he was looking at Bradley, as if he was looking at himself in an alternate life. "Can I make an appointment to speak with you about it?" David said with a forced formality. If he needed to talk to someone—and he did, he needed to try at least, didn't he?—he was sure Bradley might be the right person. A social worker was trained to deal with other people's tragedies. Bradley would know better than to offer up unwanted sympathy.

"Next week, any time," Bradley said. He didn't ask about Jessica. David figured that Bradley had heard the "change in status" line before to connote divorce, separation, a change of heart, death perhaps. David figured, let him think that for a week. Let him look back at our appointments and home study and try to isolate the points of friction. Let us, for a week, in someone else's mind, be typical.

Seven days later David stood in Bradley's office. The photo collage on the wall—filled with, it appeared, the same pictures of gawky, smiling children as he'd seen the last time—stared out at David as he stood just inside the doorway.

"Can we maybe go out for coffee or something?" David said.

"This office isn't working for you, huh?" asked Bradley, motioning to the off-green walls, to the baby pictures that reflected the room's harsh fluorescent light. He put David's file into a folder. "No problem," he said. He rose, put on a coat, and tucked the folder under his arm.

The coffee shop was a take-out joint where, at the counter, David and Bradley ordered drinks that were served in thick paper cups. The two men sat at a semi-secluded table toward the back. "Your situation has changed?" Bradley said to David. "Something's up?"

David tore open a packet of sugar and emptied it into his cup. "Jessica. Jessica is no longer around," he said. He shifted his chair so that he could see out the window at the side street. Bradley removed the papers from his folder and lay them on the table.

He didn't speak. David continued, "Since right after we saw you last, one week after, to be exact. It's not about us, not some angry spouse fight. She's just missing, Missing Person, for real." David took his eyes off the street and looked at Bradley, at himself, at himself giving a full explanation, for the first time, of all that had come to pass, and felt the way the cold words—*missing, person*—came off his tongue as if they had never been inside him at all, as if someone else had put them in his mouth for just this purpose, and his insides sank and he froze. He suddenly felt the burden of the words that *were* inside of him, and he could not speak.

"If you want to talk about it," Bradley said. "Why don't you tell me what happened, from when I last saw you, what happened." And David took a breath and looked the social worker in the eye and told him the whole story, from the moment he returned from Sun Valley and discovered the empty apartment to the moment, three weeks ago, when Detective Hallander called him into the precinct to look at a photograph, a Polaroid of a woman lying on the coroner's table. "They had a slashed-up body nothing like Jessica's," David explained. "Just unidentified and the right age. For a moment I wanted it to be her, coming back to me in one form or another, letting me know, for worse, where she was."

Bradley barely touched his tea. He interrupted only to ask a few questions, dates mostly. David finished and said, his voice thin now, "I thought you should know. I thought you should be informed before, you know, you spent more time trying to find a kid for this couple who no longer, I suppose, exists." The social worker who'd promised to be such a calm and levelheaded presence looked uncharacteristically as if he had no idea what to say. The air between them turned heavy and sad.

"Thanks," Bradley said. He paused, ran his finger across the rim of his cup. "I'm glad I know," he continued finally, nodding his head, "and truly, I'm sorry to put you through this whole retelling—"

"The retelling," David interrupted, then stopped. "The retelling," he began again, quietly, wanting to hear the end of his own thought, "is honestly the least of it." David looked at these words and saw their truth.

"I can imagine." Bradley leaned closer, his own voice quiet now. He rested his elbows on the small table and seemed to understand how little there was to say. "Or, I can at least begin to imagine. I could help you find someone to talk to, let me know if that interests you, often it helps."

"Jessica really wanted this kid, you know that?"

"You seemed to really want this kid as well. You seemed pretty certain yourself." Bradley looked hard at David, as if perhaps he might be able absorb all that David could not.

"I wanted a kid with Jessica, yeah," David said. Bradley wrote a few lines on the top paper in his folder, then sealed it shut again.

The next morning David sat on his bed and considered rising and going to work. He looked at his clock. The office edit meeting had been moved up to 9:30, Elliot's attempt to get everyone into work at a decent hour. And, given that it was David's turn to present the mock-up, he actually had to be there. The other editors were finally growing weary of David's showing-up-whenever-I-please attitude and were making clear that his mourning grace period, his morning grace period, was over.

He'd dreamed about Jessica. Another dream—a nightmare really—straight out of their real life. Jessica, in the dream, unable to bear children. Awake now, David's head hurt. He thought about his conversation with Bradley. David wasn't sure now if he'd ever actually wanted a kid, or if he'd simply craved the *family* that a child would turn him and Jessica into. Sitting on his bed, alone, David couldn't truly remember why he and Jessica had wanted a baby anyway.

He slowly made his way to the shower. Had he and Jessica really wanted a child? He asked himself this question for the first time. He thought about how, while he and Jessica were trying to conceive, first naturally and then through in-vitro treatments, they had never discussed their desire to start a family. They had never questioned the *why* of it all. They had simply pressed forward, soldiered on. This is what you did, you established a home and then you built a family to fill it. That was what they had craved. Now, on this morning when he wanted nothing more than to crawl back into bed and hope for a dreamless sleep, he wondered *what were we doing?* As the bathroom slowly began to warm up with the steam from the shower, David sat on the side of the tub and these thoughts, all these thoughts, impossible and intangible, coalesced and sank like a ball of steel inside him.

PERU 1992

It is David and Jessica's last morning in Puerto Maldonado, and David's thoughts drift to the missing American. In the bathroom, struggling to rinse the soap off his body with the low-pressure stream that passes for a shower here, David wonders about the American. *Who is he? Is he dead?* That's the logical conclusion. Imagine, David thinks. Coming to South America for a trip like this one, okay, okay, not like this one, the trekker was alone—going it *alone*, David thinks, understanding the allure, but also realizing that this is something he himself will never do again. *Being alone* is something he disavowed in front of friends and relatives less than two weeks ago. Now David tries to imagine coming to Peru and then not coming back. Say those military policemen outside Cuzco, what if they hadn't just wanted the rental car, but had wanted to create real havoc? Couldn't they easily have killed David and Jessica and gotten rid of the bodies? Who would dare question the cops' word—in a country where a citizen's safety was so often linked to his ability to keep quiet—if they said they never saw an American couple traveling that road?

David dries his body with a small towel—in Puerto Maldonado's intense humidity his body becomes sticky again almost immediately—and lets these thoughts rise and waits for them to dissipate but, instead, after they rise they fall again and hang on his damp skin, following him into the day.

"He could have been hiking and plummeted into a crevasse. They have ice hiking, glacier hiking, up north. It says so in my guidebook, the oversized one," Jessica says, sitting on the edge of their bed, lacing up her hiking boots. David's brother, Will, is the family mountaineer, ice hiking and ice climbing and going on glacier treks. David and Jessica only know the details of these sports from his secondhand stories.

"Don't you leave tracks on a glacier?" David says. "Maybe not."

"You're looking for a mystery." Jessica's voice is muffled for a moment as she pulls a sweater on over her head. "You know: Man Takes Andean Incan for Bride, Cuts Off Ties with Western World. Speaking of brides, this one's all packed and ready to move on."

David locks Jessica's suitcase with a small padlock, and then begins working on his own. "No, it's just that falling in a crevasse doesn't seem worthy of this kind of news attention."

"What kind of news attention? That news story you saw, that was the local news. Growing up in Connecticut, cats caught in trees and the death of the third-grade class's hamster got local coverage. My neighbor got a nose job and I thought about pitching it to the local station. Boy Gets Rhinoplasty, Thinks No One Will Notice."

Walking toward the door with the suitcases, David looks over his shoulder and sees his wife grab her hair into a ponytail, stretching her arms behind her. God, she looks good, he thinks, focusing on her collarbone where the late afternoon sun, coming in through the shutters, just barely catches her skin. Over the last ten days the sun has tanned her skin perfectly and evenly, as if all those years growing up on tennis courts and beaches were merely training for this, preparation to look absolutely perfect in Peru, on the edge of the rain forest.

In the lobby David signs their room bill and helps heave their bags behind the counter, where they will remain while David and Jessica grab a light meal before catching their flight back to

Lima, their home base for the final two days of their trip. At the front desk, David asks for an English-language newspaper.

"We have only this." The man behind the desk motions to an array of Spanish papers, three of them, which lie flat on the counter.

"Can I get an English paper in town?"

"Maybe," the man says. "I have not looked. Probably no."

"The *Lima Times* is the only English-language paper produced in Peru, and that only comes out once a month," says Perry, who has just entered the lobby with May.

"Oh, hey," says David, turning to greet them. "Hi, there."

"We were just talking about whether we'd run into you before we lift off," says Jessica. David tries to catch her eye, but Jessica's gaze is intent on the Canadian couple. "Can you join us for a quick bite before we head to the airport? We could use some tips on where to spend our last two days."

"We can spare a moment, and this, as well—" and from his shoulder bag Perry produces a *Herald Tribune* from the day before. "The Brit in the room next to us carted it in from Lima and passed it off to me." He hands David the paper. May purchases a Spanish paper, this morning's edition of *El Mundo*, and then the four of them head out the door.

In the hotel's café, they sit hunched over avocado salads and small plates of seafood.

"If you have two days in Lima, you'll want to head to Ica. It's not right around the corner, but you don't want to be around the corner from Lima anyway," says May, adjusting the brim of her canvas sun hat.

"You two drink, don't you?" Perry asks.

"Sure," Jessica says.

"Ica's the wine center. Two days in the distilleries is the perfect antidote to a week in the jungle. Though you'll likely end up with no memories of those two days. Ica's Pisco is strong medicine." Perry laughs. "Be sure to get to Bodega Tacama while you're there."

"That sounds nice," says Jessica to David, who isn't listening. He's busy flipping through his *Tribune*, skipping over the stories about European commerce fluctuations, looking for something more.

"News is news," says Perry, seeing the haste with which David flips the pages. "You think you're craving it, but then you realize it doesn't compare to what's happening right in front of your eyes." He puts a forkful of scallop in his mouth and motions with his head to the street in front of them. Across the road, a man in indigenous costume, marred by mud and the green-gray of river water, futilely tries to control his small horse, which clearly wants to walk the opposite direction, back toward the muddy banks that serve as the port on Tambopata Rio. The horse holds firm, leans toward the river, tightens his haunches.

David finishes looking through the front section of the newspaper, refolds it and lays it on the table.

As the waitress clears the table, May hands her copy of *El Mundo* to David. "This is the real fun read. Local land squabbles and new ordinances and petty crime reports. Do you speak Spanish at all?"

"Not a word. The no-good schools I went to emphasized Latin and French, not that I remember those anymore, either." David shakes his head. "Jessica speaks some Spanish." He smiles and kicks her under the table. "You should hear her rattle on to the locals."

"My high school Spanish is pretty rusty, but it's been getting us by—"

"And *more*," David says. "She tells me she barely speaks Spanish, then we get here, and she's speaking like a native."

"A nice little honeymoon surprise for my new husband—he thought he had me all figured out." She smiles and reaches for his leg under the table. She and David joke affectionately in front of others, as if to prove, in the presence of witnesses, that they are connected and carefree. When they are alone together, David has noticed, they joke less than they used to, as if there is no longer any need. Perhaps it is simply that they are alone *more* now, suddenly occupying the same space, building the same life.

David glances at *El Mundo*. On the front page, in the lower right, sits a photo of the missing American hiker. Bottom right corner of the page, below the fold, the resting place for B-level news. Which is more attention that the *Herald Tribune* gave the story. The *Tribune* has ignored the story completely, if they've even heard about it.

"The follow-up to last night's news," May says, noticing the attention David gives the photograph. "Nothing new, except that his name isn't on the Sendero's lists."

"Their lists?"

"The Sendero, the Shining Path, are intricately organized terrorists," May says, "with their bookkeeping, at least. They let the government know whom they've killed, most of the time. They want credit for their acts. The authorities checked the lists, the article says, at the insistence of the American's family, and his name isn't on any of them. Anyway, the Sendero don't simply disappear people."

"The only people who do that," Perry jumps in, "are the government—but they wouldn't slay an American, not an American—and the drug traffickers."

"But the drug scene is subdued these days. Quite a difference from the first time we were here. The country's steadily shaping itself up. And this American seems unlikely to be mixed up in drugs, from what I can tell. He's in business, that's what it says, big in environmentalism."

As May says this, David's eye, scanning down the article, sees a familiar name, EnvirCor, and he understands why the man's face looks so familiar. Under the photo, in small print, his name: Derek Mark Jhensen. Derek Jhensen is the founder of EnvirCor, among the first environmental consulting firms in the Northwest, a firm that, just three years ago, was the subject of an intensive investigation. It appeared that EnvirCor's plans for a few of its clients, including two of the larger-name high-tech outfits in the area, skirted some of the more prominent hazardous waste laws. Threatened with both heavy fines and the possibility of jail time for Jhensen and his partner Dan Allegra, EnvirCor had settled the case, and been made a high-profile example by the Justice Department. There was no proof that Jhensen or Allegra had knowingly flaunted the laws—but environmental policing in the area was under pressure from both sides, from the Northwest's strong environmental lobbies as well as the area's traditional business community. The Northwest's longstanding—*upstanding*—companies were as wary as the earth lovers of the proliferating high-tech corporations. And these new corporations, for the most part, were EnvirCor's clients. *The New York Times,* had given the EnvirCor controversy front-page coverage.

David looks up at Jessica, "He's a consultant, the guy behind EnvirCor. You remember that story."

"Oh," Jessica says. "Yes. What was he doing down here?"

David looks to May, who answers, "According to *El Mundo,* he was vacationing. He was an adventurer at heart. You know the type." She smiles. David tries to picture it, surviving a high-profile government investigation only to disappear in the wilds of Peru. It seemed too much, too incongruous to comprehend. "It says he's the first American to be reported missing—with no plausible explanation—in Peru in more than a decade." The table falls silent. Jessica looks at her watch.

"Oh!" Jessica stands. "I don't mean to be rude, but we need to get moving."

David looks at his own watch and sees that she's right.

The two couples exchange addresses and phone numbers, and David makes sure to get May's work number as well. As he and Jessica walk quickly back toward the front desk, ready to grab their bags and rush to the airport, David says, "I think I'll call her. There seems to be an article for me to write in here somewhere. You know, on the Quechua dialect maybe."

"Something on that missing hiker, maybe, the EnvirCor guy," Jessica says, turning to him, speaking in a slow, low voice that implies she's letting him in on his own secret. Then she laughs, grabs onto his arm. "I know you're thinking about him, your alter-ego! The infamous hipster adventurer, the 'merchandized sportsman type.' You love that. I heard May when she said it yesterday. Even down the street her voice came through loud and clear. I was like, 'Oh, man, there goes David's ego!' " Jessica is joking, David thinks. She smiles up at him.

"Hey." He fakes offense and then laughs. "It's not such a stretch," David says, and he thinks this is true. "Did you see the picture in the paper? If I let my facial hair grow, and let my face get some sun?" When David was a kid he resisted Will's intense interest in hiking, his father's attempt to lure him more into the mountains, to fishing, to camping. But David knows he could have gone that route, could have become a trekker himself, traveling with a backpack rather than a duffel on wheels.

When, as a child, did he decide not to go that route? That path would have led somewhere as surely as this one has.

J essica wants to go to Ica. She and David have landed in Lima, crawled into bed for the night, and it is all she will talk about. What is obvious, though unspoken, is that they are reliving the start of their honeymoon: Jessica complaining about the capital city, David trying to convince her that it's not that bad.

"Since when do you turn down the chance to drink leisurely for two days straight? And there's a beach resort near Ica, too," Jessica says. "It'll be our homage to the classic honeymoon, sun and alcohol, all that Club Med stuff we pretend to hate."

In the background, the Channel 4 news is on constant loop. Earlier, right after sliding into bed, David had turned on the TV and flipped between the three newscasts (passing other stations, as well, featuring bad American sitcoms from the 1980s, plus somewhat familiar movies-of-the-week, a Peruvian soap opera, and *Magnum, P.I.*) before settling on Channel 4. "*Canal Quatro, Canal Lima,*" the young newscaster says each time before going to break. Even without speaking the language, David is certain this is the broadcast he'd be watching if this were his home country and this was the TV selection he was offered each night.

For a few minutes Jessica translated the gist of each news story as it was presented. Then, bored, she tried to lure David with talk of Ica. Now, as David feigns sleep and listens to a newscast he can't understand, she rises from the bed, turns off the TV, and goes to sleep herself.

D avid tries to send Jessica to Ica herself. He presents this idea in bed the next morning, as if it's a vision he's had in his sleep.

"Why don't you go to Ica, and I'll hang in Lima?" he says. He thinks it's a great idea: She wants to see Ica and visit its bodegas, he suddenly wants to stay in Lima to meet the local journalists, maybe get a story out of this vacation. He happens to be *here*, where a story has appeared right in front of him. A guy who'd been famous just a couple of years ago has up and vanished. David wonders how much coverage Jhensen's disappearance is meriting in the U.S. Likely not much, or there'd have been a mention in the *Tribune* or on CNN International, which David has been watching on-and-off since he awoke early this morning. He could have this story before anyone else, he knows this.

Up in the States, David has grown weary of his job. *Journalism as desk job*, just one more drone, editing in an office that has had the air sucked out of it. Perhaps this story is a way out, a way for him to break from the pack, finally make his own name as a reporter. *David wants this.* And honeymoon or no honeymoon, isn't the fact that he and Jessica are both so independent—at the same time that they are totally a couple—what makes their relationship so satisfying in the first place? It only seems natural to David that in the face of conflicting plans he and Jessica should each do their own thing today.

He lies in bed and explains his thoughts in the order they first occurred to him. First, the rational. "I mean, if we both want to do different things, it seems to make sense." Moving on, when Jessica says nothing, to "Being independent is what, among other things, we love about each other, you know that." He reaches his arm around her naked body. She sits up, hugs her knees to her chest. David ends with—pleading—"I'm a journalist, how can I ignore this story?"

Only when spoken aloud does the ridiculousness of that statement ring clear to David. Jessica isn't stupid. She knows David well enough to know he's not a war reporter or investigative guy driven to get to the truth of the matter. He's a soft-core features scribe who can create a spot-on headline and likes the life and doesn't mind seeing his name in print every once in a while. But he can write, and he can report, and isn't that what any story, whether it's an all-American puff-piece or an overseas war report, entails? And for the first time in his career he has happened upon a story that somehow captivates him, should be easy to write, and just might turn into something huge and exclusive and *his*.

This is a story David knows an editor will pay for—Jhensen is already a name in the States, he's already been associated with scandal and intrigue—and it is a story David wants to write. It is sitting right in front of him. And he can't get the hiker's face out of his mind. It's the familiar look David saw in Jhensen's eyes that compels David to see the story through.

"Don't you think—" David is saying when he rolls over to see that Jessica is already out of bed and standing at the far side of the room, leaning against the doorway, looking defeated and ready to unleash her power all at once.

"Don't *you* think, David?" She's angry, her voice is sharp, she lets her head drop to her chest. "Don't you *see*? Besides the fact that this is our honeymoon and we're here to be *together*, haven't you had your eyes open?" She pauses, as if hoping to not have to go on. "This isn't exactly a safe place for a woman traveling alone. *My God.* Feed me to the lions, why don't you?" She gathers her robe around her and walks into the bathroom. David hears her brushing her teeth.

How blind can I be? David chastises himself. Jessica gets disoriented in new restaurants, let alone foreign cities by herself. *Why don't you go to Ica by yourself*: David can't believe he even suggested it. He stands up next to the bed and kicks the nightstand with his foot, as hard as he can, letting himself stumble back from the pain before walking through it and into the bathroom, where he will join Jessica, where he hopes to make things right, to apologize every way he knows how.

"Okay?" Jessica asks only an hour later, not bitter, honestly wanting an answer. She doesn't seem angry at all now, or at least less angry than David would have expected. Her ease with forgiveness is something he found difficult when they first began dating. He'd felt cheated by being rarely punished for his bad behavior—forgetting to call when he said he would, not making dinner reservations after promising to do so—as if the push-and-pull of what he expected from a relationship was somehow disrupted. Instead of their relationship being a give and take, it sometimes seemed more like a take-and-take-again. Slowly, though, instead of feeling guilty about this, he started to appreciate the way it made being a twosome less of a stress. And it wasn't, in truth, a true take-and-take. Looking at Jessica under the hotel's gleaming green and yellow awning as she shades her eyes from the morning sun, he knows she will call on him to *give* when the time is right. He wonders about the power of her position, being the person with the chits to call in.

"I wouldn't have cared about going to Ica at all if that couple hadn't brought it up," she says, "so I don't know why I got so fixated on it."

"Then let's not fixate on it now, right? We'll have fun here. Let's grab some eats." David puts his arm around her and leads her to the street, guiding her to the left, toward the busier shopping strip.

"Sometimes I feel like all we do is eat." She laughs. "The food's not bad, but, you know, considering it's not great, all this eating seems like a waste of time. If only we didn't need sustenance to survive." She's shaking her head, smiling.

"Time," David says, lacing his fingers through hers, "we've got."

But just an hour later, he seems less sure of this. As they finish breakfast, David twice looks down at his watch. He's thinking that it would only take one day, today, to do the legwork to find out if this story is doable, if it's truly within his reach. He figures that the embassy would be a likely first stop. He looks down at his watch and sips his coffee.

"You know what?" Jessica says. "They have buses from the hotel to the ruins at Pachacamac. I'm going to check them out. It's an organized tour, you know? I'll be with a group, or a driver at least," Jessica says, her voice shaking, forced but insistent. "You do what you have to do, I'll be back at the hotel before dinner. Maybe I'll even have time to sit by the pool. By nightfall I'll be tan and rested."

"Jessica. I'll come with you. How can I say no to more ruins? Pachacamac sounds great," David offers, feeling he has no choice.

"Seriously, David, I'll see you around dinnertime."

David waits to hear more, to be sure this plan, a plan which Jessica has conceived, is truly all right with her.

"Like you said, our independence is one of the things we love about each other. You had something there," she continues. "It's just half a day. Don't worry about it."

"You're sure of that?" David asks, a bit too quickly. Then, to take the edge off his eagerness, he says slowly, "I'll be back by dinner, and I'll leave word at the hotel, of where I am, in case you get back early." He thinks this plan is fine. As she pointed out, it is only half a day. And the trekker's story has practically been gift-wrapped and handed to him. What a shame not at least to *begin* to pursue it. He asks, one last time, "This is really okay?"

She nods and makes an honest effort to smile and he loves her for this, even if it is just an act. "Sure," she says. "Yes. It's like you said, why shouldn't we do our own thing?"

Except that this, certainly, can't be how Jessica thought *doing our own thing* would shake down. This: A day and a half later, at the Lima airport, David helps his wife check her luggage. The agent at the United Airlines information counter assures him that, whenever he decides to fly home, his unused ticket for today will get him a place on standby. "Great. That's good news," he tells the agent. He feels sick to his stomach, he feels wrong. He fixes his attention on the gold flecks in the information desk. He reminds himself that he and Jessica will be together again soon, and for the rest of their lives.

They have arrived far too early for the flight and have an hour to spare before Jessica needs to be at her gate. Jessica reaches for David's hand as they stand beside the information counter, unsure of where to go next. Over the past day and a half they have barely laid eyes on each other. David spent yesterday at the U.S. Embassy, where he didn't find much out about the investigation into Derek Mark Jhensen's disappearance; there isn't much to know, it turns out. But David did make what he calls to Jessica "valuable contacts" with the midlevel personnel, the same guys who function as the information center for Jhensen's family back home. "They're the pipeline," David explained. After returning from the embassy, he'd called a few business reporters he knew on the West Coast to get their take on Jhensen. And then this morning, David stopped by the Channel

4 newsroom and located the camera crew on-call in case any Jhensen leads came in. The crew was already tracking down loose leads connecting Jhensen to the drug trade. "This is going to take time," David told Jessica when he returned to the hotel in the afternoon to ride with her to the airport. "But afterward, think of what a great story it could be. Plus, in reality, it'll be something tangible, documentation of our having been here. You'll see, in the end it will be something valuable." That word again. And as he helped her lift her bag into the taxi—there was no reason for her to stay, to extend the honeymoon indefinitely, as he would need to—he lay a hand on her back and said, solemn and quietly commanding, "Don't hate me for this." And then the joke, hoping she might smile politely, "You said you didn't want a traditional honeymoon."

In the airport they shop for magazines, buying nothing. David gives her a pack of gum and a box of Sudafed, in case her ears block up in the pressure of the plane's cabin. They walk through all the duty-free shops, and inside the last of them Jessica says, "Damn, I could use a bottle of Pisco for the flight home," but she doesn't buy any. She fingers a carton of cigarettes, as if almost, but not quite, considering taking up smoking for the first time in her life. David sees her do this and thinks, *yeah, right*. When half an hour has passed, he suggests that maybe she should go to the gate, make sure she gets the aisle seat that she wants.

"That makes sense, the plane's probably full," she says.

They follow the signs to Terminal B. She shows the guard her ticket and lays her jacket and carry-on tote flat on the X-ray machine's conveyer belt. David can imagine laying his own sweater on the conveyer belt and stepping through the archway toward the gate and following Jessica onto the plane, a plane for which he actually has a ticket and on which he has been, until now, expected to take his passage home. His bags are still at the hotel, but packed and ready to go—they could easily be sent on to New York later today, by the concierge. *To stick to the plan, to leave with Jessica, could be this easy.* To simply walk onto the plane with her, *he could do this one thing.* He can imagine that being one end to this story, to his honeymoon. To follow the script, to continue along in the parts assigned to them, politely declining opportunities to deviate, *to walk onto the plane.* But he also wants to follow this story (It is right there! In front of him for the taking!) and she has given her okay and promised that she means it, and now, when there is *an opening,* a quiet between them and a pain in his gut reminding him that he is wrong, she says nothing. He does not put his sweater on the conveyer. He will not be boarding this plane.

Jessica turns to walk through the gateway, then turns back. She takes a step toward David, who is reaching out for her. "Okay?" she says. He pauses and then grabs her tightly, wrapping his arms around her shoulders, and kisses her on the top of her head, where her hair parts, and lets his lips rest there for a moment. She runs her fingertips lightly down the sleeve of his shirt. Her face is in his shoulder until he lifts it up, places the requisite kiss on her lips, and lets her turn and walk away.

1997

After six months of sleeping badly, in the bed he had shared with Jessica, David reconstructed his life in the guest room. He moved his clothes into the closet. He carried his clock radio from the master bedroom and set it on his new night table, a temporary flea-market find that they'd meant to replace once they got around to buying real furniture, pieces without this night table's shady, unknown history. He brought his favorite water glass, his jar full of change, the small, framed map of Peru that had gently rested against the lamp on his dresser. He lugged his shoes, three pairs at a time, and arranged them at the foot of his new bed. It was a good bed, polished maple and extra-firm and high off the ground, more than adequate for a guest and perfectly acceptable for David.

He left the pillows, throw rug, and lap blanket behind. He left everything that smelled like Jessica. He was sure it was this smell that kept him up at night, awake for hours, until, finally, rest came, an irregular sleep, marred by nightmares. Images of Jessica, sad and confused, standing over their bed and wondering why she wasn't in it, or standing a block from their apartment but unable to navigate her way home. He dreamed he was a boy lost on Nantucket again and woke wheezing and reaching for his mother. In a dream so vivid that David almost searched the house for Jessica afterward, he saw his wife pregnant, her stomach extending far beyond her toes. *Jessica, carrying a child*, something they had imagined together, all the time. In the dream, she grinned and said nothing.

So David left the master bedroom and moved to the guest room where, free of Jessica's smells and their shared history, he could sometimes forget about all of it for the six, seven, eight hours that he slept.

Jessica's belongings remained in the master bedroom as she'd left them. The only things he removed were the loose odds and ends that usually lay splayed on the dresser. Seeing it all—her hairbrush, her makeup, the small bowl full of safety pins and hairbands, a pile of grocery receipts—was, to David, like looking at a painful collage of her used parts. He swept the entire dresser top into a shoe box.

A larger cardboard box sat in the corner of the kitchen. Every time he spotted a clipping that someone, someone with a bad sense of cause-and-effect, might think pertained to Jessica's disappearance (WOMAN ABDUCTED IN SOUTH JERSEY or RAPIST ARRESTED IN PITTSBURGH), he dropped it in the box. None of this truly had anything to do with her, he knew this. He'd given up on believing flimsy leads and wallowing in unsubstantiated hope. Still, every time he saw a clipping that reminded him of some aspect of his wife, he dropped it in this box. He tossed in photos from magazines if the model had Jessica's haircut. He threw in clips of person-on-the-street interviews if the person said something David could envision coming from Jessica's mouth.

Now, as he moved his things out of the master bedroom, away from his memories of Jessica, David looked at this newer, smaller box, the box beside her dresser, the box of her actual *things* (her lotions and creams, her spare change, her receipts). He'd eyed them often. He'd sat up in bed in the middle of the night and focused on her hairbrush, the loose nickels and dimes (likely the last coins she'd touched), in hopes that a clue might arise. Now he saw clearly how all these bits and pieces added up to nothing. Not to a hint of where Jessica was, not even to an image of who she used to be. And, feeling the inevitability of it all, feeling the wham-bang of the loss, he lowered himself to the floor. He sat with his head between his knees, his arms looped behind his neck in plane-crash position. He strained to anchor himself to a thought, to find a way to stand and move forward. But the crash had already come and gone and taken Jessica with it—and all that was left was the clean-up, the act of reassembling the pieces. He finally got to his feet and lifted the small box and carried it down the stairs and into the kitchen, where he wedged it into an upper corner of a high cabinet, next to his and Jessica's least favorite wedding presents and most useless gadgets and the fragile, spare china, still in its packaging.

Will and Annette threw a party for Ginny's second birthday, and David attended with every intention of putting on a good face and playing along. He wanted to be a good uncle. He showed up on time and lugged along a large stack of children's books, wrapped in primary colored paper, and signed the card in big block letters. But by the time the party was in full swing— the doorbell no longer chiming to announce the arrival of yet another adult carrying a toddler under one arm and a box or bag in the other—David found himself in an unshakable contrary mood. He blamed the crowd: mostly girls and boys under the age of three and in various states of hysteria. David hadn't realized how proficient he'd become at avoiding children, at keeping himself out of situations where he'd be faced with intact families unashamed in their contentment. And now here he was.

A clown entertained the kids, who all cracked up in unison, tumbling sideways on the ground and knocking against one another. All the clown had to do was turn in the children's direction and the giggles began. David's mother, in a chic new haircut that she said helped her forget she was the *grandmother* of the birthday girl, forked a bite of cake into her mouth and looked at David. "David, have some cake, you'll feel better," she said, eyeing his obvious discontent.

"Believe me, I'm trying," he said. Briefly the children went silent, holding their breath as the clown prepared for his next pratfall. "But I'm not as entertained by clowns as I was a few decades ago." Even as a child David had preferred magicians, armed with their visual teasers and intricate puzzles and able to pull off the seemingly impossible with an ordinary deck of cards. The phrase *disappearing acts* suddenly worked its way into David's mind, but he dismissed it, concentrated on the scene in front of him.

David's father approached, full of energy, and carrying a toy cellular phone. "Have you two seen this? Will's boss gave it to Ginny." He flipped the toy open and pressed the Send key. "Want to come play?" the toy asked. And then, "Let's be pals." David's father pressed the button again and again, facing the toy toward David and his mother, showing it off as if amazed by the crude technology.

David had spent little time alone with his father recently. Both his parents had frequently visited the city after Jessica disappeared, but back then, and even now, David's father relied on props to carry the conversation, as if time and the simple fact of conversation—uttering smooth streams of words that said nothing at all—would eventually make everything better. David's father had lived his life by the tenet that there was nothing that couldn't simply be persevered through. The mere forward movement of time would beat the opposition. Put your head down and power onward. Until recently, David's life hadn't challenged this idea.

"Press it again," David said, "See if it says, 'You're wanted in the conference room, ASAP.' Or how about, 'Short all shares in clown stock due to sudden market disappointments.' "

David's father was still looking at the phone when he asked David, "What time are you on the tube tomorrow?"

"Sometime after ten A.M., I'll let you know when I'm sure."

David was scheduled to do a live interview with CNN for a segment on recent dangers to tourists in South America. David knew little about the subject—he was an expert only on the story of the one trekker gone missing four and a half years ago. *Missing*: When David heard the word these days, he couldn't help but feel that this simple seven-letter string had been keeping track of him over the past four years, waiting for the right moment to reenter his life, and the right person to take away in the process. One American missing in Peru, this was the extent of David's knowledge of the country   he had only kept up with the recent siege in Lima by reading the same papers as everyone else. But *Travel Excursion*'s publicists figured the interview would be good exposure for the magazine. And, though David felt foolish about this, he never had the nerve to turn down a TV spot. He didn't know anyone who didn't jump at the chance to see his own face going out over the airwaves.

"Look at that." David's mother motioned across the room. "You'd think Annette's parents were kids themselves. They can't get enough of that clown." She grinned slightly, then turned to David. "You know, you and Will married great women, truly, but boy, did they come with interesting in-laws. Handfuls." David remembered when his folks first met Jessica's mother, when they were planning David and Jessica's wedding. "How did Jessica end up so low-key?" David's mother had asked afterward. But had Jessica really been so low-key? Either she'd been low-key, or she'd simply had a talent for playing it as such. Either, or. He couldn't remember which. David's mother continued, "But Jessica herself, you know." She squeezed his elbow, a show of support. "She was a find."

A find, David winced. He smiled back at his mother. "Thanks. I know." He nodded. His mother reached up and held him briefly as if to remind him that he was still her son, that that truth still held. "I hurt for you every single day," she said, giving him a final squeeze.

After the guests left, David stayed to help clean up, hoping this late show of enthusiasm might atone for his lack of fervor during the party itself. While Annette washed the cake pan and Will swept, David toured the room with a trash bag, collecting the paper cake plates and plastic cups and disposable forks that were strewn through the apartment like carnage from an oddly festive battle. *The preschoolers versus the pre-preschoolers, tooth-and-claw to the death.* He started to toss a heap of discarded wrapping paper, a featherweight boulder marking the center of the battlefield, into the bag. Annette scolded him from across the room.

"We save that," she said. "Just leave it in a pile and I'll fold it later."

We save that. David looked at the heap, which was so clearly meant to be trash. Who wants to receive a gift wrapped in another person's birthday refuse? He obediently pushed the paper to the side and continued to forage for plates and glasses.

"Ginny's sound asleep," Annette said to Will.

"I can't believe she made it through the whole raucous party," said Will, leaning down to sweep cake crumbs into a dustpan.

"Did you talk to Dad at all today?" David said. "He couldn't get enough of that toy cell phone Trey gave Ginny." David paused to knot the top of the trash bag. "He said Trey told him, 'It's all the rage.' Can you hear that?" David was smiling.

"It's unbelievable, these gifts. I'm surprised no one bought Ginny a real phone. Or a beeper, a pager. Can you imagine?" Annette was shaking her head. "I'm hoping she doesn't get too used to this." Annette looked worn out, but David had seen so little of her recently that, for all he knew, this was her general state of being. Saving wrapping paper, berating the conspicuous consumerism she lived among, this had to be an exhausting way to live.

"Oh, come on! It's a three-star riot, the gifts these kids get," David said, laughing. "I mean, when even Dad's getting into it. 'It's all the rage!' Dad said. You gonna knock that? You think too many gifts are what's going to spoil that child? Watch out for my dad and—"

David ducked just in time to avoid the object Annette hurled hard at his head. It crashed loudly against the wall behind him and fell to the floor. Amazingly, the object, the toy phone, withstood the shock and when David picked it up and held it to his ear, it was still in one piece.

"What the *fuck*?" David said under his breath. He had no idea where Annette's anger had come from or what she wanted from him. Into the phone, he muttered, angry himself now, "Earth to Annette, what the hell?"

"What the *hell*? What the hell is going on with you, David? This whole freaking family of yours. You think life is just a laugh a minute, don't you? Try having an emotion some time, why don't you? Is this what you are going to do, just move on with your life like Jessica never happened?" She leaned on the counter in front of her as if unable to bear her own weight. Will walked over, stood beside her, took some of the weight on himself. "I," Annette paused, "I don't—" she said before cutting off her own thought and walking toward the door to the bedrooms.

Will began to follow. At the doorway, she stopped and turned around. "You know what I do all day?" she said to David. "I wonder how I'd act if I were you, or if Will were you. If we were the victims here. What my husband would do if *I* were taken. Would he possibly *be* so freaking oblivious? Would he?" She looked at Will, here eyes large, scared. Then she turned back to David. "I thought you were just in denial, but it's been half a year and all you've done is sulk and then act like it's all behind you. You sit here, at Ginny's birthday, without Jessica and without a child and act like you've got everything you want. Like it's all a-okay. Have a breakdown, why don't you? Be human. It's time someone told you to *mourn* already." Ginny wailed from her bedroom and Annette quickly walked out the door and toward the cries. Will motioned to David, just a sec, and then followed her.

Fuck Annette, David thought. This wasn't her tragedy.

Will came back into the room almost immediately. "Her mood's been turning on a dime, things have been rough around here, I think," he said. He gently kicked a balloon that had sunk to the floor. "It's hard to bring up a kid in a world where you know that someone can just up and disappear and there's nothing you can do about it."

Nothing *you* can do about it, David thought, suddenly angry. David imagined himself the balloon, the air slowly seeping out of him. Annette had cut right to his center, dissecting him in front of his own brother. David tried to see himself through Annette's eyes, through any eyes but his own, and he saw how firmly he'd refused to move from this point, this rockbed of total stasis. *The mere forward movement of time would beat the opposition.* Time itself would take care of things, would propel him out of this mess, he'd assumed. But it hadn't. And, honestly, he no longer trusted his own assumptions. He used to act like he could predict what Jessica would wear, how she would think. He'd been so sure not only of his thoughts, but of hers as well. All those times he'd tried to predict every little thing—*I thought you would have ordered the roast chicken. No? Why not?*

Will shut the door that led to the back of the apartment. "Don't pay attention to Annette," Will said, sounding completely convinced, completely on David's side. "It's been tough over here, too." He paused, listened. The apartment was quiet. Ginny's cries had ceased. "Silence, beautiful," Will said. He ran a sponge over the kitchen counter. "It's weird, as an infant she slept through the night, but now she wakes at the sound of anything."

David nodded, happy for the change in topic, and tried to force his building unease—toward Annette, toward this inane situation, toward his own actions and reactions—to fall away. Usually all it took was willpower and a healthy dose of what had Annette said?—of *denial* for David to return his mood to the status quo, but today it wasn't working. The hard ball of steel in his gut stayed put, refused to dissolve. All these months, David finally realized, he had been waiting for a sign, a symbol that everything would be all right, but there was no proof that a sign would ever come. No evidence that *waiting it out* was the way to go.

"You have time to hang around? We could break into the Scotch Annette's folks dropped by," Will said.

"Yes," David answered. "Sure." He left the haphazard stack of wrapping on the floor and walked toward the kitchen, hoping a drink would help.

D avid looked into the camera, spoke slowly through an easy smile.

"I haven't actually been to South America in the past couple of years, but that has nothing to do with the unrest. I'm eager to get back." He relaxed into the TV banter, put on his best TV face. This was a piece of cake. He was good at this.

"How wary should tourists be?"

"Well, Jeanne, the risk factor varies not only by country, but city by city and region by region. Any heavily touristed spot, say Machu Picchu, is going to be well protected. The last thing anyone in these countries wants is to harm a tourist. Tourism is an increasingly important source of income."

"What about the Shining Path, or the others, the group that has the Japanese ambassador's residence under siege, the MRTA?"

"The Shining Path? Don't join up with them. There are better tour groups out there." David laughed. "But honestly, tourists should stay in the touristed regions—this isn't a part of the world where it's necessarily safe to go off the beaten path. Do your research before leaving the U.S. and rely on accredited local guides once you've reached your destination. And the MRTA is no worry at the moment. They've got their hands full with the residence, they don't have time to meddle with foreigners coming down to see the local flora and fauna."

"Any predictions on whether airfares will stay this low and how their dip is affecting South American tourism?"

"Jeanne, I'm not sure there's much of an effect. We have a theory at *Excursion* that people who have the time and interest to hang out in another culture are people willing to spend money on that luxury. I'd forgo dinner all week if it meant I could be in the Andes by Monday," David said, still grinning.

David's mother called soon after the segment aired. "The lighting on you was harsh, but you sounded great," she said. He could hear her eating on the other end of the line. Crunching something, an apple or a carrot. "I'm still surprised when I see you on TV. You seem like someone else, you've got a real knack for it. I have to kick myself to remember that it's really you."

David, embarrassingly impressed with his own performance, responded, "If that were me"—glib, slick, spewing glossy truths—"I'd shoot myself."

The crowd in the restaurant on Saturday morning was loud, distracting. The noise rose and then rose higher as David looked over the menu, making decisions, while Nadine ordered the fish soup and an endive salad. The waiter didn't write the order down, didn't even carry a notepad. David never understood this. People with such sophisticated memories, he figured, shouldn't be waiting tables.

"Oh," Nadine said, "and a café au lait with skim milk."

"We don't have skim milk," the waiter said.

"Can you do a skim cappuccino?"

"We don't have skim milk," the waiter said.

"Oh, fine. I'll just have a plain American coffee, skim milk on the side." Nadine looked at David and then at the waiter, challenging him.

"We don't have skim milk," he said, as if on replay.

"Fine, bring me a café au lait with whatever whole *lait* it is you stock." After the waiter walked away, Nadine explained, "You never know. How American of me to assume they'd have something lowfat in that bistro kitchen of theirs. This *is* America in the nineties, after all."

David immediately wished he were anywhere else. He'd even take Russia in the fifties or Spain during the Inquisition, after all. He was sure Nadine was just getting started. He'd called her for a date, if that was the name for this. In the two months since the night he'd walked out of her apartment, he'd rehashed the scene a number of times in his head. Life's full of missed opportunities, he could hear his mother say. "All men pass up the good things," that feminist guru was always lamenting on talk radio. But why? Why pass up the good things? Why let some pisser of a mood, some string of bad luck, a missing someone who may right now be alive and fine—given the stunning lack of evidence to the contrary—why let anything get in the way of one more chance at a good thing?

"I just want to make sure you got your glass back that night," David had said to Nadine when she picked up the phone on the first ring.

"I'm on the other line," she replied, "how about if I call you right back?" She did, twenty minutes later. "You weren't calling about the glass. That was months ago."

"It's just," David said, "that it looked like part of a set and I hate to see a family of crystal broken up."

"Thanks, David. I found the glass when I opened the door to look for you."

And now they sat across from each other in a haute French coffee shop not far from her east SoHo apartment. Saturday lunch. "A nonthreatening date. It'll be light out, and I rarely strip off my clothes before teatime," she'd said.

David watched her pour sweetener into her bowl of café au lait and listed, in his mind, her good points, all the reasons he'd decided to give her a second chance: She was Curt's ex-wife, so there was no fear she'd want commitment; she could make conversation with an unlit lamppost; she'd expect nothing from David except behavior better than his last performance. If he was going to have to start *getting out* (he knew, for his own quiet sanity, that he had to begin to nudge his life forward again), this would be a good start. Nadine would make a fine practice run. She had undeniable appeal: She was tall and dark, with chin-length hair that swayed when she turned her head to locate every unexpected sound in the restaurant and to eye every guy who walked in the door. She wore a mesh, see-through top to a casual lunch.

She was the complete antithesis of who David expected to be sitting with midday on a weekend and, as a result, he forced himself to be excited. At Ginny's birthday party, Annette had made David feel that he should be mourning—not just mourning Jessica, but lamenting all those life accomplishments she and Will had managed to accumulate and line up in perfect order. How dare she? David thought. As a child, David had coveted his older brother's independence, the six-string guitar he got for his twelfth birthday, his kickball prowess. But how dare Annette assume David would want the bounty Will now claimed as his own? So here David sat, doing his best imitation of wanting something different.

When the food arrived, Nadine reached her long arms over her head and stretched, first one side and then the other, as if preparing for a rough round of calisthenics. Then she picked up her spoon and started on her soup.

"I hear you and Curt are buddy-buddy these days," Nadine said, lifting the spoon to her lips and then putting it down.

"It's a small office."

"Mmmmm. Lots of big personalities and appealing little assistants, to hear him talk."

David wasn't sure how she expected him to respond, and at the same time wondered exactly how far Curt had tested the limit with their assistant. David was pretty sure that Curt, with all his boasting, was simply looking to push Nadine's eager little buttons. "Do you talk about your ex on all your dates?"

"Okay, no more Curt. But I'm not going to do all the first-date small talk. You were," she laughed, "at my wedding, after all."

The wedding had been one of the better parties David attended five years ago, maybe six by now. Two hundred people at the Players Club on Gramercy Park, women smoking in long dresses on the small balcony, David and Jessica, then his girlfriend, sneaking up to the club's restricted third-floor landing and making out—and then, between dinner and dessert, David in the men's room, taking a toke of Frank Bishoff's joint, one of David's few smokes since college, and placing money (he can't remember how much, it was all forgotten by morning) on the odds of Curt and Nadine making it through a full year of matrimony. They lasted eighteen months in the end.

Nadine was still spooning soup into her mouth and talking. She was a brash antidote to the rest of David's life. But what did she see in him? Why did she return his calls, respond to Curt's prodding that she should show him a good time? David looked at the other women crammed into the café, some in jeans, some in rumpled nighttime wear—slinky pants and slight, strappy tops—dressed up but looking unshowered, as if newly rolled out of their lovers' beds, having not been to their own homes since sometime yesterday. One woman sat alone. It had been a long time since David had really looked at the women around him.

"My sister-in-law threw a fit on me," David said to Nadine when they were done with their meals and finishing their coffees.

"A fit? What kind of fit? A hissy fit?" Nadine asked. She looked David directly in the eye as she spoke. "I love that word. I love hissy fits."

"She thinks I should be falling apart at the seams. Like maybe I should have random crying fits throughout the day." Annette had implied, David thought, that his behavior—his lack of behavior—was wrong, that his response to this situation, *this entirely undefined situation*, was completely inadequate. She'd left her implied accusations with David and now he couldn't shake them.

Nadine laughed. There was a joke in here that David had missed. "Oh, David," she said when it became clear that the humor had passed him by, "crying fits wouldn't suit you at all. Can you imagine? The whole teary-eyed thing is so false these days, faux torment. People only cry in movies."

"Or at the movies," David said, surprised to find Nadine's charm working, to find himself smiling, leaning toward her. He pushed his coffee away from the edge of the table.

"Even that, the crying in the theater thing, went out of style when Katharine Hepburn left the business," she said.

David ran the actress's filmography through his mind. "No one cried at Katharine Hepburn movies."

"Did I say they did?" Nadine asked. "So what's your sister-in-law got that you should be jealous of? Your brother? You don't want him, right? I mean, you don't want to be shacking up with him. He always seemed like a bore to me. Well-meaning, but, you know." She paused. "Seriously, you could have that if you wanted. There are plenty of Wills out there for the taking," she grinned.

"Still—" David tried to keep up with Nadine. He'd never heard anyone call Will a bore before. He worked to remember what exactly had set Annette off.

"David, darling, since when did you start taking stock of what people who've married into your family have to say? A sister-in-law can be out of your life in the time it takes to sign an alimony check."

David nodded. She was right.

They paid their restaurant bill and Nadine stretched again before sliding into her jacket. Outside, David asked, "Am I supposed to walk you back to your apartment? I'm rusty on day-date etiquette."

Nadine pulled up her sleeve and checked her watch. "I need to do some shopping. Unless you've got a yen for some afternoon nookie, we can part here."

"Sure."

They stood in silence, as if waiting for the date to conclude on its own volition, until Nadine spoke. "David, we can try the nighttime thing again. Dinner—you remember, the evening meal—sometime soon. Take some time, then call me. It'll be a surprise." She pulled her scarf tight and hoisted her bag onto her shoulder. "I love surprises. Or you could not call, that would be a surprise too. You decide."

Peru 1992

The apartment is silent when David enters. At first he thinks Jessica isn't home. David has been away for two months—the first three weeks on honeymoon with Jessica, the remainder of the time spent down in Peru alone. In the nearly six weeks they've been apart, their frequent phone conversations have been short and stilted—he in Peru with all sorts of excuses (bad phone lines, altitude sickness, sources only available at strange hours, power outages, culture shock), she in New York with the city's characteristic nonchalance to fall back on. Neither of them has ever been much good on the phone anyway, but as the last few weeks wore on, their phone calls grew increasingly halting, full of guilt and resentment and false charm and ill-placed humor. Now David is back, and as he looks around his New York living room, he feels like things should seem somehow *different*. This is his first time in his home as a married man.

David is weary from the all-day flight. He can barely remember last night, which he is telling himself is only a dream. There had been a fire in Lima, sources killed. Mere hours after the inferno, an entire nightclub reduced to ash and demolition, he'd booked his flight home and made his way to the airport. And now he is finally in New York again, where Lima isn't even in the news. He can barely remember buying his plane ticket, boarding the plane. What he does remember is the moment he ran from one terminal to another in the Miami airport, stopping (*Foolish! This is how people miss connections!* he'd thought) to place a quick call to New York. He'd hunched inside the pay phone's small *cabaña* and tried to picture Jessica while the phone rang.

"I'm on my way home, I'm in the airport right now," he told her when she answered. "Honey, I'll see you tonight."

"Seriously?" she said. "Thank God. It's time."

But now he is back home and there is no welcome party. Why should there be? From the signs in the living room (today's paper spread open, a can of club soda half empty on the coffee table, two lamps lit) life has proceeded without him. There's been a whole month of Jessica's life, of the start of their life together, which he's missed. A week or two: that's how long he'd told her he'd need to get the story. But he stayed in Peru more than twice that, in the end.

He sees the light on in the bedroom, and pushes the door open. There, on the bed, fully clothed but under the covers, fast asleep and curled into herself, lies Jessica. His footsteps are purposely heavy and loud, but she doesn't move when he walks into the room. She stays put, as if she's been lying motionless in this exact position for the past month. When David walks around the bed, he sees that her eyes are wide open.

The bed creaks as Jessica sits up quickly, as if startled. "Oh," she says.

"I—" David begins to speak. He looks at Jessica, who seems so tired and drained. And beautiful. She looks beautiful, quiet. As her legs dangle over the edge of the bed, not quite touching the ground, she appears somehow stranded and somehow serene. While David searches for the right greeting, Jessica speaks, saving him.

"You're here," she says, the small words drawn out, her mouth almost in a smile, but only briefly. David sits on the bed next to her and they lightly kiss. They spend a few moments simply looking at each other, taking it all in. Then, abruptly, she looks down to button up the shirt she is wearing and says, "I thought you'd be home earlier." Her voice isn't quite accusatory, but *still*. Where does she think he's been? He called from Miami only four hours ago. Sure, his take-off ended up delayed, but only by twenty minutes. And even without delays, it would've been tough to get here much sooner. Is this how things will be from now on? Will he have to account for all of his comings and goings?

"Stuck on the tarmac," David says. "I got here as fast as I could." *Miami's as south as you can get and still be in this country*, he wants to say, but holds his tongue. He already owes Jessica so much.

And now there is silence again. He lays his hand on her knee. She tenses up and then relaxes, as if easing into the idea of having David around again.

Immediately after he'd sent Jessica home from Peru, David began investigating Derek Mark Jhensen's whereabouts. For a few days, the South American news agencies and papers had been interested in the story as well. But with no leads, and Jhensen having been neither seen nor heard from in three months, they all assumed he'd either fallen victim to nature (dumb hiker, alone in the mountains) or been drawn into the drug trade. The South American press easily believed that Jhensen, like so many stupidly curious and illegally ambitious businessmen from around the world, had noticed the profits coming out of Peru's cocaine industry (free money, white gold, Peruvian flake: "a gift from the Gods," the Andeans had labeled coca a full century ago) and decided to get involved. After all, Jhensen had previously shown a proclivity for getting tangled up in illegal activity. How far a fall was it from skirting environmental laws to growing illegal substances? It was all exploitation of the earth, when looked at from the right, or wrong, angle.

Jhensen had last been seen in Tingo Maria, a hotbed for coca growing and the site of the largest domestic coca kitchens: square, bare rooms where farmers' wives carefully dissolved the plants' leaves in paraffin and hydrochloric acid, creating the paste that would later, after a bath in acetone, turn into the white powder blow in which so many of David's friends found solace during their college years. David could see the ways this might be alluring to an American like Jhensen. Something from his youth, something a little risky to counteract the staid life he'd been living. But there was no proof.

And with no one coming forward to claim having seen Jhensen—no one from the mountains, none of the government's spies, no one close to the drug trade, the news agencies quickly decided that Jhensen was already dead. The mountains were dangerous: hypothermia, hypoxia, snakebite, guerrilla terrorists. They reported that Jhensen was already likely dead, and the United States papers gave up on the story soon as well. They all ran early articles about the shock of Derek Mark Jhensen disappearing, this well-established, high-profile northwesterner. But when they saw that there was no *ending* to this story, no pat wrap-up, no easy clues to follow, they stopped covering it. Only David and Martín Diaz, a cameraman/producer for Channel 4, thought there might be more. "People are so macho. People pretend that stupid gringos disappear all the time. But they do not, not with no trace. There is always a trail, somebody speaking up with clues," said Martín. And Jhensen was no stupid gringo, thought David.

David spent five days in Lima doing research with Martín, and then traveled for two weeks in the north of Peru where Jhensen had last been seen. "This is what they say: A man's past is the best place to see his future," Martín said before David left. In the mountains David did his best to reconstruct Jhensen's first two months in Peru, before he disappeared. Jhensen had left a trail along his way. He hadn't simply disappeared into thin air, but had traveled on a path from *here* to *here*, destination to destination, and so on, until it became impossible to determine where that path finally landed. Or which cliff it fell off. It wasn't as if Jhensen had been careless in covering up his tracks, but as if he simply hadn't taken the time to explicitly lay out where those tracks led.

Following the clues up north, David interviewed local drug trade experts, a truck driver who transported Jhensen from Caraz to the Huascarán, vendors who spotted him in the markets, a maid who cleaned his room in Trujillo (the room full of nothing but the exact things David and Jessica had lugged to Peru—toiletries, rolls of film, a travel diary, spare soap), and student organizers with whom the trekker crossed paths. David gathered lots of color, just the sort of details that Americans love in their magazine articles: local Andean myths recounted by women who'd grown up in the mountains, oral histories of the men who trekked coca over the border to Bolivia, quotes from students who'd shared lunch with Jhensen as he passed through their towns. While David found no concrete clues to Jhensen's current whereabouts, he found a likely theory. He could paint a picture, convincingly, of how Jhensen would have found himself caught up in the drug trade. The only other likely avenue (besides a natural death) was the possibility that he'd encountered the Shining Path or the MRTA. But the MRTA—more revolutionaries than terrorists, upper-class kids violently fighting for a Marxist cause—didn't kill randomly. And the Shining Path didn't kill without publicizing their acts afterward.

Once back in Lima, David got on the phone and sold the story on spec to one of the few U.S. glossies still willing, in this media recession, to run the occasional long investigative piece that they deemed, for some reason (the exotic locale, the drug angle, Jhensen's name—that EnvirCor dude gone missing!), sexy. They'd have liked an ending, but were as convinced as David that story itself could be rich and worthy. "We want details," they told David. "Can you talk to a drug exporter?" Sure, David had already spoken with one, a minor middleman in

Huaraz who didn't give his name and whom David barely believed. *But he would do*. It was that easy. Over the course of two days spent mainly on the phone to Seattle, he interviewed Jhensen's business partner and his sister. While Peru provided the story's color, it was these interviews that most excited David's editors in New York, the idea of this somewhat famous American taking a new, more delinquent, path. David was astounded how quickly the combination of *drugs* and *South America* and *wealthy American* got the press's blood pumping, especially with David on the scene already.

Aside from his consulting firm's past legal snafu, Jhensen's business, now more than a decade old, was one of the largest in the northwest, doubling its profits in the past two years as the region grew increasingly dense with start-ups and high-tech properties eager to expand fast. Jhensen and EnvirCor had now made enough money—real cash, not fake paper millions—to hire managers and directors who could run the office while he traveled. He'd always traveled, but having his name dragged through the U.S. press had made him only more eager to get away, to be somewhere else. These days, the firm was really run by Dan Allegra, Allegra explained to David, while Jhensen traveled for months at a time, upscale-roughing it, hiking and climbing in remote undiscovered locales but sleeping in tents outfitted with four-poster beds and complete with continental breakfast. Occasionally, according to Allegra (who talked on incessantly, hoping to keep David on the case, hoping to find his old friend and partner), Jhensen slept outside by ancient ruins without even a tarp, but always with a porter and a cook nearby. He wasn't married, had no kids. This "getting away" was what he'd worked so hard for for so many years. But in Peru, he'd entirely shed his entourage and had traveled without a guide, only occasionally hiring locals to point him to the right trail or carry his bags over a high-altitude pass. The idea of this particular man turning to drugs, which is where his travels through Trujillo pointed, made for a good story.

After David returned from the mountains, he remained in Lima typing up his notes, even though he knew he should be heading back to New York; there was no more on-site research to be done. Still, he stayed. Each day he spoke with increasingly tertiary sources, and visited the U.S. embassy where Tommy Kenderman, the deputy in charge of David, finally admitted, "We're as stumped as you are, there's truly nowhere left to look." David himself had already trod through Huaraz and Trujillo and Tingo Maria in the north, through much of Lima and its suburbs, spoken with local activist and regional leaders and the men who truly knew the mountains. David acknowledged that Jhensen could be just about anywhere in those impossibly vast thousands of square miles of deserted mountains—ranges marked by nothing more specific than the natural erosion and etched Incan symbols and the occasional out-of-date political slogan. There were many places that one man or his body could possibly be.

What had David been looking for? That's what Jessica wants to know right now.

"Did you find it?" she asks tentatively. When David doesn't respond, she repeats herself, "Did you *find* it?" Her voice sounds ready to break, as if this is the question she'd been saving up, the sentiment she'd been afraid to voice on all of their forced phone calls.

"What?"

"Whatever was so important it was worth your staying there." She rises abruptly, walks out of the bedroom and into the apartment's narrow aisle of a kitchen with David following her.

Jessica stands among David's things. Six months before the wedding, they'd moved in together, into this cramped one-bedroom where David had lived alone for three years. His old bachelor pad. Jessica has added a few touches, but seeing as they hadn't planned to live here for long, much of her stuff remains in boxes. She has been, essentially, living in someone else's home. For the past month, she's been living there without that someone else.

"I got a story," David says. This is the first time he's truly done this. After nearly a decade in journalism, feeling like a fraud (moving ahead because he is skilled with office politics, pleasant to have around, accurate and quick with his writing—but never because he'd gotten a big scoop of his own or found his way inside a story no one else could crack), he's proven himself. This is a sort of relief he hadn't known he was looking for. "It's over now. I'm home, it's good to be home," he says. "Come on, tell me what's been going on. I've missed this place." He reaches out toward her.

She pauses as if carefully considering what to say. "People *call*. They want to know how the honeymoon was. Or when we can come over for dinner. Or if we'll be at the museum party. And I smile—I'm on the phone, they can't even see me, but I smile just in case they can sense it." She breathes deeply. "And I say, 'Gee, the honeymoon was swell,' or 'I'm not sure this week is great for a get-together, I'll be sure to ask David once he gets home.' And to good friends, when they call I say, 'No, really, it's a *great story* he's working on, my husband, really exciting for both of us.'" David flinches, but remains silent, and Jessica continues, steady and stronger now, "And all the while I'm speaking to you, on a different continent, as if it's all great. What's the option? Call you home and feel like I've taken you off the most important story of your life, just so you can act married?" Her voice is suddenly tightly coiled, taut and ready to spring. "It's been a freaking fun summer, David."

David steps back from her sudden antagonism. They are facing each other—he in the kitchen doorway, her back pressed up against the refrigerator—in a space barely big enough for the two of them. David wonders if, when she chose to walk deep into the kitchen, she perhaps forgot that there was no emergency exit at the back of the room. "You don't have a clue," he says.

David had enough research for his story weeks ago. He had more on Jhensen than anyone else in the States; the Jhensen coverage there had been thin. David's story would be jam-packed with local color and theories, and interviews with experts, and a few quotes from Jhensen's parents, and anecdote after anecdote from Dan Allegra. David knew this kind of exclusive story might be once-in-a-lifetime for him, for the kind of guy who doesn't find himself on the path of intriguing tales as often as he finds himself sitting behind a desk.

But even long after David *had* this story, he stayed in Peru. His life in New York began to feel distant, and at the same time remarkably permanent. That life wasn't going anywhere. This opportunity to live in Peru, however, was momentary. Martín and the others at the station (guys who came to dinner and yammered about politics and soccer and the local energy problem) didn't ask about David's life back home. He'd thought they'd be fascinated by his American existence, by all the hot, hip American advantages (True democracy! Plastic surgery! Texas!) that David took for granted. But the U.S. held no allure for Martín and his pals. To them, the U.S. was simply another corrupt country not worth visiting. Martín knew that David had a new wife, that she was here in Peru until a month ago. But Martín didn't ask for details; he rarely mentioned his own wife, who lived with her family outside the city, in a house where Martín stayed when he could get a full twenty-four hours away from the station. Peru was a country that prided itself in family, but which, at the same time, prioritized the *here and now*. Martín lived within the confines of whatever story he was working on that very minute. To David—who had been living outside the boundaries of his own day-to-day life ever since Jessica returned to the U.S.—this was a sort of relief.

So David remained in Peru. He would have Jessica for the rest of his life. This is the vow they had signed off on, for better or worse. So while in Peru, at night he went drinking or dancing with Martín or Marguerite or alone. *This is what Jhensen did.* He went away and immersed himself and became part of all these different, distant worlds, the greater world—there is real appeal to this. David could feel it. He thought about how easy it was to spend your whole life in your hometown, in some small nook you'd created for yourself or fallen into and were too distracted to claw your way out of. Jhensen spent months at a time thousands of miles from any discernible nook.

David could sense the appeal, firsthand.

During the days, David took long lunches with Tommy Kenderman at the white-tablecloth joints near the embassy. He spent a number of afternoons at the studio of a young artist, a friend of Martín's. Cienfuegos was in his early twenties and habitually clad in Adidas track shoes and slim corduroys and wiry dreads and, as Martín made sure to mention, he had crossed paths with Derek Mark Jhensen.

"I thought he would buy a piece; he came here to look. Rich Americans like my work," Cienfuegos told David on David's first visit to the artist's studio. "I had a exhibition in Los Angeles, it has been two years ago." Cienfuegos was anxious, nervy. On the walls of his workspace hung canvases covered with bits of debris (food labels, newsclippings, frayed wire, sea glass, parts of bedframes) mirroring the piles of trash on the beach outside his window. In Barranco, the posh suburb that many of Lima's artists called home, the road to the beach was lined with large, sprawling stone residences, some hidden by well-kept gardens, many guarded by armed security men posted outside the iron gates. But the beach itself was piled high with small mounds of trash. In place of sand dunes sat heaps of food containers and soda cans and broken bottles and food crates. Bits of unidentifiable appliances, plastic fused to metal. "Some people say, 'Oils and canvases are expensive, so he turns to trash.' People talk, I don't care," Cienfuegos said, taking a drag on his cigarette.

"Derek was going to come back but he didn't," Cienfuegos told David the second time they met, out of the studio, at a dance club where Martín and his pals spent their late nights.

J essica stands at attention in the back corner of the kitchen. David picks up a water bottle from the counter. "There was this artist," he says, pacing his words. "Did you even go to the beach that day? That day we got back to Lima after leaving Puerto Maldonado, when I decided to investigate Jhensen and you went off to do your own thing? Did you take that bus tour to the beach? It's outrageous, it's a dump, literally a dump, the beach in Lima, a fucking dump, and this kid, this little club kid artist boy found some beauty in it all, you know? He saw enough—"

"Five weeks later you suddenly ask what I did that day? Your timing sucks. Okay, here's what I did: I took a crappy tourist van with a scrawny girl-guide who sported a whole season's worth of Maybelline and five-inch heels and I went to Pachamamac because the goddamn tour was the only thing going on that day and I wasn't going to sit around waiting for you, and I wasn't going to hang out in Lima and absorb all the fucked-up karma of that city. And then I took the tour bus back and waited for you to return from your little day of investigating, all satisfied and apologetic. But you came back chock full of your journalistic bravado and Encyclopedia Brown investigation plans. As if I were just a fawning little office intern who really gave a shit. You know? Why fight that? Why get in your way?"

David doesn't remind her how easily she'd acquiesced to his staying down there, how many openings he'd given her to speak her mind back *then*, when there was still time for him to change his mind, to board her plane to New York. She'd said nothing at the time. And now, as the silence grows, their eyes locked, neither willing to look away, David finally speaks, says what he needs to. And what he truly means.

"I'm *sorry*." I love you, he thinks. I love you, I'm sorry, I love you, the words a silent mantra, willing a response in kind from Jessica. A response which David is certain he doesn't deserve. In Peru, he'd felt her buried resentment grow as he'd lengthened his trip, as he'd resisted coming home.

"Do you know what it feels like to be left behind? I've been playing the worn-out role of the scorned housewife, sitting home waiting. Do you know what it feels like? It's my worst fear, David." Her tone is steady now.

Her worst fear? David knows she can imagine worse; they talked about worse fates just recently, while she was still in Peru. *Plummeting in a crevasse*. Being sacrificed off a mountain top, falling victim to South American terrorists—aren't these fates worse? Not from the look on Jessica's face, hard and angry and scared. "I'm so sorry," David tells her. "I love you," he says.

"I know," Jessica says. "I know that."

In Lima, at night, Martín took David to El Floridita. From the outside, the club looked like a tourist disco. The back-lit sign featured a drawing of a pink flamingo. Inside, the long bar was lit with blue neon light. A small spiral staircase led down to a basement where a mirrored disco ball was strung from the ceiling. The walls were hung with deep scarlet bedsheets. A DJ spining from turntables balanced on plastic milk crates. A bar in the corner. David was reminded of parties in high school when someone's parents were away and a keg was rolled into their half-finished basement.

On David's first night there, Martín fetched him a beer and then wandered off, leaving him alone. David didn't want to dance—he was clumsy, he had no rhythm—but a woman pulled him into the crowd, smiling and nodding as if already aware that he and she had a spoken-language barrier, and he found it easier to give in than to resist. She set him in motion, helped him move in time to the music. Once David had it, got the hang of it—marveling at first at what Jessica would think (she'd like the sight of him out here, she might pull him close, whisper in his ear, incredulous and maybe excited, or perhaps simply confused, *but you hate to dance!*) and then letting himself fall into the Latin techno beat—he could not remember why he had not wanted to dance, why he'd thought he had no rhythm.

At three that morning, David was still dancing, exhausted and happy. When he finally sat, Martín said, "Almost time to go home. The young kids will go crazy soon. They start to come down from their highs." On the edge of the crowd Cienfuegos moved frenetically to his own beat. Martín continued, grinning broadly, "This is fun, no? You, gringo, I saw you smile—as rare as an honest politician in Lima. That makes me a hero, no?"

"That makes you a superstar, at least," David said, conscious of his own lazy smile. He'd tried to remember the last time he had fun without intending it, without planning it ahead of time, without forcing it into its place.

Jessica's presence seems so small compared to the women

David had danced with in Lima. The women at El Floridita were all expansive gestures and rhythmic energy.

David reaches out to Jessica and is surprised when she comes to him. He holds her tightly, and then pulls away slightly to look at her face. She shakes her head. David leans back against the kitchen cabinets and scans the room—the trash can catches his eye. On top, the postcard he'd sent just ten days ago. He'd expected to beat it home, international mail being so unreliable. The picture-side of the card, sporting a cheesy Technicolor image of the president's palace, is facing down. It was hilarious, David had thought when he bought it, glorifying such a corrupt government with a cheery mass-market image. He'd picked up the card on his way to an interview with a university professor, an expert on land management, who'd had dinner with Jhensen early in his journey. On the way to the interview, David bought the card and then sat in a coffee shop, just outside the university's grounds, and felt the pressure of what to write to his wife. He imagined all of all the campy clichés a guy could write. He could make Jessica laugh, if he wanted, out of all this. He could make her smile, he could still do this. God, they'd had fun together in Cuzco and the jungle. He could match the text of the postcard to the trite tourist image on the front. *Wish you were here!* came to mind. But he stopped himself. He knew this was an opportunity. Regardless of the fact that he assumed this postcard wouldn't reach Jessica for weeks, until after he'd likely be home, he knew this was a small opportunity to smooth things over and make all that would follow just a bit less difficult.

David had eyed the ornate iron gates that secured the single-family houses lining the block, and he thought about why he was still in Lima, and he thought about Jhensen. He took the cap off his pen and squared the postcard in front of him, and when everything was in place he wrote on the back of the card in a large, sharp script. "One man missing, another missing his wife," he had written. Across the street, men and women in business attire had streamed onto a rickety municipal bus. The espresso-maker behind him rattled and then stopped. *One man missing, one man missing his wife.*

Just ten days later the card's inscription faces up at David from the kitchen trash. Jessica follows David's gaze, and then looks up at David again, as if daring him to take the card out of the garbage. *She's thrown it out.* After he called to say he was on his way home? Who knows.

"This isn't how I'd planned to welcome you home. I'm glad you're here. I am," she says.

"I wasn't going to stay in Peru forever, you know that," David responds. "I should have come home ages ago. I'm sorry." David watches himself talking in circles, apology-as-mantra, and knows this isn't enough, but doesn't know what else he can do, what Jessica wants now that he is here and his misdeed is done.

Most nights in Lima, David went out to El Floridita, to the movies, wherever. For so long he'd dreamt of living the perfect status quo, and now when he'd gotten his hold on it—marriage, the right friends, a hip and steady job, all the pieces locked in place—he was, it seemed, avoiding it. Jhensen, too, had stepped out of his life to try something new, in Peru, where it all was so different. David wondered about the paths he himself sped past on the road to this easy life in New York, a life which suddenly seemed not as inevitable. Does Jessica wonder about this as well?

Most nights he went out in Lima, but last night David had opted to stay in his hotel room to get some work done. He'd sat on the bed arranging and rearranging his research and interview notes. He wasn't sure how to conclude the Jhensen article. David reread his interview with a Peruvian journalist who had spent three years in the north studying the drug flow. "The local coca farmers are fleeing now," he'd said. "The government has cut down their trade, they can't make money. But there are still fields there, to be harvested by a person willing to risk the trek over the Andes. There is a place for a foreigner to come in, an observant and resourceful foreigner. A brave foreigner," he'd said, alluding to the Shining Path's continued influence over the north. The terrorist group controlled much of the drug trade in that part of the country, keeping an eye on the coke's movement and a hand in the profits.

Yes, this would be a fine story, David acknowledged as he sat on the bed, surrounded by notes and maps and press releases and a few receipts Jhensen had signed along the way and that David has been lucky enough to get his hands on.

David was jolted by the ring of the hotel room phone. He listened, waited, cracked his eyes open and saw, on the clock, that it was five in the morning. He'd dozed atop his research. He sat up quickly. It was five in the morning: an hour that never brought anything, he was sure, but bad news. *Jessica*. It would be six in New York. It had been two days since he'd called her. He lunged across the bed for the phone.

Martín was mumbling, as if already midsentence and drunk. His voice was barely audible. The light-tight blinds in David's room were shut and he didn't know if the sun was up yet or not. "What? Hey, Superstar. *Que?* You there?" David sat up straighter and oriented himself. He was tired, his head hurt, his eyes had yet to fully adjust. He could make out only the dark shape of the TV across the room. "Martín?"

"*El fuego*, David." Fire. "El Floridita. But you are okay. You are not inside the club." Martín took a deep breath. "Go back to sleep."

David's cab made it to El Floridita in less than fifteen minutes. Outside the club, David could barely determine what kind of trauma had taken place. Police barricades and the early hour kept the area clear. There was little crowd. As David neared the scene he eyed the cops, the few bystanders, the thickness of the air, the approaching morning. Only when he was almost on top of the barricades did he see the bodies. As if in a movie, the corpses, a dozen or so, lay parallel and were covered with sheets. A row of columns, like numbers or cornstalks or drinks set out on a bar, one next to the other, so the bartender had only to glide the bottle of rum or tequila or Pisco in a perfect line to slowly fill each of the glasses with minimum effort.

"Oh, man," David muttered, frantic. "Oh, *man*." David quickly reasoned to himself, worked out a proof: Martín was not dead, Martín called him on the phone and thus must be alive. And behind a camera, standing just inside the barricades, David spotted Martín, and called to him.

"Gringo," Martín said, walking quickly toward David and putting on a good face, as if David already knew the bad news and was in need of consoling. And slowly, silently, David began to cry, his tears heavy and silent, because whatever he was here looking for, whatever had kept him in this country, he was sure now that it was gone.

At just past 3 A.M. something inside (could have been a cigarette, Martín said, maybe the stereo equipment, eventually an investigation would clear it up) started a spark that caught on the sheets lining the walls of the basement. Under the sheets lay nothing but drywall, and the room went up in flames almost immediately. The only escape route was the small spiral staircase up to the upstairs bar. There was no smoke detector, fire alarm, sprinkler system.

"*Hombre*, it is a club, you know? The *policia*, yes, they are angry, there were too many people inside, the numbers should have been regulated. The fire would have started by the stairs, barricaded their path, like the shut door to a safe," Martín explained. "That is how it looks." No one in the basement survived.

Less than an hour ago, fire extinguished, the bodies had been carried up one by one. Thirty-six corpses. Martín listed names familiar to David. *Cienfuegos*, Raul Andiamos, *Marguerite*. The bodies had been found clustered in the small entryway to the stairs and in the center of the floor, away from the flaming walls.

"Cienfuegos, a kid," Martín spoke. "Okay, they tell me, I don't think they could have known what was happening. You lose consciousness like *that*. This is something to hope for."

David imagined how Cienfuegos would have rendered the scene. Flames erected from spare donut cartons and eggshells and wires, frayed wires rubbed smooth by the sand of the beach. David imagined himself, on a night when he was not so tired and did not go back to his hotel early to simply read over his notes, on a night when he too went to the club and was crazy dancing, partying until the flames felled him, threw his body onto one of the heaps, the heap the middle of the room, probably, away from the flaming walls. David tried to block the thought, to picture daylight, to picture tomorrow, or yesterday, when everything was all right.

"Go back to sleep," Martín said. David did not move. He could easily have been inside this club. "David, do you understand? It is okay." David saw the rubble in front of him and the bodies, the police.

Martín continued as if sure of himself, defeated but certain, "David, understand, this is a country where we lose people. Go back to your hotel."

* * *

David did go back to the hotel. He slept for two hours—a surprisingly easy sleep, as if his body knew that this trek was over and it was time to stock up on energy for the next—and then he grabbed his duffel from the closet and tossed his clothes and notes inside. And when there was nothing left to pack or straighten in the room, he quickly checked out of the hotel—as if making an escape—and hailed a taxi for the airport, where he nabbed a standby seat on a midday plane out of Lima and the next thing he knew he was huddled inside a phone booth in the Miami airport, shaking, speaking to Jessica.

I'm coming home, he'd said, his voice hiding his hurt and his desire for forgiveness and the thudding awareness of all he had risked. He has so much at stake.

David could have lost it all—everything he has just run home to—in a country he shouldn't have still been in anyway. His future is here, in New York. And now, with Jessica in front of him—she is the one who is shaking at this moment—his American existence suddenly looks so good. Is he too late? He opens his mouth to speak, to explain, but Jessica stops him.

"David," she says.

He nods, waits.

"We're both here now, you know? I want to move forward. Can't we just do that?" Jessica says.

"Yes," David responds, eager to put last night, and the last month, behind him. He knows he'll finish the article, it's nearly done anyway. They'll spend the hefty paycheck on a new home for him and Jessica. They need to get out of this cramped bachelor pad anyway. With a place of their own and some time together as a couple, David thinks, Jessica will forget this; she will forgive him. Everything will be okay.

1997

When David arrived home from work on Tuesday, he found a package outside his apartment door. The plain brown wrapper would have screamed *sex toys* if it hadn't been bound with high-glare foil ribbons. Jessica's mother's signature wrapping. Since Jessica's disappearance, her mother, Elaine, had been in the city often, staying with friends or at midlevel hotels. When Elaine came to town these days, more often than not she didn't even let David know she was here. She did, however, always make a point to ring Hallander and Gilchrest at the precinct, leaving them a number where she could be reached. Just in case. David knew this because the detectives, with whom he checked in every two weeks, told him. "I have a mother-in-law, too," Gilchrest said. Yeah, David thought, but you've still got the wife, the asset to balance out the mother-in-law debit. And now David could only think of Elaine as red ink.

He brought the package inside with him and put it, along with the mail, on the counter.

On top of the stack—David flinched, winced—a postcard from Jessica's dentist. *Time for your spring cleaning! Tick tock!* A notecard from a parallel universe where Jessica not only continued to exist, but had potential plaque buildup. Below the postcard, nothing but two bills and a thin housewares catalog boasting early spring sales.

Elaine's package contained a tin of her homemade dusty pecan cookies. Elaine was always bringing the cookies by when Jessica was around. She claimed Jessica loved them and always had. In truth, Jessica hated the crumbly biscuits and tossed them in the trash as soon as her mother was gone. Sure, as a kid she'd faked an appreciation: The cookies were the only thing her mother ever baked, and she figured the encouragement might spur Elaine to try whipping up something else, something that tasted good.

But she hadn't, and when nobody told her how bad the cookies were—"Low in sugar!" Elaine bragged on occasion; I can tell, David would respond silently—she assumed David liked them as much as she thought Jessica did. After David and Jessica married, Elaine sent the cookies often, prompting David and Jessica to joke about regifting them to unpleasant coworkers or leaving them out on the counter to ward off bugs. "Even roaches would rather starve!" they'd joked and laughed, going as far as to offer the cookies to Welford Manahan when he complained that his building had mice. "We've got a tin of cookies that will drive rodents away," and then they'd all laughed. But they never told Elaine and the cookies kept coming. We fooled her too well, David scolded himself. Then he wondered: If Jessica had pretended—*for her whole life*—to crave those cookies, what else had she faked? David couldn't imagine what her other charades might have been. Were the cookies merely a warm-up?

David looked at the new tin. This was the third batch Elaine had dropped off since Jessica's disappearance. Taped to the top of the tin was a business card: *Dr. Julianne Graham Dunn—Channeler.*

And a note in sloped, narrow letters: "She's been quite helpful, maybe you should pay her a visit. Be well—Elaine."

Pay her a visit. David put down the note. Pay being the operative word. *Helpful?* David hadn't seen any new evidence. David considered dropping the card into the box full of clippings in the corner of the kitchen, but instead dropped it in the trash.

D avid had received calls from a dozen supposed conduits-to-the-beyond—psychics, channelers, seers, people with hacking coughs and *unexplainable hunches*—in the first few months after the disappearance. Did these people scour the police files? Regardless of the fact that Jessica's case had been kept out of the paper, the psychic phenomenon experts caught wind. Did their sixth sense include an awareness of all the news that wasn't fit to print? The first time David found one of their messages on the machine—"I see your wife, and I see a field, and in the field there is a building with a flat roof and no windows, and, it looks like, a blue door"—he'd called the precinct, as if it might be a lead. The detective wrote it down and said, in an even, patient tone, that he'd keep an eye open for windowless buildings with blue doors in open fields. David understood the attitude that lay beneath the cop's words and chastised himself for even calling. From then on, when the messages came in—"I see a 1976 green hatchback with tinted windows" or "I see a gravel driveway" or "I see strawberries on a plate" or "I sense hostility and a river" or "There is a man nearby" or "I can feel her living aura"—when these messages came in, David pressed the machine's delete button before the speaker had time to finish the sentence. "She has a cat in her lap," one prophesizer began. David pushed the delete button. Jessica was a dog person.

Maybe it was a function of the passing of time, or perhaps it was simply the season, early March and starting to thaw, but suddenly, six months after Jessica was last seen, people—people whom David knew (people who could not be classified as telemarketers or psychics or relatives)—began to call again. Sally Dickenson—*"Hey, Jessica, I hope it's not my fault and I didn't leave you the wrong address before"*—even Sally called. She told David that Welford Manahan was trying to gather crew for a late winter lunch.

Recently when David had seen Sally she'd felt compelled to discuss Jessica and had proven oblivious to David's hints (shifting feet, wandering eyes, constant waves to people he didn't know across the room) that he'd rather not talk about Jessica. Proven oblivious? Sally was smart, sharp, eager to help. *Not oblivious*, just unwilling to let David change the subject or ignore it all together. *She just wanted to help.* Or to find a compatriot in her own grief. Still, David liked her. She'd been one of Jessica's favorites, and Jessica had been a fine judge of people. So David agreed to lunch with Sally and Welford and *the crew*. When David arrived at the restaurant, Welford motioned him to the seat across from Sally.

"Sorry I'm late," David said, sliding into his chair and leaning over to kiss Cate, next to him, on the cheek. "Deadlines."

"Absolutely," Welford said. Then, by way of an introduction to the two at the table David didn't know well—Thad Stillman and a woman named Marna dressed in head-to-toe taupe—"David's our token award-winning journalist. He's an editor."

"Oh! Do we have quotas now?" Sally Dickenson asked, sipping an iced tea. There were six of them at the rectangular table, with Cate and Welford holding down the ends.

David scanned the menu, one concise sheet filled with outrageously pricey tidbits. *Hamachi on Daikon* or *Homemade Duck Prosciutto* or *Venison with Lingonberries*. He could feed a Third World family for a year on one of Welford's lunch tabs. Feed a whole village.

"David, if you're into game, go for the bison. It's great, it'll incapacitate you for the rest of the day," Welford suggested.

"What I'm really into is bacon cheeseburgers." David grinned and laid his menu on the table. "But since you're paying, go ahead and bring on the game."

David thought about how, if Jessica were here, this is where she would knock his knee under the table and then maybe make a joke, aloud, about buffalo appearing at such a swank hotel restaurant. Something *about the cost*, maybe. I can just hear her say it, he thought, and then, not a moment later, he nearly did. But it wasn't her voice. It was Sally Dickenson's.

"Bison," said Sally. "I'm always thinking, I know it's a delicacy, but for forty-three dollars you should also get a pair of shoes made from the hide."

"When's the last time you bought a pair of shoes for forty-three dollars?" Cate asked.

David felt the conversation inch away from him and he struggled to find his place within it. Marna leaned toward Cate and winced. "I know!" Marna said. "Lespinasse just added a thirty-two dollar soup to their menu. It's a crime." She paused. "But it's delicious."

Welford leaned across the table and threw a lifeline to David, an attempt to save him from the female banter. "How *are* things?" he asked in a conspiratorial half-whisper.

"Things are fine, actually, fine," David said, reassuring and upbeat. He knew how easy it would be to drag down the mood of the whole crowd, and this wasn't what he wanted. What any of them wanted. On the other side of the table, Marna was now talking about her baby, her husband in L.A. on business this week, her nanny search, her attempts to retile her master bath.

Wood panels lined the restaurant's walls and David let his eyes rest on one of the perfect cherry slabs. The last time he'd been here was for a fashion industry press event, the showing of a resort collection right after he'd started work at *Excursion*. He'd leaned against one of these walls and ended up discussing, with an editor from one of the women's monthlies, how soft and perfect the wood was, as interesting to look at as any intentional work of art. At the time, that conversation had seemed important.

"They've got two works—one Zuniga and a Tamayo mixograph—stuck in customs in Mexico City." Thad Stillman was explaining why Sotheby's had contracted his law firm. "They won't let them out. And the Tamayo's only a mixograph, not even a one-of-a-kind."

"Save room, we're ordering the spun sugar for desert!" Cate said when there was a pause in the conversation.

David's eyes rested on the walls again. Living this life is an art, he thought, one that he had studied and enjoyed but that, for the moment, was no longer his. He was looking for a distraction, had been since the moment he walked in, hoping someone else would arrive and join them. But who? And he realized, as he looked at the women at the tables around them, he was looking for Nadine. He was wishing someone would show up, someone not sporting Ferragamo shoes, someone without Chanel sunglasses perched on her head and, while that description would suit Jessica fine (she'd have arrived at this lunch in a simple sweater, her hair sleek in a ponytail, perhaps, and she'd have whispered into David's ear, "It's a good free meal, put *that* on our list"), the person he was wishing for was not Jessica. Her name hadn't even crossed his mind. Because she wasn't going to show up. At least not here. Maybe today she was somewhere else eating her own luxe lunch. But at this moment, Jessica wasn't what David craved.

At home that night, David stared into the refrigerator. At lunch they had all talked about how big the portions were, how obscene, how they never had room left for dinner after eating bison and steak tartare and heaps of spun sugar at noon. Each and every one of them left a third of the meal on the plate, complaining about how they couldn't eat another bite. This was the ritual. Now, five hours later, David was hungry again. He opened his fridge and crouched to look deep inside. Three types of mustard. An eight-month-old jar of cornichons, an industrial-sized tub of mayonnaise, left-over take-out roast chicken, apples long past their prime, packets of soy sauce and duck sauce and Chinese mustard, a pot of apricot jam, a chocolate bar from David couldn't remember when, the cookies from Jessica's mother that he hadn't worked up the nerve to throw out, half a turkey sandwich from last week, wilted lettuce, congealed salad dressing. You are what you eat—or maybe what you've *left behind to rot*—David thought as he pulled out a stale package of stone ground crackers and a jar of dijon mustard, promising himself that tomorrow he'd buy some real food, tomorrow he'd work on figuring out what real, living people stocked in their cabinets.

J essica's mother's psychic had spotted Jessica in Eastern Alberta. In a vision. And Elaine called David to report this.

"Did she spot Jessica?" David asked. "Or just her aura?" David thought he spotted her aura all the time, but usually it was just a coffee stain or shower curtain mildew or someone else's body odor. "Because if it's her aura, I'd be happy to just leave it alone."

"She spotted her, and right where she spotted her there have been three serial murders. One serial murderer, but three victims, at least. It was on CNN International, on the computer. I looked it up. They recently caught the man. There may have been even more victims that they don't even know about. But one of the victims they found a few months ago is still unidentified and that's what Juliann Graham Dunn saw."

"Are you okay?" David asked. Was Elaine being serious?

"I told the police. They're looking into it. They are going to call Canada, or whatever the procedure is."

"What exactly did the cops tell you?"

"That if this unidentified victim had matched Jessica's description from the start, we'd probably have heard about it earlier. But she's my girl, I know it's her. She's really gone, David." Elaine's voice was soft and earnest and yearning, and David heard how hard she was trying to believe herself. And he heard how hard she wanted, *needed*, to hear David support her as well. *She and he against the disbelieving police*, this seemed to be what she was aiming for. But David couldn't rally to the cause.

He knew two things for sure. First, the body in Canada wasn't his wife's. If it were Jessica, the police would have made the connection themselves already. Second, he agreed with Elaine about the fact that, yes, Jessica really was gone. But not dead. Like a shock that had been with him all along, David realized he knew this now for sure. How could she be dead? There were no signs, no body, no struggle. She's my baby, he thought. She's alive, just not looking to be found. *She's alive.* Could he have held onto her tighter, kept her right here? He could have been a more attentive husband, but who couldn't? Whatever it was that had set Jessica off, David knew it wasn't a spousal misstep. It wasn't only him that she'd left, if she'd left. And he'd loved her. He loved her.

He remembered something he'd heard once, an offhand comment from a Peruvian in the mountains, pieced together in broken English: People who don't want to be found aren't. *She's gone.* He tried out these words, and let them round out in his mouth, let them come sharply into the air, into the room. *She's alive*, he listened to these words, trying to decipher in their stresses, in their affect, their *truth*—whether it was to be trusted or whether it was merely something he'd found a way to believe. And he understood: She could be doing *this*, he thought, looking at himself, at his desk, poring over his memories of the past and looking forward at the same time, figuring and figuring out, finding ways to move ahead in the right direction, on a new trail. Or maybe not. He sat with this image for days, trying it out until it settled in and felt right. If Elaine was being allowed her own certainty in her own misplaced theories, David figured that gave him leeway to believe the sharp thoughts making the rounds in *his* likely misguided head.

And then, with Elaine so sure of her daughter's death that she could easily place Jessica's face on any conveniently unidentified body, David, sure his wife was alive—but gone to him—could suddenly picture her nowhere. But he could imagine a time in the future when he might look around and see Jessica, really see her, or some shadow of hers, everywhere.

How easy it had been to think he'd known her: *to really know someone else*. He considered this possibility and its defects. There had been, he reminded himself, good times. Right now he could barely even remember her. But later, someday? Someday, when she'd been long gone, maybe he would notice her on the street in the form of another woman, or coming out of the school where she taught—*Oh, no, Jessica was taller than that*—or perhaps two rows in front of him in a movie theater, possibly on a ski slope—*But wait, Jessica always favored her left-side turn*. He might hear her in a voice on the radio, or next to him in the supermarket, or across the street and suddenly gone. He could imagine the structure of a building reminding him of her shape, the veins of a leaf, a certain wall color might bring her to mind.

Lemon yellow, the color she'd insisted they paint the kitchen and that now reminded him of his loss every time he walked toward the fridge with his eyes open and the lights on. In the future, when she was so far gone that the people she knew would somehow be out of his life, when he'd stopped *questioning*, he could imagine locating her, some small arcane impulse of hers, when he spotted, out of the corner of his eye, a car parked at an awkward angle.

The second time Elaine called, two days later, she was even more convinced that the body in Canada was Jessica's and she wailed into the phone. She was mourning, grieving. And David, the skeptic, emotionally selfish, sure of his own theories, caught up in his own ruses and day to day distractions and absolute truths, would not allow her grief to draw him out. He shielded his center and rushed Elaine off the phone, "Elaine, I'm not even sure what you're talking about anymore. It's just a random body."

A day later, in his office, David closed the door. He reached for his atlas and flipped to North America, page B78. He inked over the places that Jessica would never be, dead or alive. He blackened out North Dakota. He put the Florida panhandle in shadow. He made a large X over the state of Texas. He covered Baltimore and Las Vegas with opaque dots. He thought hard about Illinois, so nebulous, and decided to let it go for now. Alabama. He felt comfortable negating Alabama in black ink. Ditto for Oklahoma. He raised his eyes past Maine to Canada— which for the first ten years of his life he thought was merely a really big state—and paused. This was why he had opened the atlas, wasn't it, so he could confront Canada? So innocuous on the page, so wild, big and blank, devoid of the masses of boundary lines and rivers that made the U.S. a wrinkled mess. You wouldn't know it was home to, to what? Certainly not his wife's body. This certainty—Jessica wasn't an anonymous unclaimed victim, not in Canada, not here—was something, finally, that he could assert to himself without question. Something on which he could slowly take hold.

SEPTEMBER 1991

David squints at the sun, which rests a few fingers above the horizon. It's not late enough in the day to really catch fish, but still, David and his father sit in a rented canoe, in the middle of the pond, with their lines in the water. When the silence between them has gone on too long, one of them reels in his line and casts again, the whirr of the running filament taking up the space created by the silence. *Look,* David's father says, motioning with his head to the shore to the left of them, far away. *They're building on that lot. Nothing has ever been there.*

Here, at this far end of the pond, reeds rise straight out of the water, and the shore itself is piled high with wild grasses and small saplings. Larger trees are set back further. And to the left, where David's father has motioned, sits a large expanse of open land like an immense, lush, manicured lawn. It is private land; David can't imagine why it took so long for someone to develop it, to build a house, which is apparently what's going up at this very moment. This is the pond David's father fished on when he was a young man, and now it is where, in the early fall, he likes to come with his sons.

That land could have been yours for the price of a movie ticket thirty years ago, David says to his father.

If only I weren't so fond of movies, David's father says. *I saw some great flicks in the early sixties.*

David sits in the front of the canoe, looking over the prow of the boat, his back to his father. So he only hears the man's voice—doesn't see him—but he doesn't need to see him to know he is smiling. David hears a good-natured groan and he turns. His father holds an empty hook. *Something took my worm,* he says—they are fishing for bass and brown trout using nightcrawlers—*and I didn't even feel it.* He reaches for the styrofoam canister of crawlers, then stops. *Hand me the tackle box? I think I'll try a lure. Maybe I'll have more luck.*

David hands the box to the back of the boat and then looks forward again, at his own line, limp in the water. He hears his father shuffling through the lures. Slowly David reels his line in. It is good to be away, to be on a boat in the middle of the pond. It is good to be in a canoe, a vessel that can only comfortably seat two, so that a boy and his father can make a clean getaway without his mother or brother or girlfriend tagging along. Jessica is back home in the city. A guy and girl, just because they have been dating for a year and a half, don't need to spend every waking minute together. But still, David feels guilty. And he feels like, out in a boat with his father, it's the kind of moment, in the movies at least, where there is revelation, insight. So he throws his line back out, looks straight ahead, and says, *Jessica and I have been going out for over a year.*

Sure, his father answers. His father isn't a judgmental man; he likes Jessica. He assumes, David knows, that if David is dating her there must be a reason. She must be worthy.

I feel like I'm supposed to know what happens next, you know? Supposed to know whether I want to marry her. But I don't know. And one of these days I'm going to have to figure that out, I mean, if things keep going in this direction. I'm going to have to fish or cut bait—David can't keep the bad figure of speech out of his mind. He waits in silence for his father to tell him *how* he will figure it out, what the answer will be— and resists the urge to glance over his shoulder, to see the look on his father's face.

Finally, David's father speaks. *You'll cross that bridge when you come to it,* he says. David turns now and sees how dead earnest his father is. The sun is visibly sinking and the lines in the older man's face, a healthy face—this is what the word *hale* was invented for, David thinks—have fallen into shadow. David's father gives his words weight, speaks them slowly. This isn't a flip metaphor specific to today, when he and David are on the water. It is a bit of advice David has heard from his father before—on dry land—often. David's father has lived his own life by this tenet and he has, for the most part, done well, built an enviable life, avoided major confrontations. If this is the goal, he has accomplished it. It is the kind of life some people would have a hard time arguing with.

Don't worry, David's father says, *you'll cross that bridge when you come to it.*

But how will David know when he's come to it? Maybe it's already here. Maybe he'll get to the river and there won't be a bridge. Or, he considers, maybe he's already stumbled onto a steamer ship when he wasn't looking, and taken passage, and now, without realizing, he is on the other side. Would that be a problem? Perhaps not. Things have been going well with Jessica. *Smooth sailing.* Maybe that is enough.

David feels a small tug on his line and rapidly begins to reel it in. The boat rocks lightly as the fish pulls and the wind kicks up. David's line spins easily and as it cuts smoothly through the water he begins to forget that, just a moment ago, he had so many worries and was so desperately casting out for revelation.

Maybe I have a fish, he says aloud.

Or maybe you've just had your bait taken. His father laughs hard, and with a relaxed cast throws his own line back into the pond.

1997

Samantha handed David the fax and said flatly, sarcastically, with all the attitude that seemed to help her get through the workday, "Looks important. It's foreign. *Quel excellence.*"

David nodded and placed the fax on his desk and continued listening to Elliot argue, on the other end of the phone line, that they were paying too high a rate to their freelancers. "They'll be able to retire sooner than I will, and in higher style, if we keep tossing them cash for these little throwaway pieces. The expenses! Next, they'll want to be reimbursed for their luggage."

"If you cut out the perks," David responded, "they'll write for someone else. They're not writing about Zermatt simply because they have a passion for the written word."

David started to push the fax aside so he could get a better look at the layout beneath it—but stopped when he saw the characteristic scrawl of the handwriting on the fax's cover sheet. "I've got to go. I'll think about our rates," he said to Elliot as he lay the phone down in its cradle.

The top sheet was a handwritten note from Martín Diaz. In the nearly five years since David had finished reporting the Derek Mark Jhensen piece, he'd hadn't been in touch with Martín except for the occasional card to keep each other updated with current addresses and fax numbers.

"You'll be interested, I think so," Martín had written in his blockish, sloppy hand on the cover sheet.

What followed was a single-spaced page of carefully arranged notes. It started with a short description of the recent takeover of the Japanese ambassador's residence in Lima by the MRTA, the Movimeinto Revolucionario Túpac Amaru. This was nothing new to David. He, like anyone in the States, couldn't avoid the daily front-page headlines about the affair if he'd wanted to.

But the *New York Times* coverage had been sensationalistic, from the outsider's point-of-view and with all the inherent misunderstandings that marked every U.S. paper's Latin American coverage. Martín's recap gave just the basic facts with none of the fear and scare tactics that marred the North American versions of the story.

At the end of the fax, Martín wrote: "DMJ located, in the first month of the siege, at MRTA safehouse. Seen by outsider working as advisor, an expert on financials and transportation. Understands business, he is speaking Spanish but not using his name. Still the outsider is certain it is him. Definitely an American. The man at the safehouse is definitely a gringo, and since it is not you, who else could it be?"

David pulled up his computer Rolodex file and scrolled through for Martín's name. While David searched, his phone rang. He let it go, let it roll over to Samantha's line. He wrote Martín's number on a scrap of paper. *An American with the MRTA*: It would have been all over the press up here, if the press knew about it. The MRTA was underground, and any American who'd joined up and gone underground as a member would have been reported missing by his family, *and Jhensen was the only American recorded missing in Peru.* If *A*, then *B*, David reasoned. Man, this information from Martín could be true. Samantha poked her head into David's office.

"Your mother-in-law is on the phone. You'd better pick up."

"I'm not in," David said. The MRTA was the kinder radical group in Peru. Unlike the Shining Path, they didn't kill without reason. They were just the sort of scare-the-rich to feed-the-poor types that an American do-gooder, an environmentalist, might go overboard and sign on with. A guy like Jhensen: fed-up with the government, already disenchanted by its rules and legalese.

And what American could it possibly be other than Jhensen? Not some college kid on vacation, not doing the *financials*, not with a knowledge of transportation. Jhensen was a businessman with a specialty in the environment, in skirting the law. Everywhere he'd gone in Peru, he asked questions about the government, the land, agriculture policies and city planning.

"I tried that. She says you're not returning the messages she left for you at home and she needs to talk to you *desperately*. Her word, not mine."

"Samantha," David snapped. He looked up. "If I'm *not here* then it doesn't matter how desperately she needs to talk to me. Get it?"

"*Got* it. What swam up your pants this morning?" Samantha said and left.

David fingered the scrap of paper with Martín's number and felt suddenly out of place in his sterile office high above Sixth Avenue. In his hand was a small link to Lima. I could be there, he thought.

David picked up his phone and began to dial. He got as far as the country code before he placed the receiver back in its cradle, stood up, and walked across his office. This lead from Martín came out of nowhere but made sense. Men don't just disappear. *Nor do women*. The thought fought for his attention. This Jhensen lead was probably real. He could feel it. Martín was smart, perceptive. David leaned out the door, toward Samantha's cubicle.

"Samantha, I need the research guys to dig for anything current on the MRTA down in Peru. Not just the recent Japanese embassy stuff, I need background, local stuff, whatever, if they have access to it."

"I can do it," Samantha said, appearing over the wall of her cubicle. "Sounds interesting."

Again, David picked up his phone and dialed. The voice on the other end answered with a quick, nearly unintelligible "Canal Quatro" and David recognized Martín's rasp.

"Hey, superstar," David said into the phone.

"Gringo," the voice replied warmly.

I'm back, David thought. He steadied himself and took a slow breath. Martín was speaking, telling him to hold on. "Just one minute, I'm glad you got my note," Martín was saying. *This is my chance*, David thought. This story, this old story, might have an ending after all. An end, an answer, something welcome and long-awaited and finally within his grasp.

"Give me a few days to check the facts, that it really is your hiking man," Martín said to David. "You know the way people say they saw something and then they think about it again and say it was something else? I like this lead—it sounds like him, no?—I like it very much, that's why I sent it to you. I still think it is true, but let me make sure. We'll talk in a few days, then you can get all worked up. Then you can come down here, work on your tan." He let out a deep laugh. "You need it, no?"

The day after receiving the fax, David was still waiting for Martín's promised follow-up call. He lingered in his office late, organizing his story files, double-checking his writers' contracts, tempting the possibility that his phone might yet ring. When he'd stalled as long as he could stand it, he finally stacked the papers on his desk, shut off the light in his office, took one look around, and closed the door. The rest of the floor was mainly quiet. People were either gone already or had their heads down, rushing to get their work done so that they, too, could flee toward home. As David walked to the elevator bank, all the office doors he passed were closed.

David was alone as he rode the elevator down to the lobby. He could almost hear the *psssshaw* of the elevator descending through the mostly vacant building, through the after-hours air. David stood stooped in the corner of the car and thought about the stack of work on his desk and about Martín and about finally getting out of here. When the elevator doors opened, he found himself face-to-face with Elaine.

"David, please," she said. "I thought we should talk. I need to talk it all out and you won't take my messages."

"I can't, I don't have time tonight," he said, trying to get his head around the situation (Elaine, here, in his office building lobby!) and patting the duffel that was slung over his shoulder as if it were full of wildly important work he was bringing home rather than what it actually held, his running shoes and gym shorts. He walked briskly, then less briskly, toward the back door to the street. To his right, by the security desk, a maintenance worker quietly buffed the floor in slow, spirographic circles. The overhead lights were dimmed to a half-power blue. David turned back toward Elaine. "Look, we can talk. Another time," he said. He knew he was hurting her, was being unkind, but he couldn't help himself. He had nothing to say to her, and he wasn't ready to face whatever it was she might have to say.

"David."

He paused and turned to her, the strength of her voice halting him. He looked at her the way any stranger happening upon her in this lobby might, actually registering her features and the emotion behind them. She appeared so totally put together for someone who was convinced her daughter was dead, recently slaughtered. When had David last seen Elaine? It had been at least a month. Three months? The last time he'd seen her she'd looked frightened and disheveled and lost. Now he was thrown by the way, in the meantime, she'd regained her composure. She was half a foot shorter than David, but standing here with all her strength she appeared his equal. "David," she said. "She's gone. And we're not getting her back, and the least we can do is try to figure out who she was, why she was, to give it all some meaning. Give me an hour, will you please? You can't give me an hour?"

This kind of touchy-feely talk usually drove David to nausea. *Why* she was? Give it all some meaning? *Create your own.*

"David?"

"An hour, I have an hour," David said.

He lightly took hold of her elbow and led her outside where he hailed them a cab. Elaine gave the driver the address of the apartment where she was spending the night, where she assured David they could talk quietly, undisturbed.

When they got to the apartment, Elaine turned nervous. She filled glasses of water from the tap and added ice cubes until the liquid almost spilled over the rims. The eager face she'd held up so well in the hushed, dimly lit lobby began to fall, slowly coming unstuck. She set the drinks on the elaborate coffee table in front of David and then immediately raised the cups in the air again, as if the tabletop and the glasses were repellent magnetic forces. She put the glasses on the counter and searched noisily through the drawers in the kitchen. For what? David sat silently, couldn't imagine what his mother-in-law needed so urgently. David looked at his watch. Elaine returned with two coasters, painted with tulips and inscribed with the flowers' Latin names. She placed the glasses on the coasters. "It's not my tabletop," she said. "I don't want to leave marks."

David nodded. Elaine was staying here, at a friend's apartment, while that friend was in Paris. And in another ten days this was where Elaine would throw a memorial service for Jessica. This much she had explained to David on the cab ride here. He'd been silent ever since, unsure what Elaine wanted to hear—and what he wanted to say.

She'd come to her own closure, she'd told David. And now she was going to have a memorial service. She wanted to talk to David *first*, before firming up the plans and setting the date. But when he refused to call her back, she'd sent out the invitations anyway, just a day ago.

"Excuse me?" David said. This was all so unreal.

David looked around the vast room, this friend's apartment. It seemed like a cold place for a memorial service. *It seemed like a cold room even for living in.* Everything was white. From the rugs to the walls to the suede-covered couches. The shelves, elaborate built-ins with a low gloss finish, like milk, were filled with books arranged by size and held in place with ivory bookends. Had any of the books ever been opened? Most likely not. In a bad movie they would be hollow and filled with the family heirlooms.

"Look, she's gone," Jessica's mother began, carefully. "And we're not getting her back, and the least we can do is try to figure out who she was, to give it all some meaning." Her speech sounded well thought out, rehearsed beforehand and edited in private.

David looked at the woman across from him, a woman he knew more through Jessica's stories than through any direct contact. He knew about her, but he didn't know her. Jessica had always stood between them, acted as a buffer. There was no love here. Maybe there was compassion, shared histories of a sort, but there was no love. Elaine sped up the cadence of her speech as if aware she might lose David.

"You raise a child, you don't know who you're going to get in the end. It's a toss-up, a work-in-progress until the day you die, or the day they—" She cut herself off. "You only know what you've got for the moment." She talked on, steadily: "And then, maybe, you can only blame yourself. She started to shut us out, you know. Early, early on. Oh, sure, they say it's age appropriate in junior high, back then, but to look at your child and not have her look back? To watch her turn into a stranger?"

David knew this much. For Jessica's whole life, as far as David knew, she had turned on her mother, showed her mother her hard side every chance she got. A side David only saw when Elaine was present. "Girls and their mothers," David's own mother, a mother of sons, had told him, "have their issues."

When Jessica lived alone, when she and David first began dating, she had pictures on the wall of her bedroom, photographs of herself as a child, smiling. When she moved in with David, the pictures she put up were of her and David, together. Or of landscapes, pictures she'd snapped on vacations and weekends away.

"Jessica was her own person. She was happy," Elaine said, "so it cut deep when she shut me out."

Don't, Jessica had told her mother when she was thirteen and waiting next to the court for her tennis match to begin. Elaine had reached over to straighten the pleats of her daughter's skirt. Jessica looked down into the strings of her racquet and said, *Don't. Just watch. Or go home. You could go home, you know.* And when Elaine persisted, insisted on reaching out to hug her child, a small momentary gesture after the match was over, Jessica having won, an easy win that should have been difficult, Jessica pushed her away. *Get off me*, she'd said. *Go away.* She'd looked around with a fake nonchalance. And then, under her breath but as if for the benefit of anyone who might be listening, *I don't need a mother hanging on me. Just go.*

David thought about the one childhood photo that Jessica had hung in their apartment, which still hung on the guest room wall. A picture of Jessica in tennis whites, the racquet nearly as big as she.

Like all the mothers, Elaine continued, she showed up to the tennis matches and ballet recitals and athletic events to watch her daughter, to see what her money had bought. It was that day, when Jessica said *Don't*, in a tone so much harsher than her usual *I can't* or *I won't* or *No way*, it was that *Don't* that cut right into Elaine. David thought about Jessica turning away from him in bed when he'd touched her breasts, red and worn from the infertility treatments. "Please," she'd said. "No," as if adding another brick to the wall.

Don't is what Jessica had said to her mother. Later, Elaine would understand how cruel any thirteen-year-old can be, the way almost any action from a young teenager—a girl trying to figure out what is expected and how to fit in and where her place in the world will be—the way any action from such a girl can be read as malicious, malignant. "There had been so much silence in the house," Elaine said. "I thought her moods were our fault." Silence? David started to speak, to question, but he stopped.

Look at both sides, Jack said to Elaine in bed that night, as if mediating a dispute between his law partners. *What? You wanted your mother around when you were a kid? Jessica will come back to you.*

We're her parents.

Then act that way, let her go, Jack said, getting out of bed, taking the top blanket with him and settling into the armchair in the corner of the room where he spent the rest of the night, waking up early—even before Jessica rose for school—to prepare for the merger he was mediating that afternoon.

"What's the point, Elaine?" David asked. His voice was harsher than intended. Why rehash Jessica's past? he wanted to ask.

"I don't know why it matters." Elaine's tone turned a corner, from pleading and insistent to weak and worn out. "*I don't know* what matters. She's been running from me ever since she was thirteen, running toward her own perfect life without me. I didn't know my own daughter for the last twenty years of her life. Now she's been taken from us, and what do I have to hold on to?"

David breathed deeply. Had he been any closer to Jessica than Elaine was? Sometimes, the way Elaine insistently called, stopped by, sent care packages—the way she tried so hard to reclaim Jessica, sometimes he felt like the tie between mother and daughter had been Jessica's tightest bond. Like repellent antipodes on the same battery. Had he or she ever known Jessica?

"She was a good kid," Elaine said, sitting back in her chair now, letting her eyes close. "She was always trying to match up, and she did match up. Geez, she was fourteen and already trying to keep up with the Joneses. When we expected rebellion, when she was turning us away as parents, instead she became the poster-perfect teen, without our help. While other parents were pressuring their kids to study, to pile on the extracurriculars, to trade their tattoos for sweater sets, Jessica was ahead of the game. She put all the pieces in place by herself. As if this, her solo act of perfection, was her crowning achievement in defiance."

This, David thought as Elaine told the story, this was a little bit of the Jessica he knew. A little bit of himself as well. The striving to fit in, that fear of being different. The discomfort in having a scar or fissure or hair out of place. The way that, for David, Jessica's disappearance had been a double whammy: the slam bang of his wife being gone, and the social and societal kaboom of being the guy who was weird, who had the missing spouse, who stuck out in a crowd, who was deserving of pity. The concerned glances aimed toward him when people thought he wasn't looking. At least in public, it would have been nice to fit in. The ways he and Jessica had kept their infertility problems to themselves, to their immediate families. He could understand Jessica's compliance as a teen; she always worked to smooth things over.

For a moment Elaine was silent and the room felt large, its white expanse like a film still David had stepped into.

David shook his head. He saw what Elaine was doing: trying to pinpoint what went wrong, where *she* lost Jessica as a child. Now that the adult Jessica was lost to Elaine for good, she needed one final moment to cling to. David looked hard at Elaine.

"I'm sorry. I thought—" she said, pausing suddenly, as if waiting for David to interrupt. But he didn't. His silence was airtight and complete. Elaine went on, "I loved her so much. I wondered if maybe, combined with the Jessica you know, maybe we could remember her as she really was. Maybe that's one way to keep her with us."

Really *is*, David thought.

"We have to piece together her story, to carry it on. And I'm hoping that, along with everything you know—"

"No," David said. Jessica carried it on. It was her story.

David reached for his bag and watched Elaine search for some sort of concluding words.

"No," he waved Elaine away, made an excuse, found his way to the elevator where, on the way down, he leaned over and heaved, dry heaves, sharp and sudden and empty, nothing coming out of him.

At home that night, in David's mailbox, Elaine's memorial service invitation was already waiting. The address on the envelope was carefully hand-calligraphied. The invitation inside looked engraved. David noticed the font, a smooth typed cursive that clashed with the stiff ivory card on which it was printed. David noticed all this—the paper stock, the print style, the embossed border—before reading the words themselves:

In Memoriam
Please join Jessica's family for
an afternoon dedicated to celebrating
her life, vitality, and legacy
Monday, April 21
One o'clock in the afternoon
1250 Fifth Avenue, Apartment 11 F

Jessica's mother's name was signed at the bottom of the card along with a phone number for RSVPs. David ran his finger over the card's words. *In Memoriam*, as if her life were a closed case. Elaine was determined. He grabbed a beer from his refrigerator before heading to the living room to read the handwritten note Elaine had included in the envelope. He sat on the couch and unfolded the paper.

David—

I wanted to discuss this with you before mailing the invitations, but you've proven impossible to reach. I hope you'll attend. I know you and the police don't believe, as I do, that

*her body has been found, that she is gone, but in my own
mind I know what I believe and what I need to do. She
would have wanted this and she would have wanted you
there. Please get in touch soon so we can include you whole-
heartedly in this event.*

   Elaine

David put the letter and invitation back in the envelope and
dropped the entire package into the box—his Jessica file, a random stack to which he rarely added anymore—in the corner of
the kitchen.

Martín finally called David to follow up on the fax, and his
new information left David no more time to brood over Elaine's
memorial service and her stories about Jessica. If Martín's new
information were right, Jhensen was outside the ambassador's
residence, but still in Lima, one of the point people at the
MRTA safehouse—likely running the show, since all of the
MRTAs with any experience were *inside* the residence—waiting
for action, remaining quietly in hiding, undercover, until his
services were needed.

During Martín's first phone call, and here again during the
second, the Peruvian made no mention of who his sources might
be. David knew better than to ask. He had learned early on
while creating his network of sources in Peru, a network of new
friends as well, that any personal history these people might
have outside of the immediate here-and-now was their own,
and wasn't necessarily relevant to their interactions with David
today. David imagined Martín's face and thought, *He'd have*

been a rabble-rouser in his youth, maybe an MRTA member him-self. Maybe in the MRTA still. Most likely an objective observer with a lot of old pals.

All of the members of the MRTA, or almost all, or most of them at least, lived underground and out of sight. They were middle and upper-middle class, many of them plucked straight from the university when their gut told them to *save the people, give back the land, feed the masses*. They sacrificed their identities and birthrights and all of the privilege they'd grown up taking for granted, to go undercover, underground, with new names and freshly severed ties to their past lives and a passion for change that, all their efforts notwithstanding, might never come.

After David hung up the phone, Martín assuring him again that his information was reliable, he sat alone in his office for nearly an hour. He shut his eyes, rested his feet on his desk, and imagined Jhensen as a revolutionary. He imagined the American trekker, a serious pleasure seeker—or so David believed from all he had uncovered—sacrificing his self, his own identity, for a cause completely foreign to all he had ever known. David tried to picture how that would look, that total change of course—*This sacrifice of oneself,* could an American, a white American with cash to burn, even *comprehend* that, coming from a country and a demographic where injustice was, by definition, *someone else's problem?*

Except this: Jhensen had come up against the government, the U.S. government, himself. He had fought the big American bureaucratic behemoth and lost. Why not fight the smaller, but infinitely more evil, Peruvian head honchos? And if fighting the U.S. government had turned Jhensen into a bad guy, fighting with the MRTA—a group whose main mission was to forcibly spread Peru's wealth, to bring the land's spoils to the impover-ished majority—would re-create him as a bit of a hero. For the first time since the arrival of Martín's fax three days earlier, David allowed himself to completely believe that this path to the trekker was absolutely real and waiting to be followed. He pictured breadcrumbs, trail markers on trees, street signs all pointing *this way, this way, this way*. Come and get it. Answers right *here*. From the start, the Jhensen case had been like a jigsaw puzzle that David hadn't quite been able to complete, to make fit. And here was Martín, handing David a new piece, perhaps the final piece. Like a puzzle that actually might be solved and, in doing so, like a how-to primer on *finding*. A chance to prove that finding a person was possible.

When David emerged from his office it was lunchtime. He took the elevator downstairs, walked outside, down the steps to the subway, and before he had time to understand exactly what he was doing, he was at home, standing on a chair in order to reach the top shelf of the spare closet in the master bedroom, a room he had barely entered since moving into the guest room more than a month ago. From the top of the closet he pulled down two boxes filled with everything there was to know about Derek Mark Jhensen. David hadn't touched the boxes in the nearly five years since he'd written the original articles and, now, as he lifted off the tape that held the first box closed, he felt his hands shaking. There is a life in here, he thought. Then, a moment later, he knew exactly what was feeding his giddiness. The life, a life he'd constructed inside this box, that life was still out *there*, waiting to be found.

David laid the contents of the boxes—newspaper clippings, interview transcripts and tapes, notepads filled with phone numbers, pages describing people and places—on the bedroom floor and slowly began to reconstruct the trail into a path that might lead to the MRTA, that might lead to today. David picked up the typed pages that contained the transcript of an interview with the truck driver outside Caraz who claimed to have transported the trekker. This is what David liked about the story all along: how Jhensen had left clues, traces. He hadn't been purposefully surreptitious. It was as if his disappearance was merely a random byproduct, the way the signs were interpreted when you simply moved on without leaving a forwarding address and a book of stamps.

He went to pull down a third box, and caught a glimpse of something else—in the corner of the closet—small and bound in tan leather, and for a second David thought, *a clue* (a clue!), but he realized almost immediately that it was not a new clue at all. It was simply Jessica's datebook, returned by the cops after-the-fact, after they'd had it for a week or two (and copied the pages surrounding the day of her disappearance, and gotten their smudged ink fingerprints on the papers), and then tossed by David into a closet corner where it wouldn't taunt him. David reached for the book now, as if to add it to the stack of Jhensen material. As if the clues Jhensen had left might rub off on Jessica's story, might provide, finally, the answer. He reached for the book, small and square and Jessica's whole world inside without a single piece of evidence about what happened to her. He was struck by how little Jessica had left: just a quiet stop, a silent and painful vacancy. He looked at the pile of Jhensen research and found comfort in the mere fact that he *had* this research, that in the case of Jhensen he'd found *something*, this stack of papers and notebooks that he could now hold in his hand and shuffle and organize.

David spent the entire afternoon at home sorting and, by the time it was dark outside, he had sifted through all the papers and re-stashed those that were no longer useful or that had led him down false roads in the past. He stood at his fourth-floor windows and watched the street below. Traffic stood still behind a cab letting off a passenger. A young woman stepped out of the cab and walked a few steps east before correcting herself and walking the other way, continuing west. She swerved to avoid a crowd of men walking in the opposite direction.

David reached to the side of the blinds and pulled the horizontal slats closed. Then, instinctively, he crawled into the master bed, a bed he hadn't slept in in more than a month, and he slept deeply, dreamlessly, until he woke with a hard start early the next morning.

David was the first person in the office. He called the corporate travel department, but no one was in yet. What would he say to them anyway? He wasn't sure when he was leaving or exactly where he would need to go. Samantha arrived right on time, a sure sign she was planning to skip out early, and dropped a pile of phone message slips, from the afternoon before, on David's desk.

"Here." She stood in front of him, waiting for him to say something. Instead, he began looking through the slips. She spoke again, "Next time you plan on taking off for half a day, you might want to let me know so I can tell people when they call." He still said nothing. She handed him another pile of papers. "This is the research you asked for, the Peru stuff. If you need anything else, you can get it yourself. I'm busy. Curt has me fact-checking. He might actually let me write something, too." And she was gone.

"Elliot, Elliot. Hey, Elliot!" David saw the managing editor walk by and began following him down the hall. "I need to talk to you." David caught up with him and now they were walking side by side.

"Cut the energy level." Elliot made a hatchet motion with his left hand. "Since when are you a morning person? Regardless, it's nice to see you here on time." He motioned for David to follow him into his office. Elliot sat behind his desk, and David took one of the chairs in front of it.

"Look," David said, and then stopped. This was the kind of talk he should have planned ahead, like asking for a raise or offering a resignation. He was about to demand an indefinite amount of time off. "I'm going down to Peru. For a while." His voice was strong, declarative. He thought perhaps he should be ashamed of his impulsiveness, should be offering some greater explanation, but, instead, he looked Elliot in the eye and said, "I guess I just, you know, thought you should be aware of that." David rose to leave. Elliot reached out to stop him.

"Excuse me? David." Elliot motioned to David to sit again. David did, and Elliot continued, "You want to tell me what this is about? I'd bet hard cash it's not a vacation, vacations don't get you this agitated, no second honeymoon if you ask me." The minute those words were in the air between them, Elliot realized his mistake. "Sorry, David, I didn't mean—"

"What?" David said. "Oh, sure, don't worry about it." David felt the spell, his own exasperation, excitement, broken for the moment. Elliot cleared a space on his desk as if making room for whatever David had to say. David thought about Martín, the MRTA, Lima.

"It's Derek Mark Jhensen," David said. "One of my sources spotted him with the MRTA, you know—" but how much did people know? "—the group inside the Japanese ambassador's house. In Lima. But I don't even know if it's him. It's like, I *know*, but not for sure. He's outside the residence right now so maybe I can get to him, get some closure to the story, whatever, but it's all down there waiting for me, however it shapes up, and instead I'm here, putting a glossy spin on 'Where to Eat in Bruges.' " It was David's turn to apologize. "Not that there's anything wrong with that, with all this. Tourists in Bruges have to eat something, so, you know, that's definitely an issue that someone needs to address, I guess."

"*Shit*, David." Elliot was two beats behind. "Derek Jhensen is a terrorist?" Now Elliot was clearly intrigued. When he swore, which was rarely, it was meant for emphasis, to prove how seriously he was engaged in the exchange at hand.

"Terrorist? Fuck *that*, Elliot, the MRTA, they're revolutionaries. They've got an actual cause, you know? Fujimori is jailing dissidents just for the heck of it, and finally these guys are fighting back. And it seems like Jhensen to join a fight," David took a breath, tried to catch up with the heated, high speed of his own voice. "Yeah, they've got machine guns, but nonviolence doesn't work in that part of the world. It's been *tried*."

"So what? You're going to storm into their revolutionary headquarters to get the real story? Brilliant."

David was surprised by Elliot's hostility. Just two months ago Elliot had found the clip on Jhensen and Isla del Sol and thought David would be interested in investigating. So why the shock now? "I'm not storming headquarters. Chances of my finding any trace of where the MRTA are holed up is unlikely anyway. I'm going to head down and ask some questions—I don't know what I expect to find. But there's a story there, and if anyone's going to find it, it should be me. I'm simply telling you so that you don't wonder why I'm not at the office," David said.

Elliot nodded, began to loosen up. "I'm not going to fire you, get a grip. I'm just trying to get a hold on what you're planning and whether it's foolhardy. Heck, David, you hit me with this me before my morning coffee, what do you expect? Answer these questions for me, will you? Are you going down there to write an article? Are you pitching it to me? Or are you just looking for time off?" He paused. "And here's what I really want to know: Is this safe? I ask you as a guy who honestly likes you, David, not as your boss."

"I'm going down there"—David hadn't thought much beyond this, but continued—"and thinking maybe, hopefully, there's an article in this, there's surely an interesting story if it's really Jhensen down there. But I don't think the story's a *Travel Excursion* kind of thing. So no, I'm not pitching it to you. And yes, I think it's safe. There's a pretty big handful of U.S. journalists already down there covering the hostage crisis, and nobody's even been bruised."

"Maybe it's not for *Excursion*, but maybe. You're on staff here, so unless you're quitting, you owe us a first look. On the off-chance we want whatever you write, it's ours. Agreed?"

"Sure."

"And we can't do without you indefinitely. Take vacation, talk to Muriel about how much you've got left, and take one extra week unpaid if you need it—if we print the piece we'll pay you for that time, sure—and let me know where you can be reached and when you'll be back. You need to stick around at least through tomorrow, to get your work in order before you take off. We're not changing the world, but we have an issue to close." Elliot had his arms crossed and was sitting up straight, at attention. "Think it through, all right? This whole decision seems a bit rash. There's no reason not to do your research thoroughly up here before nailing down your flight plans."

Before he was even out of Elliot's office, David began calculating a to-do list and estimating how soon he could be aboard a plane bound for Lima.

* * *

W hen David got back to his desk, Curt was waiting. "Hey, man, what's this?" Curt waved the invite from Elaine. "You're not involved, are you? Am I supposed to go?"

"I'm not involved. I'm just an invited guest myself. Who else got one?"

"Everyone. Name anyone. Even Nadine, who only met Jess, like, once, maybe. I think your mother-in-law invited everyone Jess ever mentioned."

David had figured as much. Elaine didn't like her parties small. Despite her grief, she'd probably hired a party planner to orchestrate the shindig. Probably the same scrawny, neurotic guy who'd arranged the details of David and Jessica's wedding— until Jessica put her foot down and insisted they bring everything down five or six notches. Or maybe not. Perhaps Elaine, for all her attention to etiquette and appearances, would get this sort of service exactly right.

"It's just a crazy idea of your mother-in-law's, I take it? Unless there's some new sign of Jessica I don't know about," Curt said.

"No, nothing." David was glad Curt had asked.

"So it's just Elaine acting out. But come on, I do think we should go."

Would David go? Would he play his part in the charade, help pass hors d'oevres and solemnly accept condolences from distant family members? Buy into the idea that Jessica was gone forever? It would mean the world to Elaine. She'd made that clear. David knew Curt was right. David knew he should go.

"We'll grab some drinks first, make a day of it," Curt said. "We can show up to the event completely sloshed. Whatever you need, I'm there with you. We'll do it our own way."

"I don't think I can," David said. "I won't be here. I'm going down to Peru."

David booked a flight to Lima as well as a room in a high-rise hotel between the San Isidro district and Lima Centro, a high-rise favored by journalists and visiting dignitaries. David gave Curt a key to his apartment and asked him to pick up his mail and to fax him at the hotel if any of it looked urgent—*if any of it pertained to Jessica*. He called his parents, called Will. He called the police and gave them his phone number in Peru, just in case. *Because maybe it was like that watched pot*. Maybe the minute he left the country Jessica would return and wonder where *he* was. "Didn't you get my note that I was running out to the gym and would be back in eight months?" and then they'd have a good laugh about Elaine's cockamamie theories about the Canadian serial killer and her determined search for closure. No, it was tough to imagine that this scene with Jessica would happen. She'd had plenty of time to return already. But *still*.

David zipped up his bags and checked his phone messages one last time before walking out the door.

MAY 1993

To the left, Will hugs a boulder. He climbs under and above the large rock, his fingers curled into its cracks. A few yards away, in front of the rock wall, David stands on solid ground. Jessica is ten feet above him, on the other end of the rope he holds, silhouetted against a blue-gray sky. She balances her toes on a small crevice and finds enough traction in the rock's small nubs to cling on with her fingers. David can see her thighs starting to shake. She looks up at the rock face above her and then cranes her neck down to look at him. *I can't go any higher,* she says. *I don't know what to grab onto.*

He makes sure that the rope is taut. That it will hold her if she falls.

David says, *Reach to the—*

I can't go any higher. Her legs, thin but sturdy and muscular, are really shaking now. *I can't stay up here anymore.*

Will hears Jessica's pleas and stops his bouldering. He walks toward the wall and at the same time coaxes Jessica to reach high and to her right. David continues to hold tightly to the rope, pulling it against the carabiners on his waist harness. Will has spent this morning teaching David and Jessica how to climb and, more importantly, how to belay, how to man the ropes, how to act as your partner's safety net.

I want to come down, Jessica says, not quite insisting.

Reach up to your right, you've got nothing to be afraid of, the rope will catch you, Will says. Jessica reaches out her arm and loses her footing all at once. Her body swings free away from the rock. The rope strains in David's hands as he concentrates on standing square and firm, his heels solid in the hard dirt beneath him. He controls all of her weight and balances his own against it while she steadies herself in midair.

Will puts his own hands on the rope, directly above David's, and slowly begins to pull, easing Jessica up the wall until she is high enough to reach the next hold.

Got it? Will says.

Jessica does have it, and when she is higher up and on steadier rock she laughs, briefly. David has never heard her voice, always round and high-pitched, come from above him before. It throws him slightly, disorients him. She laughs again. *It's definitely easier when you pull me up, but I guess that's not really climbing?*

Whatever it takes. Will nods and then, after making sure that David has a strong hold on the rope and Jessica feels secure and ready to move on, goes back to his boulder.

Jessica continues climbing, more determined now. Reaching farther, aggressively, for the tiniest holes and cracks. *You're a superstar,* David says to his new wife. Each time she moves a few inches up the wall he adjusts the rope. He likes this. This is Will's wedding present to them. Almost a year ago, when they got married, Will promised to take them to a mountain inn for the weekend to teach them to climb. *You've both got climbers' bodies, long and lean,* he'd said. *I may look flexible,* Jessica had responded, *but I can barely touch my toes.* Will's wife, Annette, has come along for the weekend as well, but is spending the day at the inn with her bike and a book.

I think this is fun, and terrifying, Jessica says from her perch. For a moment she is resting and looks amazingly relaxed as she balances on the rock. Like she suddenly has a feel for this sport that, only a minute ago, she was willing to give up on.

It's not terrifying, I have you. And when David says this, he realizes he really does have her. If he were to get distracted and let go—and if her fingers slipped at that very second—she would fall to the ground. He can imagine being distracted by a dog's bark or an unexpected spasm or a mosquito. How high is she? Fifteen feet? Eighteen feet? How serious would her injuries be? He thinks of the faces that Will climbs, sometimes eighty or a hundred feet. Someone is always at the end of the rope with the power to let go.

Jessica moves up the wall, slow and steady, like she has a rhythm in her head. Her legs are at awkward angles for a moment. Her left foot slides up the rock to test a hold just below her waist. David concentrates and controls the rope tightly. The slack is pooled at his feet. He wonders how it is that in a world where so many people climb rocks and extreme ski and fly in single-engine airplanes, everything, most of the time, comes out okay.

Jessica manages to get both feet onto a natural ledge in the rock. Almost to the top of the climb, she rests again, tucks her hair behind her ears, and straightens her harness. Even from so far below, David can hear her breathing.

Hey, Jessica says.

What? David looks straight up the wall to Jessica's perch.

Stop staring up my shorts. She laughs and then, nervously, looks farther up the wall at the vertical path before her.

PART THREE
1997

"Eh, man, I cannot believe you are back," Martín said as he sat across from David at lunch. "It takes a good story, and we get to see you again. I think so." He flagged a waiter. "You will drink, it's not too early?"

David nodded and Martín ordered two beers and a bottle of water.

In Martín's face David saw the passage of time, his skin was looser on his bones. The entire city was different. Driving from the airport to the hotel, and then to this restaurant, David had been greeted by none of the menace that smothered him and Jessica when they'd arrived in Lima for their honeymoon. The sense of dread on the street was nearly gone, eradicated by President Fujimori and his anti-Sendero, antiterrorism actions. Amazing: An ambassador's residence in takeover, seventy-plus hostages captive inside, and Lima seemed *more* at ease. "Anything new at Canal Quatro? I can't believe you're still there," David said.

"What? Nothing is ever new. The Japanese fiasco has been *loco*. You know why we are here for lunch? It's the only place that is not now full of Americans and Euros with tape recorders and video crews." He handed a manila folder across the table to David. "It's the interview with the man I mentioned, who gave me the information. It's all I have, and he will not talk to you. But it should get you somewhere. I don't think we need to talk about it? There is nothing more I know." David fingered the folder, placed it in his lap.

Their beers came, along with plates piled high with chicken, green vegetables, potatoes. Martín grabbed a spoon and served himself. "In the States, things are good for you?"

Good? David's internal barometer of good and bad had been broken for so long he no longer even thought to consult it.

"Things are good, you know," David answered.

"And your wife?" Martin said offhandedly while poking through his food with a fork, spearing a small sliver of meat.

David opened his mouth to answer Martín's question and saw how, like a child in denial, he had all the lies ready, in wait. *She's fine, she's the same, she's at the doctor's, she wants to get a pet, she gained a few pounds but has lost it already.* Even better: *How's my wife? Who knows?* Or the truth, phrased in a way to halt all future questions, *We're not together anymore*, said with such authority that there'd be no need to explain. He could do this. In New York, he hadn't had to, everyone already knew the news. He imagined it had circulated on the cocktail circuit like alcohol poisoning—the initial thrill, *Oh my God, she WHAT?*, then the lingering hangover. Now David opened his mouth to speak, but when he looked up he saw Martín continue to eye his food, piling a small heap of vegetables onto a slice of bread, trying to keep it balanced, concentrating.

"Well, you know," David said. Martín nodded and ate the vegetables.

"You should stop by the station," Martín said. Martín continued to move the food around his plate. David thought about how easy it had been to say nothing. *Everyone in their own little box.* So why had Martín called David down here?

"You should make a stop at the station," Martín said. "It is not the same place. Now, it is all *mujeres*, the women are doing everything." He picked up his beer as if to take a drink, and then put it down. "Sometimes I think Marguerite would be happy to have these girls to side with in the editing room when we talk dirty." David tried to picture Marguerite, but all he saw was the pile-up of body bags that last night outside El Floridita. "But mostly," Martín said, "I don't think about that. There is too much a man might dwell on that happened a long time ago, and a man cannot live that way." He reached into his pocket, came out with a cigarette and a box of matches, and lit up.

W hile Lima was somewhat peaceful, David's hotel was in a state of eager agitation. Hopped-up journalists, over-caffeinated and perennially drunk, jammed the lobby. At the front desk, when checking in, David had run into Robby Carver, whom he's only seen occasionally since they started out at *Time* together, right out of college. "Nothing doing at the residence today and, it's like, you can only wait outside the gates for so long for so many weeks in a row, so we're making our own fun," Robby had said, offering David an invitation to dinner. "When did you get in?" Robby asked.

David had planned to spend the evening rereading the folder Martín had given him. He'd flipped through the contents in the taxi after lunch and found nothing more than an interview with one source (no word, David noted, on how this source got his information or whether it was reliable at all) as well as a number of clips, in Spanish but with rough English translations, about the way the MRTA worked and the hierarchy of their organization. David wanted *more*; he hoped on a second read these clips would prove deeper. At the same time, why rush it? He feared rereading the papers and finding that there was, in fact, nothing more in them, that he'd come all the way to Peru on such a flimsy lead. Why rush it? Robby was a welcome face, an old friend in a foreign country, and David said yes to dinner and now here he was.

"You haven't been over to the residence?" Daryl Krauss asked. Daryl covered South America for a West Coast news service. There were five of them at the table in the back room at El Benner, a wooden-table ceviche spot where prices were high and what you got was, as Robby claimed on the way over, "simply the freshest fish and most decently poured wine around."

David shook his head.

"Don't bother," Robby said. "I can fill you in on all the fine atmospheric details and save you the trip. No joke, all of San Isidro is a madhouse. There's a circle of military-induced lunacy surrounding the residence." Robby motioned for the bartender, then turned back to David. "*Cervesa?*"

"You working for *Excursion* down here? Or is someone hiring you to do a real article?" Serena Conover, the Lima bureau chief for one of the Chicago papers, asked after being introduced to David.

"*Excursion*, kind of."

"Oh, seriously? Fuck this," Robby said shaking his head. "The tourist rags are covering political unrest now? Mother Mary and Jesus, I'm scared."

"I'm surprised they sent you down here, with—" Serena paused, shrugged "—I've heard they're cutting back. Like everyone, I guess." She'd heard this where? Was *Excursion* planning to cut back on the frills, or were they going to cut staff? "But you never know," Serena continued.

"It's actually personal. A guy I know heard rumors that Derek Mark Jhensen, the missing EnvirCor exec, I did an article on him a few years ago, is—" David paused, wondering how much to reveal and then realizing that these reporters had been here since the beginning of the siege and might be able to help out, "in Lima, he's been spotted in Lima."

"The EnvirCor founder? I thought he was gone for good." This was Daryl Krauss.

"Oh, shit, David, that article that paid for all your nasty habits back *when*?" Robby licked the condensation off his beer glass. "You know, that's a nice idea, the guy hanging around Lima, but no one leaves their real life back home to shuffle their feet in this hellhole. This is the place people flee *from*." Robby sat up taller and laughed. "Unless he's one of the hostages, or—oh, yeah—maybe he's donned a red bandana and signed up with the MRTA and is *holding* those hostages. *That's* a story, David. From corporate exec to guerrilla in one middle-of-the-book spread."

David flinched. Robby seemed to notice. "Davy boy, nobody gets hooked up with the MRTA while on vacay."

"Where'd you get your info about this guy?" Daryl asked, sounding only half curious.

"Just a local news guy I used to know. He didn't have any details."

"Don't believe what the local news guys tell you. They don't know a thing. They're completely restricted," Daryl said. "The only free press you get in this country is the half-fucked job the dry cleaners do. And it's not even free, just cheaper than what you get back home."

"No, I know, I know," David said, playing along, saving face. "But I figured I'd look into it, you know, why not? Any idea where the MRTA safe houses in Lima are?" David asked.

Daryl smiled, "If we knew, they wouldn't be safe."

Art Nuñez—a normally quiet, reserved guy, the fifth reporter at the table—explained, "They're usually right under the government's noses. The house they attacked the residence from was next door, separated by simply a chain-link fence." Like Robby, Art was a familiar face to David. Three years ago they'd met at a crowded media party thrown by a mutual friend (a has-been editor hanging on to the young up-and-comers), and had talked South America over bad well-drinks in the corner farthest from the bar.

Art continued, "Ring the residence by a half-kilometer and I bet you'll walk by a safe house. But you'd never recognize it. Probably got a nice old couple living there as cover."

"Hey, Curt Helprin still working with you? I owe that dude a call," Robby said.

"Yeah, he's around," David said. Curt was likely at the *Excursion* office right now, David figured. Just a few days ago Elliot had griped about the high fees *Excursion* paid its freelancers. *Shoot*, if Serena Conover was right and Elliot was looking to cut back, he'd save a bundle by firing the fuck-up of an editor who rarely showed, who came to work only to flee to Lima for his own purposes. *Shoot*. David thought about what a scarce, expendable presence he'd been in the office recently.

Art was saying something in Spanish to the waiter (Maybe *that* was the problem with the info Martín had given David that, even on second look, told David almost nothing—maybe the gist of the papers had been lost in Martín's translation, scribbled in the papers' margins). Robby leaned forward and spoke to David. "Serena," he motioned with his head to her, next to David. "She was inside the ambassador's residence when they stormed it, pled to stay actually, but they forced her out with the rest of the women that first night." He caught the waiter's attention and then turned back to David. "Oh, heck, maybe she has some leads for you. Hey, Serena, you didn't spot a preppie northwesterner named Jhensen leading those young MRTA boys in morning drills?" Robby laughed, thought this was rip-roaring hilarious. The rest of the table was too busy—serving themselves from the platters that had just been placed on the table—to notice. David grinned.

David noted how completely authentic, how rich and complex, this food was. In the stew, full of squash and corn, David tasted fresh ginger and cinnamon, flavors with an intensity that only comes from spices ground a moment ago in the kitchen. The earthiness of the potatoes reminded him of the kind of meals he'd had in the country, up north, while on Jhensen's trail.

While they ate, Serena told David about her night inside the siege. "The garden's where the action was," she said. "The party was a Japanese luau, it's always the best fete of the year down here. Colored lanterns, waiters passing food while some of the women, the younger drunker ones, went barefoot in the grass— the residence keeps up quite a lawn—to prevent their heels from sinking in." David pictured the bright lawns of his suburban American childhood. All over the world, even in South America, these lawns had come to signify good times. "The takeover happened in an instant—a split second. The sound of a car bomb and within no time the crowd was lying on the ground. That's what you do when you sense danger, you know?" Serena said. "You throw yourself face down on the ground. Genius." David pictured the crowd at Cate and Welford's, the usual crowd, throwing themselves to the floor, prone on Cate's Persian carpets while revolutionaries stormed in through the polished hardwood doors in search of, what? Vermouth?

Serena continued, "People were in piles, masses. Fujimori's sister was inside, found refuge under the piano. That was at eight-twenty. The MRTA took names and positions, had to know who everyone was. With the exception of me and a couple of other journalists, it was a world-class lie-fest. I mean," Serena said, "you don't try to pull one over on a guy with an Uzi, but, understand, all the military personnel who were guests at the party, they ripped the stripes off their sleeves even before they hit the ground. There was a cacophony of flushing toilets, everyone associated with the government getting rid of their papers. The residence sounded like a convalescent home for folks with bladder infections.

"There were fourteen captors, and even with the bandanas over the lower half of their faces, you could tell that most of them were teenagers. That's scary, teens with guns." Serena looked straight at David as she spoke. "The guests were panicky, but the MRTA, they were perfectly calm. No, I guess they were a bit hyped up, having blasted into the place and not injured a soul. Amazing. Even at the time I thought that. Not a single injury."

David interrupted, "But some of them already inside during the party—I thought they snuck in dressed as waiters? That's what the *Times* said." He pictured the boys in uniform who passed appetizers at Welford's parties, the well-clad bartenders from whom Jessica would beg an extra lime for her drinks. He tried to picture Jhensen, at the MRTA safe house right before the siege, helping the young rebels get ready, straightening out their bow ties, showing them how to serve hors d'oeuvres the way a trained caterer would.

"That's what's been reported, and I believe it, but they had their waiter costumes off and their fatigues on by the time I caught sight of them. Fatigues and MRTA scarves tied over their faces, and the most outstanding arrays of ammunition strapped to their chests. We all lay on the ground for forty minutes—the military cops were firing through the windows, causing more danger than the rebels."

At the table behind Art, two couples, the age of university students, shared a bottle of wine, oblivious to the group of fast-talking Americans. They were accustomed to this by now, David figured. Tales in a foreign language about local hostages and military intrigue, this was now part of their daily landscape. David tried to imagine Jhensen caught up in it all, training the young rebels on how to act like waiters, how to work the party, how to treat a hostage in the moments before and after blowing their scene to pieces.

Robby handed his now empty plate to a passing waiter. He said, "Serena was released with all the women on the first night. They guys who've been let out in the months since, especially at the start, said it was pretty much a party inside for a while. Chess, dominoes, soccer, charades to pass the time. Sounds like the MRTA are pretty interesting folk to pal around with when you've got nothing else to do—"

"—and a gun to your head," Daryl said, looking away.

Serena said, "But it's gone on too long. Ninety days and counting. Who'd have thought Fujimori would make it this long without folding?"

What good does it do to count days? David thought. He looked to the bare wooden walls of the restaurant, to Robby's gregarious face, to the spots of food marring the wooden table-top.

"Don't think we're being flip," Art said. "It was hellaciously intense, covering this shit for the first month, but you can only take it for so long. A city can't stay in stasis forever. Regardless of the situ at the residence, at some point the rest of us, those left on the outside—we've got lives to lead, we've got to continue to survive, you know? The siege at the residence has gone from being a *situation* to a fact of life here. Like Robby said, even the hostages were partying inside, until the depression set in. They really thought they'd be out of there by now."

"At first, that the atmosphere around here reminded me of ten years ago in El Salvador," Serena said, "which at the time seemed unique and pervasive, but now I'm not so sure."

Walking back to the hotel, David lagged a bit behind. Art slowed his pace until the two men were walking side by side. "I heard about your wife," Art said, his tone even, declarative. "Any news on that? Did it ever get settled?"

"Nothing." David said. "Nothing. One day she was gone and nothing turned up since. Not a trace in the last seven months." Then, he doesn't know why: "She grew to hate Peru anyway. I don't think she'd be thrilled to hear I've returned." Was this true? He paused. She'd never outright told him that she hated Peru, but *yes*, he was certain she detested the country, or had grown to detest it as their trip here together had faded into memory. The honeymoon, David's temporary abandonment of his new wife: the chit she'd had to call in until the day she disappeared. The word *Peru* like a not-to-be spoken slur in their household. David said to Art, "We were here on our honeymoon."

Art nodded and put a hand on David's shoulder as they walked. "I can't even imagine it. You're a strong guy, you know? I was pretty sorry when I heard. I nearly phoned you, but I figured you'd have your hands full with closer friends and family. But really, I was really sorry. It seemed so crazy."

And into the vacuum that Peru had represented—a place where no one knew David as the poor guy with the missing spouse, as the paltry has-been husband, as that tragedy-next-door—he was surprised to find such sharp comfort in Art's questions, in this concern, this reminder from someone he barely knew.

* * *

Over the next two days David avoided Robby and the rest of the journalists. He steered clear of the residence. What he couldn't steer clear of were his thoughts of Jessica, of his conversation with Elaine—all those years of Jessica's life before he knew her.

His head hurt and he was tired, but he didn't need more sleep, hadn't come to Peru to rest. He left the hotel, removing himself from the temptation presented by the bed and its feather pillows, and caught a taxi. Calling on the few Spanish words he could cobble together, David set a price with the driver for the ride to Lima's Barranco neighborhood, on the waterfront. It was the closest thing to fresh air in the Lima vicinity, and maybe with a little oxygen in his lungs David would be better equipped to start finding some answers. The beach here, in Lima, was a funny thing.

"*Vaya vía el océano,*" David said. "*Es más rápido.*"

And the taxi followed the line of the water, and at the foot of the Puente de los Suspiros in Barranco, still a beautiful neighborhood, still serene, David got out.

The haze, today, felt particularly oppressive. David crossed the street, followed the sidewalk to the beach entrance. A basketball court was set up on the sand, to the left. An actual court floor, made of fiberglass or plastic or something else hard and remarkably flat, was laid out in the sand. A full-sized pick-up court, with only three men playing. The water was steady, a constant stream of knee-high, slate gray waves. David walked to it, only twenty yards or so. He leaned down and touched the pale surf and then turned around to look at the beach, which played host to the basketball court and its three players and a hard flat layer of dark, wet sand, and nothing else.

The last time David was on this beach—situated directly on the edge of Barranco, an area that was home to many of Lima's luxe hangouts—trash had been piled high. The dumping site for homeless refuse. Got a load of wire to spare? Used-up light-bulbs? Party streamers past their prime? Drop it on the shores of Barranco. *Send us your filth, your dirty diapers.* David kicked his foot in the sand, as if he might hit upon some small bit of for-gotten personal debris, some message in a bottle, but came upon nothing but more hard-packed sand.

"*Actuador!*" one of the ball players hissed.

"*Usted está oculto,*" his opponent calmly replied as the game continued, the sound of the ball against the court sharp and loud.

David left the beach and walked straight up the main road, taking a cursory look down Avenue Pedro de Osma. He used to have a friend who lived there, an artist, but the artist was gone, his things would have been removed. David sat on the steps of Casa Edén, still apparently an upscale lunch hangout for the underworked intelligensia. Men in well-tailored suits—expen-sive suits, David tallied up their prices as they walked in the doors, suits that any of David's banker pals in New York would be jealous of—walked in and out of the heavy revolving doors. On the roof of the two-story building across the street, a private security guard paced, his gun slung tightly over his shoulder.

A kid in uniform—not the uniform of the military, he'd seen a handful of these walk in—a bellman or waiter, came out through the door and leaned against the wall of the building. He lit a cigarette.

"Is a dreadful day," the boy said, his accent strong and his words fractured. David looked up, nodded. "You are an Ameri-can?" the boy continued.

David nodded again.

"Journalist?"

David nodded again. Given the political climate, there probably weren't many nonjournalist foreigners in Lima at the moment.

"I was at the residence. Not this year, for the party last year. I was a waiter. A good job, a lot of money for one night. This year I do not work there, I work here." The boy paused. "You can interview me if you want."

Fabulous, David thought. He'd happened upon a source with miraculously bad timing. The kid had been in the embassy a year *before* the siege, exactly. Still, this minor connection to the events was likely enough to win this kid his fifteen minutes in the American press. David was reminded of his sources, the last time he'd been in Peru. All filled with circumstantial evidence and backstory and ideas, but no real facts. They'd all told him what might have happened to Jhensen, given what they knew about Americans, about Peru, about one or two little conversations they perhaps had with Jhensen when they crossed paths. And from these odds and ends, David had pieced together a very possible scenario and presented it in the article as a sort of truth about what had happened to Derek Mark Jhensen. David had fallen for believing that this kind of plausible story could be substituted for a real answer. For a life.

"No, thanks," David said to the boy. "Unless you know something unique about what was going on in there this year?"

"No, *No sé cualquier cosa*, nothing. I worked at the party last year."

"A man's past is the best place to see his future," Martín had once said. David could go back to Jhensen's past, he knew this. Because maybe he'd gotten the past, the man's history, all wrong. He knew that you could follow the past all you wanted, but if the past, as you know it, was false, where did it lead you?

To an utterly confused present? To a misconstrued idea of a future? Idea. Had he gotten Jhensen's past wrong? David thought not. He'd had research down here four years ago, had followed a hard-evidence trail that had led in a specific direction. Toward the drug trade, with no sign of the MRTA in sight. Sure, when Martín suggested the possibility that Jhensen had signed on with the MRTA, it sounded like something Jhensen *might have considered*. But there was no evidence. Martín and his sources had provided nothing to contradict the drug-related theory that had been proven, however loosely, by David *back when*. So why was Martín trying to throw David off that trail?

David sat for some time on the stoop of the Casa Edén, watching packs of thin, mangy dogs wander by in *V*-formations, like wild geese, grounded. As he lingered, this is what he began to picture: Jessica, asking him what he was doing here, chasing down the story of a man whom he'd never even met, whom he only knew from photographs and secondhand tales. Or this: Jessica saying, *okay*. Jessica understanding why David was here and (Oh, David wanted this, now he really wanted this, they should be agonizing together, they should be going through *this*, through her and all the questions, *together*, back before it was too late, back when she herself could have told David her story) her sitting next to him, and explaining it. Showing David his own intentions, his own reasons, the reason he was sitting on this particular set of marble steps in this particular part of the world during this particular international crisis amid his own personal siege.

David turned down Martín's offer of a ride to the residence for the noon press conference. Going down to the site and becoming a part of the throng would get him nowhere. But *shoot,* he'd been in Lima for five days already and come up with nothing. And while his story might be different from the one being uncovered by Robby and Daryl Krauss and Serena Conover, *like them* he had to leave here with a story. He'd come all the way down for *just that,* after all. Here, there was supposed to be some form of conclusion. *To finally nail something down:* for that he'd desperately chased a tiny lead.

David's old contact at the American embassy was no longer there. Nick Cevallos, the new guy in charge of handling random senseless inquiries from pesky journalists, ushered David into his office. In fact, he already knew of David. "In fact," he said, he happened to have a copy of David's original article on Jhensen in his file cabinet.

"I know the MRTA inside out," he told David. "I wrote my dissertation on their roots."

And then David told Nick what *he* knew—the tip Martín had forwarded to him, the other research he had—carefully omitting Martín's name and even his occupation, information Nick didn't need to know and which Martín would be happy to keep out of the hands of *any* government. When David was finished talking, Nick nodded and gave him a much appreciated nothing-you've-said-is-outrageous kind of glance.

"It could, seen in one scenario, make sense that Jhensen would be with the MRTA, underground within the organization," Nick said. "The levels run deep. But see, if he is an MRTA, he might as well be dead. You'll never spot him, none of us will. Other than Cerpa, no members are identifiable by their own names. Their identity is the first thing they shed."

David could see the comfort in this, in the rare chance to become someone else after twenty or thirty or forty years in your own skin—he pictured Jhensen, shedding his Gore-Tex for fatigues; he pictured Jessica (where? in what skin?). As if proving that Jhensen were truly alive and living an alternate life would somehow prove that Jessica were still alive as well. Step one: Prove that missing people can be alive and healthy. Nick continued, "And they bury their identities so fast and deep that even a top-level investigation would be hard-pressed to turn it up. And I'm talking a Peruvian investigation, after they've caught someone, may be able to track down a clue or two. Jhensen, he may have even blocked out his own name by now—"

"Come on," David said, "he lived with that name for almost forty years. He might have shed it, but it's still with him, deep down."

"Okay, I'll grant you that, but how long has it been since he was last seen? Four, five years?" David tried to imagine a time span that large, right now when day-to-day emotional survival was taking such a toll. David had only known Jessica for six of her years. "Four or five years, that's a lot of days in a row. So if you honestly think he's with the MRTA, an impossibly long shot of an idea anyway, you might as well stop looking for Derek Jhensen and try reimagining him as Commandante Jaime or Commandante Manuel or something, with a beard and without, with matted hair and a scarf tied over his face and a campesino's accent."

"He spoke Spanish with a distinctly Euro affect—"

"Last time you heard." He paused. "The MRTA started out as a rural guerrilla group—but the Shining Path already ruled the mountains, and with a kind of violence the MRTA don't even touch. So the Shining Path drove the MRTA back to the cities, which is where they belong anyway. Other than Cerpa, the kids are all somewhat-spoiled city brats atoning for the rich sins of their parents. Robin Hoods, urban snobs turned good. Well, their version of good. Which is, I always say, why I think you journalists get along so well with them. Birds of a feather." He smiled. "Just kidding."

David grinned; he was in on the joke. He said, "So if he's with them?"

"It doesn't seem like a likely theory, given the little you've told me, no more likely than the drug theory you espoused in '92. And at forty-something, Derek Jhensen is practically a grandfather compared to most of the MRTA, barring the few leadership members. I'm saying, don't get all caught up in this lead of yours just because you can't disprove it."

David had yet to meet a theory that he *could* disprove, which was the problem. But this MRTA theory was beginning to seem less and less likely. Didn't it? Sure, Martín's papers had contained a description of the average MRTA member: from a middle- or upper-class suburban background, university educated (many plucked from the university while still students, enlisted at age nineteen), rebelling against their upbringings. They shunned their solid, well-to-do families and found a connection to the land, to *the people*. They just wanted to help. Up to this point David could follow Martín's logic: It would make sense for Jhensen, the suburban Seattle son-of-privilege, nature boy, trekker, educated international environmentalist, to fall in with these other Robin Hoods—shucking not just his upbringing, but his currently cushy way-of-life. But this was an *idea*, not a theory with evidence to back it up. This was an idea Martín seemed to desperately want to believe, but which barely stood up to Nick's gentle questioning. Martín wasn't after a theory that was true. As Lima slowly turned into a wasteland, Martín was looking for a hero, and Jhensen seemed to fit the bill and certainly wasn't going to speak up to deny the position.

Nick stood up and made for the door, as if ushering David

out. "There's no more I can do, unfortunately. I'm with the embassy, and this isn't the kind of thing we can necessarily get involved with."

"He's an American citizen." David himself was standing now, halfway out the door. "Isn't it up to you to find and save him? Or to at least help out?" Weren't there officials *somewhere* who were mandated to actually locate people?

"Find him? If there's evidence of wrongdoing against him, evidence he's dead, sure. Save him? If he is with the MRTA, and you're the only person who's come here claiming so, and we identified him, we'd be putting him in his grave, the deepest darkest living grave in the heart of a Peruvian prison. For life, probably. Is that what you want?"

At night, there was a steady buzz on the street. Instead of hiding in their homes after dark—the last time David was here, with Jessica, the quiet on the streets at night had been pervasive and chilling—people were out. With the hostage crisis under way, people had forgotten their fears for their own safety. People were uniting, celebrating the possibility that change might be on the way.

David watched the energy in the streets rise in sharp peaks, all kicked off, months ago, during the first week of the siege on a night made famous when protesters paraded down Lima's main drag, playing instruments and carrying Peruvian flags and hoisting placards demanding a peaceful settlement, demanding that the government consider the captors' requests, demanding that the government free the political prisoners locked tight inside Peru's prisons. A handful of marchers had carried their pet doves. David was in New York at the time, and one of the tabloids ran a photo of a man with his arm outstretched toward the camera, a scrawny gray dove posed on his finger, enlarged in the camera's eye. It had to be the most unintentionally threatening picture of a dove ever snapped. Curt Helprin got a good laugh out of the whole thing, cutting the pic out of the paper and taping it to David's office door over the caption "Killer Doves Seize Japanese Ambassador's Residence. Threaten to Detonate Semiautomatic Olive Branches and Peck Old Geezers to Death."

The city was alive and distinctly different from the city David and Jessica had visited. Lima was now filled with Mobil Marts and McDonald's and Dunkin' Donuts and neon-lit *pollerias* with iridescent chickens marking their logos. "There is too much a man might dwell on that happened a long time ago, a man cannot live that way," Martín had said. David walked faster, taking in the street as he approached Channel 4's offices, scanning the storefronts, which had lost their flavor, which now resembled nothing more than sixties tract housing units. How could a whole neighborhood up and disappear? As if an entire way of life had taken flight, for good.

And still, the city thrived; all new, the streets survived.

It was late, but David caught Martín in the editing room.

"Superstar." David ran in, the stress showing in his voice. "Questions for you."

"Always, what else is news?" Martín asked, not looking up from the editing console, the tone of his voice making clear that he did not have time to talk. His shoulders were bent over his work, protecting his segment-in-progress.

David pulled a chair next to him, close. "I looked through all those notes, *again*. There's nothing conclusive, not even a lead to call. Just lots of interesting stuff about the MRTA, and a hint that Jhensen *may* or *may not* be involved. I don't know what to believe. Come on, man."

Martín continued to scroll through the film, jotting down notes as if he hadn't heard David's little tirade.

"You've got to let me in, man. I'm stranded here. I've got nothing to go on in those Jhensen papers, and everywhere I look around here, I'm lost." He thought of Jessica, disappearing with no signs, no trails to follow. "If there are no hard leads to prove that Jhensen is with the MRTA, if you've got me hooked on this story with nothing to back it up, you've got to *tell me*. All the reference points are gone and I'm starting over with nothing." David knew he sounded desperate but made no attempt to lower the pitch of his voice. All the reference points were gone. The familiar buildings, even, had gone missing. He thought of the ways so many travelers try to ground themselves by catching sight of something familiar in their foreign surroundings. The way he and Jessica and so many people they knew created entire lives by surrounding themselves with the known. But when had they decided *that* was the ideal? "I need a lead, Martín. I need to know what to believe. There's nothing in those notes to actually tell me where the guy is."

David thought about how convinced he'd been, four years ago amid his stacks of hard-earned reportage, that Jhensen was in the drug trade. This theory hadn't been random. He'd had clues that time and he'd followed them. He thought about how easily now—when his own life was full of holes, when he was doubting his own instincts—he'd fallen for this new baseless theory.

Martín remained silent. As David opened his mouth to repeat himself, Martín spoke, loudly, as if wanting to be sure he was understood. "I thought you were the man who wasn't looking for answers. I thought you were looking for a story."

David thought: That was last time. That was before.

When David had packed his bags to fly down here, he had thought it would be easy. He'd thought he would arrive in Lima and Martín would hand him proof of Jhensen's whereabouts, and then David, armed with this proof and a map, like a treasure map, *pot o'gold HERE*, he would track down the American, take him out for coffee, and transcribe his whole story. He'd have called down a photographer to take nice pics of Jhensen in his MRTA garb ("Excuse me, Derek, would you mind holding the semiautomatic a little lower? A little to the left now. Oh, great, that's better, thanks, *gracias*." Click.) outside the U.S. embassy or on the deserted waterfront or next to the Presidential Palace. What a *fantasy*. And how easy it had been to fall for it—fantasy being something that David's life was lacking, and which Peru (in Martín's apparent estimation, at least) could use a dose of as well.

After dinner, David, feeling sad, aimless, walked slowly through the lobby toward the elevators, where he was stopped by a desk clerk who handed him a message. From Elliot. David should call him.

It was late. He tried Elliot's home number first. Elliot picked up the phone and over the line David could hear his chair—a heavy dining room chair—scrape against the hardwood floor as he undoubtedly pushed it away from the table, all the while saying, "No, no, don't call back. Let me just head to my study. It's quieter in there." David lowered himself onto his hotel room bed, fingered the buttons on the phone as he listened through the receiver.

The light outside David's window was gray and thin, growing so dark that in a minute David would need to turn on a lamp. He pictured the layout of Elliot's apartment; he'd been there twice. From the dining room, back through the foyer, past the bathroom (elaborate, like a guest bath at a banquet hall, stocked with pretty pastel soaps and lush, fringed hand towels), this was the route Elliot would walk to the study.

"Sorry, David," Elliot's voice broke back in. "We were at the office today, assigning stories and edits and such." David heard the sound of Elliot doodling, pen to paper. "And, honestly, we need to know when you plan on coming back. I know I told you to take some time if you needed it, and I wouldn't push you—" *Yes, yes, you would, you're pushing me right now,* David thought as Elliot spoke—"and I had thought we could spare you, I did, but when it comes right down to it, we hired you, like everyone at the office, to fill a position that needs to be filled. This on top of your other missed work—it's understandable, sure, you needed some personal time—is adding up to more than we can afford from one person. So if you won't be coming up soon, if this is going to turn into another open-ended leave, we'll need to hire someone, at least temporarily, as you can imagine, to edit your sections."

At least temporarily? David nodded, knew that Elliot couldn't read the nod over the phone line, and said nothing. Elliot wouldn't fire him. Not yet, would he? No matter how much pressure he was under to cut back? He might place David on unpaid leave, force him to take a sabbatical while his temporary replacement fulfilled his three-month or six-month contract, but no, Elliot wouldn't fire him, David hadn't done *enough* wrong. Elliot *knew* David, knew the stress he'd been under. But Elliot did like to be in control.

"And it sounded, last time we talked," Elliot continued, "like you weren't coming up with much on your story, in which case, maybe you're ready to head home? We won't hold it against you if you come home." Elliot laughed, briefly.

David sat at the foot of his bed where the hotel sheets were balled in a rough, haphazard knot. Atop the TV stood four empty one-liter water bottles. The door to the closet was open and his clothes were, for the most part, still in the neat piles he had originally stacked them in. And out the window, in this last hour of the day's light, he could see nothing but the soot-stained walls of the office building next door, streaked with the stains of rusty rainwater and dingy condensation. Enough of this, David thought, seeing his way out.

"I was getting ready to come back anyway," David said, doing his best to sound like a valuable employee, like a guy who might not be the *first to go* if you were the man in charge and looking to make cutbacks. "It's no problem." He paused, "I'll give you a call when I know for sure exactly when I'm arriving." New York could be beautiful this time of year, the April sun turning the air downtown, in his neighborhood of brownstones and town-houses and small backyard gardens, yellow and warm. Outside his office window on Sixth Avenue the winter clouds would have lifted for good in the last week. The climate in New York could turn on a dime this time of year. Perhaps David was strong enough to go home empty-handed, smart enough to go home while he still had a job. "Don't be ridiculous, I was already on my way," David said.

He looked at his watch, at the small square where the three should be, which announced the day's date. He would make it home in time for Elaine's homegrown memorial. He should do this, he knew that. He should be back in New York.

The next morning he packed his suitcase and left it on his bed, anticipating a hasty departure at some point in the next twenty-four hours. David took the elevator to the ground floor and strode straight through the lobby to the street outside. For the first time in days he was going to actually *see* Lima. There was a pre-Incan graphics exhibit at the Museo Nacional. He'd go there first. For the first time in days, he was looking forward to coming back to the hotel in the late afternoon and grabbing the customary drink at the bar with Robby and Art and the couple from the *Times* and whomever else was stuck in this hellhole of a city digging up dirt where there was nothing to find but recycled dust.

PART FOUR
1997

David was surprised to actually find himself at the memorial. He'd cut the timing close. After flying overnight, he landed first thing in the morning, took a stop-and-go cab back to his apartment, slept for an hour, showered, eased into an appropriately dark suit. He looked himself over carefully in the mirror. He didn't want to look thrown-together. Today was solemn and serious and demanding appropriate respect. He arrived just as the service was about to begin, and now slid into the back of the room.

Nearly one hundred guests were already packed into the Fifth Avenue living room and much of the furniture had been removed, replaced by a few rows of folding chairs and plenty of space for people standing. Flowered wreaths and scattered potted trees brought a remarkable warmth into the previously frigid all-white space. David took his place toward the back, in a corner, where he had a straight-shot view. At the front of the room, Elaine had set a small podium and two vases of flowers, peonies and lilacs. She approached the podium and as she opened her mouth to speak, her eye caught David's. Noting him there, noting that he *was* there, she seemed to breathe out, deeply and with a nearly imperceptible nod of appreciation.

The speeches were short. A ten-minute introduction by Elaine, talking about the need to create closure when none was handed to you, telling a story of Jessica as a child (trying to cut paper hearts but unwilling to believe that you had to cut along the *folded* side, that the other sides of the paper wouldn't work). And a story about Jessica as an adult, about the moment Elaine realized her girl *was* an adult, the first time Jessica brought David home to meet her. It had been, in David's mind, an unremarkable day, stopping off at Elaine's Connecticut house for a quick dinner on their way up to Vermont, where they were meeting friends to ski for the weekend. But now the story came to David over the heads of the seated guests and arrived like a peace offering from Elaine, something in return for his willingness to indulge her today's activities.

The pastor from Elaine's church said a prayer and led a hymn. Jessica's uncle, her father's brother, talked about continuing as a family while not leaving those who are *gone* behind. As he talked, Elaine slunk her way to David.

"Do you want to speak?" she whispered into his ear.

He shook his head, and she didn't press him. He was here, after all.

The entire ceremony lasted only forty-five minutes. It wasn't the kind of service where people tell funny stories and the old friends laugh rather than cry. It was simple and quiet and reverent and, David noted, it was the kind of afternoon that would have suited Jessica fine. Together, in the first year of dating, he and she had attended a memorial for Billy Tornensen's father, dead at sixty-four from a sudden heart attack. It was a church service and while Jessica was neither religious nor a close confidante of the Tornensen family, she'd cried during the hymns. "For Billy," she'd said, explaining the tears as she wiped them away.

Today, after the speeches ended, David wandered through the

crowd, nodding *Thank you*s and *It means a lot to us* and *Can I catch you later*s to people who tried to engage him as he made his way to Elaine.

"It was perfect," David said to her, taking her hand in his and holding it tightly as they spoke. And it was perfect—not meaning that this was what Jessica's disappearance called for, but meaning, honestly, that if Elaine insisted on throwing a memorial, if she was going to find her own closure, this was a tremendously appropriate way to go about it. He gave her that much.

"Thanks," she said. "I think we did okay." She smiled to the best of her ability. David let go of her hand and let her continue talking with the couple at her side, an older couple who looked familiar, a great aunt and uncle, David thought. Two of the caterer's assistants cleared the rows of folding chairs from the center of the room.

David swung through the kitchen where his own parents were helping arrange the food, and then said a quick hello to Curt and Sally and a large group of friends lingering by the windows, before making a hasty exit. This wasn't his event and he suddenly found the whole thing chilling. He felt oddly removed, like the dutiful wedding attendee who loves the bride and groom, is glad he's at the reception, but abruptly finds himself wanting to object to the union.

O n his return from Peru, David had found only one message on his home answering machine. He'd expected the tape to be full—all the people he'd forgotten to tell he was leaving town and telemarketers and maybe a few hang-ups too. But there had only been Nadine. She'd called three days earlier and left a message inviting him out for drinks whenever he got back.

He'd seen Nadine across the room at the memorial service,

when he first arrived, but lost track of her in the crowd and didn't have the energy to linger until they could talk. After his quick escape, he went home to nap and then, in the evening, finally returned her call.

"Scratch the drinks," she'd said. "You seem to prefer seeing me in the daylight hours anyway." She suggested they check out the MOMA's permanent collection at lunchtime the next day. "Nobody ever makes time for the permanent collection," she'd said. "Poor neglected permanent works of art."

And now—just three days after touring Lima's Museo Nacional—David stood next to Nadine and tried to make sense of another seemingly mindless Jackson Pollack. David had fled Lima, for the second time in five years, with barely enough time to pack.

"I never feel anything when I look at this stuff," David said, standing in front of a drip canvas from a few decades ago. *I could do that*, he almost said aloud, then stopped himself, realizing that this was what every tenth-grade comedian said about abstract art. It was similar to the way people frequently looked at infants in strollers and said, "I wish someone would wheel *me* around all day!" All those stupid cliché comments that come to mind and which most people are ordinary enough to then say aloud. David stopped himself.

"Mmmm, Pollock doesn't move me either, but some of his stuff is easy on the eyes," said Nadine. She shrugged. "Heck, he worked out east at the beach, didn't he? Which makes *easy on the eyes* and *lacking in emotional movement* seem only appropriate." She laughed, linked her arm through David's and led him to the next gallery, Pollock-free and lined with late-era Kandinskys. "Better?" she asked. "At least there seem to be discernible figures—"

"—which is what the true connoisseur looks for in art, I'm

sure," David said, a bit too loud. He smirked and Nadine continued to laugh and pulled David with her toward a bench in the middle of the room.

She and David sat and pretended to read the exhibit programs they held. She smoothed a hand through her hair. "At least we're out of the dreadful humidity for a moment—if museums are good for nothing else, at least you're guaranteed a climate-controlled environment."

David thought about Peru's dry heat, the way the peasants who crowded around Lima, in the shantytowns, would pray for any kind of moisture whatsoever. He put an arm around Nadine and said, "Come on, let's finish this room and get out of here." They rose from the bench and walked, skimming the outside of the gallery, giving each of the works a cursory look.

"Remember those things? On your wall?" David asked.

"What things? On what wall?" She wasn't looking at the artwork. David followed her gaze and his eyes fell on a security guard using a napkin to polish his shoes. The large man—*soft* is the word Jessica used to describe men who sagged slightly at their middle—had his entire dense mass huddled to the ground around his own feet. "What did I have on my wall?" Nadine looked back at the art in front of them.

"That weird painting. The size of a small movie screen, huge, kind of. Geometric. Matched, I think, your rug—"

"Oh my God! Cate's sister's painting! The eggs! I still have it. She won't take it back. I'm going to have to move and mistakenly leave it behind." She smirked and continued walking. "Why can't I have a friend whose sister is a *talented* artist?"

They took the escalator down to the museum's first floor and rested in the sculpture garden. David sat upright on a bench. Next to him, Nadine lay on her back, her feet hanging limply off the bench's end. With her long, lean limbs laid flat, parallel to the ground, there was something natural and beautiful about her. Today she sported all earth tones: a cropped khaki trench over an olive skirt. Her shoes were the same dark color as her hair. After they'd sat quietly for some time, Nadine said, her voice easing upward toward David, "Did you plan to come home just in the nick of time for your mother-in-law's home-made memorial for Jessica? You scared the heck out us all. We thought you weren't coming back. It was a nice shock to see you actually there."

Shit. David shifted sharply on the bench, his movement causing Nadine to sit up. "Elaine doesn't know I how close I'd cut it, does she?" he asked.

"I certainly didn't mention anything."

Through the courtyard's windows, David saw a school group moving up the escalator, single file. The kids held sketch pads and thick pencils and hoisted backpacks over their shoulders.

"I knew a painter in Peru," David said to Nadine. "Used the garbage from Lima's beaches to create stuff."

"Big whoop," Nadine said, her face still to the sky. "No offense, but everyone was doing trash art in the eighties. Been there, seen that. Unless this guy had a fabulous new take on it all."

"No, same grungy stuff." Cienfuegos's art hadn't been so different. So why did David care? Yeah, it had been the same grungy stuff, but he liked it. Why hadn't David *bought* one of those canvases Cienfuegos was so desperate to sell? David and Jessica had had the money, even back then. Would it have clashed with their newlywed lifestyle—overseas debris pasted to the walls? And now, who knew where those canvases lay. Proba-bly in a warehouse, lost. Or trashed in a dump, dust to dust. "And I barely knew the guy," David admitted. "Down there, you think you know people, everyone is so open, or at least they act that way, like there's no subterfuge, so you meet someone once and they're all warm and it's suddenly some sort of lifelong friendship. It's a cultural thing. You know." He thought about Cienfuegos dying in the fire, about how easy it was—how simple—to get weepy over the death of someone you barely knew. Like the instinctive, knee-jerk tears invoked by the death of an animal in a big-budget movie. David wished Martín were here with a cigarette to offer. Maybe nicotine really was the savior of our race.

David eyed the abstract sculptures they sat among. "Did you stay long at the memorial after I left?" he asked.

"I was there to the bitter end. I kept an eye on things, as usual."

"Do you think it was," he considered what word to use, "okay?"

"It was nice. I thought it was nice. Honestly."

David didn't say anything, was afraid of how he might sound. Defeated, perhaps, pitiful.

"After you left it turned into a, well," Nadine continued, "not much of a service at that point, more of a cocktail party. Jessica must have had quite an upbringing. Elaine served little tea sandwiches, your mother was actually passing some of them, and tea of course, and really fine wine. Who were all the people I'd never seen before?"

"Like who?" David had at least recognized almost everyone in attendance. Faces from a long-ago life.

"Like, people I didn't know. People your mother-in-law's age."

Who didn't Nadine know? Likely Elaine's garden club pals, decked out in floral sheaths and big straw hats, their husbands (the few who'd stuck around, who hadn't taken up with younger, more monochromatic women) in solemn dark suits. They'd all apparently arrived early; they were in the front row of seats.

"No one faulted you for leaving," Nadine continued. "It can't have been a carefree easy afternoon for you."

On his way out of the service, David had caught a final glimpse of Elaine—talking with her friends, leaning on one of them, quickly tucking her well-coiffed hair behind her ears—and for a second David saw Jessica, the woman Jessica would have turned into in twenty, twenty-five years.

Nadine suddenly stood up. "You know what? Let's get out of here. Sculpture gardens creep me out, if you know what I mean."

"Absolutely." David rose and followed Nadine. His knees ached as he stood, they'd been sitting on the low bench for a full half-hour.

"Curt hung out late at the memorial, you know. Damn him, he looks good. Like he's either getting to the gym more often or perhaps his Hair Club for Men membership is paying off."

"Very funny." David nudged her. Curt had always had a full head of hair.

"Curt says they're expecting you back at the office today. They love you there at that little magazine."

"Less and less these days. Probably *not at all* now."

Nadine looked at him. He said, "I was supposed to be there this morning, but I still haven't stopped by. I'm headed there next, maybe no one will notice that I'm a good half-day late, though that's doubtful."

"Maybe you should run—a good old collegiate sprint, arrive out of breath and full of excuses," she suggested. "I'd join you— I'd love to pop in to say 'hi' to the old *Excursion* troops—but I have a feeling I've already got enough of a reputation over there." Nadine smiled. David was about to protest when Nadine cut him short—"Don't tell me I'm not the butt of all your office jokes. I wouldn't believe you anyway."

Outside the front of the museum, they got ready to go their separate ways down Fifty-third Street. David pulled Nadine close and held her. She felt warm and giving, appropriately giving, platonic and honestly compassionate and nothing more, as if they both knew that the moment for them to have had a romance had come and gone a while ago. "You know," David said, wanting to thank Nadine for acknowledging him, for openly acknowledging him, for taking him places, engaging him in conversation, "you're great," he said. "Thanks."

"For being great?" Nadine let out a laugh, as if changing the topic of conversation. "That comes easy, no need to thank me for it."

"Of course not."

Now she pulled away slowly and squeezed David's arm. "Heck, I wanted to see some art, and I wanted to make sure you were still alive and kicking. Truly, people are worried about you."

"They've got a funny way of showing it," David said under his breath, before he could stop himself.

"Oh, you mean *not at all*? What do you expect? You want sympathy cards? I'll send out the alert. We'll have our own big memorial service, group therapy David-style, pale ale and expensive vodka and an electric guitarist this time."

David laughed, shook his head. "You know what I mean."

"Sure. And in the meantime, I'll let people know you don't need life-support yet." She smiled, looked around as if to make sure the day hadn't totally taken off without her. "Okay? We'll talk soon?" He nodded. She let go of his elbow and walked away, heading east.

David walked west. He'd been away from Midtown for just a week, but it felt like much longer. He looked at the buildings as if he'd never seen them before. He reached the corner of Fifty-third and Sixth and, while waiting for the light to change, he spun a full circle. Damn the office tower in the southwest corner, so clean, so corporate, so American. When he was halfway through his spin, facing back toward the museum now, he strained his eyes, trying to see Nadine walking away from him. But no, she'd be too far away already, was too far away already, for him to sneak that last undetected look.

The museum was only six blocks from David's office. He'd called in the morning, but neither Curt nor Elliot had been in yet. Nor Samantha, of course. She'd get in *just in time* and then complain that *most people wouldn't even get out of bed* for the salary *Excursion* paid its assistants. But in truth, today David was, as usual, the staff member most guilty of tardiness. It was 3 P.M. by the time he stepped out of the elevator and onto *Excursion's* floor, where two of the interns stood by the reception desk, sipping frozen coffee drinks from soggy paper cups. "Hey." David nodded as he walked by.

David kept his head down and walked quickly to Elliot's office. Elliot's secretary stopped him. "Elliot's been waiting for you. He's in the conference room, editing photos. He'll be back in a sec," she said.

David motioned to the inside of Elliot's office. "Can I—"

"Sure," the secretary said. "I'll let him know you're here."

David walked in, sat in one of the chairs across from the desk. On top of the desk was an early copy of the next issue. Its pages lay perfectly flat. The first make-ready of the month, it must have come through today. David leaned across the desk and grabbed the issue.

The table of contents, redesigned for this issue, looked elegant, minimalistic. The articles were listed chronologically by page number and divided into departments. The earlier issues, which listed the articles by region of the world, had been nearly impossible for even the magazine's staff members to decipher. *Travel Excursion* was figuring itself out. David continued flipping the pages, stopping to look at the way Theo Chung's photos of Istanbul looked on the page. Oddly Technicolor, David noticed. *God*, it can't be that lush in real life. Was *Excursion* touching up photos *that* much now? His concentration was caught by an ad on the facing page—for some kind of financial service, but even reading it three times he couldn't tell exactly what—when he heard Elliot in the outer office.

"Finally," Elliot said, walking in and sitting at his desk. "You got back okay?"

"I flew overnight and then I had jet lag all day yesterday," *and my wife's memorial*, he left unsaid. "And culture lag. You know how it is. I got here as soon as I could think straight."

"Sure." He nodded, sat down, continued talking as if David had never left town, left the country, left the hemisphere and returned on short notice. "We've got a double issue coming up, and need you on the listings pages where Curt's got his hands full, and we may be able to use you for the cover package. Oh, wait—" He yelled for his secretary. "Do you have a copy of the mock-up?" And she appeared in front of David with a sheath of photocopies. David remembered Martin at the restaurant in Lima, handing him the manila folder that contained so much less than he'd expected.

"So now—" David began to ask Elliot what he was supposed to do next. But *he*, David, was supposed to know this. He thought of the listings pages, editing assignments that even those interns could do. "So I'll talk to Curt, take a load from him?"

"Great," Elliot said. "How about if you do that right now, get a jump on."

David took the photocopies back to his office, but barely glanced at them. He had been doing a lot of nothing during the past week in Peru, but still, he was tired. His body felt like it had been pushed and pulled and pasted back together. His mind felt as if it had taken off on all sorts of excruciating mental excursions without him. Now, sitting at his desk, he found himself absentmindedly drawing circles with his fingers on the pages in front of him.

"Aha, the rumors prove true." Curt strode into David's office and stood, arms crossed, in front of David's desk. "You were spotted this morning at the MOMA, with Nadine, so I was pretty certain that you were slowly making your way toward the office."

"Spotted?" The lack of anonymity in this city never ceased to irk David.

"By Nadine. She called in a few minutes ago."

"Oh."

"I can't believe Elliot called you back here. I told him not to, not to call you, but, well, you know Elliot." Curt sat in the club chair. "His intentions are good, but anyone with enough cash to buy themselves a managing editorship doesn't really need to listen to people like us who actually know the trade."

"You told him not to call me back? Who was he going to bring in to do my work?" David knew he'd been slacking off, but he could still handle the listings. Easily. "Who was he bringing in?" David made no effort to control the irritation in his voice.

"Who? No one, honestly. Chill, man, the masses aren't out there begging to edit travel magazine photo captions. Your gig is safe for now. I just thought it was time for you to stay on one thing for a while, you know?" Two photo researchers walked by the open door of David's office, chatting noisily. Once they had passed, it was quiet again and Curt continued. "I figured you should come back when you were done down there, not when Elliot started to get antsy that his staff was running wild."

"Sure, sure."

"I mean, David, I don't want to turn all Shrink-of-the-Week on you, but it seems like an emotionally stupid thing to whisk a guy who himself just—well, not *just*, but less than a year ago— lost his wife off the trail of some guy he might actually *find*. Sorry to be so blunt."

David nodded, his head facing down to his desk.

Alone in his office, David took his atlas down from the shelf and flipped it open to New York. This was his home. But in the atlas, as viewed from above in topographical detail, the city was barely recognizable. David wanted to get closer, to zoom in, and, remembering something, he reached into his desk drawer and pulled out a city street map marked with bus routes and subway lines. He followed the path he'd taken today: from his apartment to the museum to his office. With a pen he marked the route he'd taken so many days in the past, from his office to the deli to his home. He marked the route he and Jessica would take, when wandering to SoHo on a Saturday afternoon, their route from there to Chinatown, and then he chose a bus route, marked on the map, that would take them home. He marked a path leading from their favorite uptown museum, across the park to an old brunch standby, then south to the spot of a nice afternoon bar, where they might pop in for a drink. Finally he found the routes he took when he was a teenager, in the city for the day, exploring New York for the first time with his friends, arriving on the train and disembarking at Forty-second Street, a thick white line running through the center of the map. He traced this line and then refolded the map and carefully slid it back into his center drawer, as if stowing an important piece of evidence.

At home that night, David decided this: He wasn't going to edit the back of the book listings. He was in no mood to, and he wasn't going to let Elliot force pity assignments on him. Elliot had, after all, suggested that David might edit the cover package for the upcoming issue. Why hadn't David pushed him on this? Insisted he be assigned the cover? David was back, and he was ready to dig in, to earn his living. And this time he was going to pay attention, pick and choose his life as he went along. He was going to trust his own instincts.

Is this what Jessica had done, finally taken stock, needed to step away to chose a path of her own? But what about this path? It wasn't necessarily wrong—for David at least. He hadn't been miserable, hadn't closely looked at his life for long enough to know whether he was. But wouldn't a guy know? And what if this hadn't been right for Jessica? How does a person look at her duplex apartment and do-gooder job and husband—David made a fine husband, was nothing to scoff at, no one to argue about, he saw this—and their stuff, more stuff than one apartment could easily hold, how does someone look at all that and claim it isn't right? People, people they knew, didn't do this. But what if they did?

How easy it had been, to go with the flow, to want the life you already had, to convince yourself of this—along the way, letting the small satisfaction of *having it all* substitute for something bigger. *Accumulating the things,* as if by setting the trappings in place you earned a happy life among them.

David's apartment had remained at a standstill since the moment he'd left for Peru. Being home now was like traveling back in time. The clothes he'd worn the day before leaving were still draped over the armchair next to his bed. His dinner leftovers were still wrapped in plastic in the fridge—though they certainly looked long past their expiration date. The magazines on the coffee table were left open to the pages he'd last read.

David tossed the leftovers in the trash and took a fresh beer from the fridge. He lay on the couch and turned on the TV, flipping the channel to CNN, sure that they'd be featuring a complicated foreign tragedy that would take his mind off his own predicaments. Instead, in front of his eyes he now saw a close-up of Lima, of the Japanese ambassador's residence. David squinted, moved closer, made sure what he was seeing wasn't a mirage from the deep recesses of his own brain. No. It was real. The residence, in Lima, in chaos, a chaos completely different from the day-to-day havoc it had been in when he left. This was different. Quieter. Solemn. As if something had already taken place. There was a sense of smoke clearing even though the picture was frozen, unmoving.

David had traveled all the way to Lima to cover a story related to the hostage crisis, came back spur of the moment to New York, and two days later, the crisis was breaking, the story erupted. All hell was breaking loose, finally, in Peru, and David was sitting on his firm, square couch drinking a beer. David stared harder at the TV screen, absolutely sure now of what he was seeing.

* * *

The Peruvian government's raid on the Japanese ambassador's residence happened in an instant. Fujimori's forces had been waiting inside intricately dug tunnels underneath the residence. Tunneling *in*! A method the MRTA themselves had used just seven years earlier to free their own members from the Canto Grande prison. At the time of the raid, eight of the fourteen revolutionaries were on the ground floor of the residence, playing soccer directly above the main tunnel. Right under these players' shuffling feet, the soldiers set off the bomb that started the attack that, when complete, only twenty-two minutes later, left all fourteen revolutionaries and two soldiers and one hostage dead.

The morning after the raid, David headed out early, not to the office, where he should have been, but to the newsstand two corners away, where he gathered all of the New York and international newspapers. Armed with these papers he returned to his apartment and sat in his living room reading the news accounts. According to the released hostages, once the government troops entered the residence and aimed their weapons, the young MRTA members immediately dropped their own guns and raised their arms in an effort to surrender. They were shot. They never had a chance. On the afternoon of April 26, one hundred forty members of the Peruvian military stormed the residence and set free seventy-one of the seventy-two hostages (the seventy-second hostage falling victim to an errant military bullet), leaving the residence itself looking like a shattered, has-been battleground, littered with the mutilated bodies of the grotesquely dead.

This, David thought. This was a tragedy. On all the news channels, the coverage was the same: Fujimori, inside the residence, walking among the dead bodies, grinning. David cringed, couldn't take his eyes away. What struck him were the bodies themselves. They should have looked asleep, he was sure, slumped in slumber. Gunned down, yes. On the ground, absolutely. But they'd been interrupted during their daily ritual—like clockwork, those games of soccer, according to the released hostages. The MRTA had been surprised by an ambush that, in its entirety, had lasted barely longer than a moment and, as a result, a well-placed shot or two should have felled each of these unprepared captors. There should have been little blood. Instead, there were pools. Each time the tape was replayed, David's eye fell on one particular body, a man in MRTA fatigues, one of his arms and one of his legs completely severed. Let's hear Fujimori claim *that* was a necessary part of freeing the hostages, David thought.

On the TV news reports, international journalists stood in a line in front of the eerily still residence. The building's façade was now marred by dust and debris, but its lawn was still lush and green, as if spared the trauma. The journalists wore flak jackets, their hair as stiff as helmets. David watched carefully, looking for Martín. But there was no sign of Martín or any of the Peruvian crews on U.S. TV. *No sign of Jhensen, either.* David laughed at the thought. As if Jhensen would be there. If he was alive, wasn't this hoopla *just the thing* he was likely escaping? For this kind of internationally televised, sanitized show, Jhensen could have stayed home. *Jhensen wasn't there*, wasn't a dead corpse inside or a living MRTA member watching from a safehouse next door. *Jhensen wasn't there.* David had known this all along. And he had seen enough. This wasn't his story anymore.

David grabbed his bags from where he'd left them at the foot of the stairs (he hadn't unpacked since his return from Peru, hadn't had the energy or the urge) and lugged them upstairs.

Martín had tried to build Jhensen into a hero, and David had been eager to go along with it. *Is that what Martín wanted,* David wondered, when he'd linked the missing American with the revolutionaries a month ago, during the early days of the siege? Back then, the siege had seemed to represent a hope for national redemption, no matter how misguided. And Martín lived in a country with a hero vacancy. A country with, at the moment, a need for someone to believe in. But they didn't have anyone at hand. In the absence of a real hero, had Martín decided to present to David an American on a platter—gussied up as a revolutionary working for national change, a romantic image in a beard and bandana—hoping David would be the vessel for this other American's sainthood, for Peru's national dream? Jhensen was gone, really gone, no trace David could see, so had Martín figured *why not*? Why not make positive use of his disappearance.

Why not? Because for all David could see, the idea of Jhensen's being with the MRTA had never been more than a dream. The problem is—David shook his head, as he unpacked his bag and rehung his clothes in his closet—Martín handed me *his* hero, his dream, not mine, not one for me to believe in. The whole story of an American shedding his identity in order to aid the peasants in a country he barely knew? Sure, it smacked of satisfaction. Hero satisfaction. Why not go with it? *Because,* David answered his own question without hesitation, the person may be missing, but whoever he was or is or *could have* turned into continued to fill that space and carry on. How dare we presume to fill it ourselves.

David's clothing still smelled of Peru. He unpacked his linen pants and hung them in the closet. They hadn't weathered the trip back and forth well and were now creased in all the wrong places. Even the T-shirts he hadn't worn smelled musty from the travel. David unfolded a button-down that he never wore in New York—it was an off-orange hue that he either liked or despised, he wasn't sure which. He'd figured that maybe he'd get some wear out of it in Lima. But no luck. He lifted the shirt out of the bag and raised it in front of him for a better look. As he raised the shirt, from out of its folds a letter fell to the floor. It was a sealed air-mail envelope, but without a stamp, without a postmark. On the front, David's name was carefully printed, as was his Lima hotel's address. He lifted the envelope from the carpet and let his eyes rest for a moment on the familiar slant of the handwriting. For a moment, just the fact that the scrawl seemed long lost, missing to him, he thought it was Jessica's. But almost instantly he realized he was wrong.

D avid held the paper lightly at the edges, as if it was fragile, as if it might self-destruct, and read the letter straight through, twice.

I saw what you wrote about me four years ago, heard talk about your attempts to track me, your aimless attempts to put my life—me, who you don't know, can't imagine in your tiny mind—on paper. You asked the right questions of the right people, and where did it get you? I've been in Peru the whole time. In Lima you've walked by me on the street and not even looked up. You've tried to place me with the MRTA, tried to transfer your own cheap, idealistic revolutionary dreams on me, where you hoped they would stick.

You were wrong. You picked the wrong guy. Only the basest of your little hypotheses smacked of the truth. Me? It's easy for a man with initiative and a set of wheels to make a fast-and-rich living in Peru. Illegal feel-good exports, tax-free, in a

community that minds its own business. Call me selfish—
sticks and stones. I picked through all the bullshit that was
handed to me up in the U.S. and hit on a route that works.
Not the noble quest you imagined. Not the noble death. I live
well.

You can obviously do what you want with this letter. But
look at it: Nothing more than a barely readable scrawl from
a stranger to a man who, in his lame efforts to search and
label, resembles a dim skeleton of the guy that stranger once
was. You followed my footsteps, walking my path like you
were testing your own escape, but you never made it. Who's
the missing man now? I thought it only fair to finally end
your empty hunting efforts. I didn't want your failures on my
conscience.

D. M. Jhensen

David read the letter as if committing the words to memory,
and then closed his eyes and breathed in, long shallow breaths.
He didn't know how this letter got into his luggage. It could
have been placed in there anytime he'd been in Peru, while his
bags were in the hotel room. Or at the airport? Could you do
that? No, the hotel's address on the envelope seemed to be a
hint that it had been slipped in his luggage while he was at the
hotel, in Lima. But there was no way to know for sure. David
looked up, listened, as if expecting Jhensen to slip out from
under the coffee table or the couch, to trip over a power cord,
announcing his presence. But around David, the longer he listened, there was only silence.

David read the letter again, the words aloud in his head this
time, and thought, *pity*. Pity. Because there *was* something
romantic and satisfying about Martin's idea of this fleece-and-

Gore-Tex northwesterner losing himself in a South American cause. Yes, Jhensen was right about the "cheap, idealistic revolutionary dreams": The idea of Jhensen with the MRTA was a story that would have fulfilled every armchair renegade's revolutionary fantasies. Pity. At the same time, David was thrilled to be right for once. Just this morning he'd gauged the situation clearly and come up with the correct answer (placing Jhensen anywhere but with the MRTA), and there was something sharply satisfying knowing that. David's original instinct, his article placing Jhensen firmly in the tax-free fast-and-rich drug trade, had apparently been right.

You've walked by me on the street. David thought hard, looked at the pictures of Jhensen that were stored in his mind, mental images of the photocopies distributed by the embassy nearly five years ago. David never saw this man, never noticed him at all. *He'd walked right past Jhensen.* He tried to conjure the faces in the hotel lobby two days ago as he checked out. He could recall nothing. He hadn't even looked at these faces, the strangers in the lobby. Any of them could have been Jhensen.

You've walked by me. Had he walked past Jessica? What if this happened? *It couldn't.* Or maybe it had already. It couldn't have.

No. For all he hadn't known, he knew Jessica well enough to know that even if, for whatever reasons, she'd had the strength, the oddball will to walk away, she couldn't simply walk by David on the street without making a movement, without taking notice, without wandering to his side, slipping her hand under the hem of his shirt to lay it against his skin. For all he hadn't known, there was so much they had shared.

He held the letter tight. It was written on notepaper, ripped from a grid-lined notebook, in small letters filling the front of the page. His instinct, when he first saw the signature, was to forward the page on to Jhensen's family. It seemed only right. Except for this: Jhensen's family had likely found some form of closure on their own, *they must have*, some better story to believe (better than this one, certainly, for sure). David would be doing them no favors by handing them this proof of Jhensen's self-serving existence. Jhensen could contact them himself if that was his intention. David wasn't going to be his conduit of bad news.

He refolded the letter along its original creases and absent-mindedly lay it in the Jessica box, now almost full of clippings and photos and loose odds and ends, which still sat in the corner of the kitchen. He had previously discovered, on his own, most everything Jhensen purported to reveal in his letter. David thought about Jhensen's talk of escape. He thought: It's possible to get a *fresh start*, to begin again, without traveling so far from home. Jhensen wanted to label David as wrong and misguided, but it was Jhensen, as well, who didn't know who he was talking about.

"Hey, man, you're not supposed to be here." Curt grabbed David by the elbow and sped him down the hallway, forced him into his office not far off the elevator bank. Curt's office was the same size and layout as David's, but was so cram packed with travel memorabilia and PR gifts (snow globe paperweights, Amazon rain forest mobiles, movie posters, a neon life preserver) that it felt like a tiny hidden lair. Curt shut the door behind them.

"Not supposed to be here?" David asked. "It's Thursday, we don't work on Thursdays now?" A man goes to Peru for a week and the whole world changes.

"I wish. It's almost four already. I thought you weren't coming in today. I called in sick for you. How's your fake cough? I've got a good hack I can lend you, you know, if you don't have your own."

Called in sick. That would explain the skewed look the receptionist had given David as he strode past her, just before Curt eyed him and secreted him into this office.

"At around noon, when you still weren't here, Elliot started getting suspicious. That happens. So I told him you called in sick, that you'd left a message for Samantha. She barely even made it in today herself. I swear, if I thought we could do better I'd replace her. What the hell happened to you? I've seen subway delays, but you don't look like you've been underground for the last seven hours. Day three of your jet lag?"

"I had some motivation problems, but I'm back." The room was silent and David felt his words settle around him. He sat in a chair against the wall.

The TV that sat atop Curt's file cabinets was showing the Peru footage. "I assume you've seen this," Curt said.

"Yeah, I've seen it all, was glued to it all last night and this morning."

"It kills me, them not releasing the bodies to the families."

"They're what?" David had missed this bit of recent news. He leaned closer to the TV. Curt sat behind his desk and fingered the edge of his computer keyboard.

"They just announced it, no corpses for the families. The government is burying them in city graveyards, anonymously, no markings so no one will know where the head guy is, so they can't turn his grave into a shrine." David looked around Curt's office, the entire gizmo-filled space like a Shrine to the Barely-Working Editor. "That's gotta be tough for those poor families. It's crack, a load of crack, these people losing their kids and then being forced to mourn without a body," Curt shook his head.

David turned to look at Curt, who was distracted by the TV. Amazing, David thought, amazing the things people continued to say to him without really thinking.

The subway moved in fits and starts. The car went express for three stations ("This train will not be stopping at Twenty-third, Twenty-eighth, or Thirty-third Street. For local stops, please disembark at Forty-second Street and take the downtown local) then stopped dead for five minutes in the dark tunnel between Forty-second and Fiftieth streets. Next to David, passengers twitched. The sudden stillness of a subway halted between stations could rouse even the perennially asleep. Slow breathing and nervous jitters. David leaned against the car's doors and looked out the window across from him, at the black of the tunnel wall.

So many people wonder what other ways they might have lived their lives. The way David had tried on the steps of those boys on the street, late at night; the way he'd slept on the sidewalk like the homeless and missing; the fact that he'd followed Jhensen's path through Peru. Jessica had taken the life that was handed to her. Would another life have been better? By all accounts this life (the tennis clinics, the ballet lessons, the second telephone line, the paid-in-full college education, fresh fruit twelve months a year, premium cable channels, financial stability, a husband who fit the bill) was as good as it gets. But accounts often missed the point.

Across the car, a passenger counted her rosary beads. Another looked to the sky, as if pleading with the subway deities. On TV today, Peruvian families had carried brightly decorated crosses to their loved ones' unmarked graves. The authorities had buried the fourteen MRTA in a smattering of municipal graveyards, high on the hilltops above Lima's slums, with no evidence of which body was in which anonymous plot. The graves had been dug in the dark of night, but by sunrise small illegal shrines (flowers and plastic idols) had sprung up around the freshly piled dirt. Even without knowing which bodies were buried where, the families each chose their spot and mourned.

The subway train started again with a quick jolt, as if coming to its senses. David grabbed the handrail and steadied himself. He stayed put when the train doors opened at Fifty-ninth Street, the station he'd been waiting for. He fingered the invitation in his pocket, took it out for a look. He could get off the train here and arrive at the right time for this cocktail party. But the party would go on all night, and be repeated next weekend, and the weekend after.

David exited the subway at Seventy-seventh Street, and walked less than a block to the hospital's entrance. Inside the building's foyer, David looked for signs. To his left, in the gift shop, a kid in a smock tallied the day's receipts. Stuffed bunnies leaned against the shop's glass walls as if pleading to get out. In the foyer itself, it might as well have still been midday. The fluorescent lights shone bright, and the nurses and doctors and orderlies chatted among themselves, wide-eyed and chipper. Fresh off the extended subway ride, David looked weary and worn. He'd barely asked his question before the woman behind the desk smiled and answered, "That way," to the maternity ward and nursery. David imagined he looked like a father who'd been up all night coaching his wife through labor. Like a man who had gotten so tired out in the process that he'd forgotten which hallway led to his new child, and his wife.

He nodded to people—strangers in those familiar green scrubs, in lab coats, in tweed blazers and wool slacks, in knee-length skirts—as he walked, he made believe he belonged here. He briefly worried he might get lost. "That way" wasn't much of a direction. But the hallways were marked with signs. This was the ward people wanted to find. And there, just like in the movies, was the large glass window looking in on today's deliveries. A dozen newborns in separate little glass cabinets. My God! How do the doctors manage not to mix them up! Next to David a woman stared and then walked away. Overhead announcements, air streaming through the vents: the noise of the hospital was constant.

David looked first at the babies, and then at the sterile nursery itself. The bare walls, the linoleum floor, the heavy doors. The electrical outlets, the window glass, the impossibly complicated machines at the ready. They appeared to be brand-new. This ward was where David was born. Seventy blocks from where he now lived, around the corner from Curt's new home, three blocks from Cate and Welford's. The newborns all lay on their backs, their faces open to David. David had gone from *that* to this without, really, all that much thought.

"You know one of them?" A nurse stood next to David. She smiled. He figured she asked this question a couple of times an hour.

"All of them," David said. And then, "You know, tough to tell." He nodded, made an effort to smile. The nurse grinned, as if she got the joke, and then she entered the room. On the other side of the glass, she scrubbed her hands and checked a list on the wall.

David imagined raising a newborn, himself or as part of a couple. He pictured himself getting a new start with some woman whom, perhaps, he'd yet to meet. He could almost see it. He could nearly imagine that happening.

*   *   *

David was more than two hours late by the time he got to the party, which was loud and packed and certainly in full swing. As he slunk out of his jacket and left it in the spare bedroom, David caught a glimpse of himself in a mirror. He'd worn the orange shirt that he maybe hated, maybe loved. *Fuck fashion*, he thought. *Why not be a trendsetter?* He stood in the doorway between the bedroom and the living room and watched the other partygoers drink, mingle, tap each other on the back, kiss each others' cheeks as if all part of a well choreographed dance.

Across the room a bottle of wine was spilled. "Don't worry, it's *white!*" David saw the wine tumble and heard the hostess's exclamation all at once, the hostess in a full, 1950s-style cocktail dress and bare feet running to the scene of the spill with a paper towel in her hand.

In the absence of Jhensen and the hostages and the MRTA—these distractions had been so nice for so long, but were about to disappear—David was left alone with his day-to-day life again. He thought about the people he knew *here* and their assumptions that you could build an entire life between and bordered by distractions. No more Derek Mark Jhensen to search out. No more situation at the residence to lay in wait for. No more—he looked up, at the empty space next to him, and he could imagine Jessica, facing him, eating a wedge of lime with her fingers and laughing apologetically, nervously, when she noticed him notice her licking her fingers. He could almost see it. And he knew, no more waiting for Jessica. Jessica wasn't out there waiting to be found. Detective Hallander had been insistent, months ago, when he'd spotted David one last time across the street from the precinct, *looking in* as if to will evidence to seep out the windows, that "In ninety-nine cases out of one hundred, when there's no evidence two months later, there's no evidence ever. The certainty that we've found all there is to find may be the only closure we get here." There was no evidence to prove anything about Jessica ("No evidence a crime was even committed," Hallander had put it a number of times).

Perhaps, in this life, there was such a thing as a second try, a do-over. Maybe Jessica had grabbed at hers. Stepped out of her life and lunged for another one. He pictured that life. He conjured an image of Jessica in a house (white, clapboard) on a beach (no, a mountain, she loved the mountains, with a lake nearby) finding her second chance, her new path, the right way (*This way, This way*, nailing the signs up as she goes along) knowing that eventually David would find his own way past all that remained unsaid, unrevealed. This was an image he knew he could hold onto and live with for a long time to come.

Across the room, Welford Manahan looked up from his conversation, caught David's eye, and nodded in greeting. David gave him a quick forgiving wave (*No, no, don't leave your conversation, I'll catch you later*) and then entered the party. His first stop was the bar, and then drink in hand, he leaned against the wall near the corner of the room. Perhaps David could believe that wherever Jessica was—if she was—she, and he, might be better off in the end. Perhaps this was her intention, perhaps this was the truth.

"Hey, stranger, you look handsome tonight."

David turned, saw Sally Dickenson beside him. "Thanks." He smiled and sipped his cocktail.

"Nothing like a stiff drink to take the edge off this crowd. Have you just arrived?"

"Sure, right behind the fashionably late. Did I miss anything?"

"Like what?" Sally laughed. "Same old. It's good to see you

out, in orange nonetheless. You should get a look at the sushi spread in the kitchen. Want me to go fetch you some?"

"No, thanks, I'm not sure how long I'm staying."

"Don't leave without a good-bye." Sally lightly touched the hand that held his drink, shook her head, and walked off.

David looked out over the party and thought, I don't need to do this anymore. He made his way back to the bedroom, grabbed his coat, and headed to the front door. On his way there, he passed the bar. While the bartender's back was turned, David instinctively grabbed a fistful of limes and a bottle of gin.

The Peruvians were right. Just because there was no body, no *evidence*, didn't mean there was no *end*. Didn't mean you couldn't mark the moment and move on. David buttoned his coat tighter and sat on the dank ground, this small hilltop in Central Park. Hidden in the dark, surrounded by trees and brush and New York's faint late-night sounds, David could feel the city moving around him. David pictured his map of the city, tucked into his office desk drawer. The park, right between Jessica's school and their home, directly between the apartment she'd lived in when they met and the first home they'd lived in together. They weren't big on biking in the city (loop after the same loop in this contained park), didn't scale these boulders the way Will did, but still, as a center hub in the city, the park was a bit of a focus point in David's and Jessica's life. It was the expanse they circumvented in subways and cabs, that they skirted on all sides on a daily basis. David thought of those photos of Jessica, taken two Thanksgivings ago on his parents' porch, in her outdoor clothes surrounded by trees much like these, her cheeks pink from the November wind.

On the dirt in front of him, David stacked the limes into a pyramid. He took a long sip of the gin, welcome in the night chill, and then placed the bottle next to the pile.

He and the Peruvians and how many others, these families with their loved ones gone and no bodies to mourn? Being asked to accept what they weren't being allowed to see. Attempting to refute the old saying that seeing—catching sight of the dead body, looking at a death certificate, laying eyes on a headstone—was believing.

David sat next to his own makeshift shrine and, through the trees, watched the city's pedestrians hurry along on the well-lit park path below. In the glare of the streetlights, the nearly empty park became alive. Two girls, not dressed for the night breeze, clung to each other as they chatted and walked briskly, their high heels making stark tapping sounds against the concrete. Not far behind, three young guys walked on the edge of the path, kicking up leaves and sticks. David figured he could leave this perch, he could make his way down the small hill and join them, walking any of the paths that converged in this park. He tore off two twigs from the tree above him nearly ready to bloom with a collection of spring buds and small leaves holding tight to the branches. The blooms appeared a pale yellow in this half light, a bare hint of color fighting to stay alive in this surprise spring chill. David took the sprigs and stuck them into the pile of limes, allowing the branches to tower over the fruit. The branches stood tall, like the bright flowers the Peruvians had propped at their loved ones' graves high above Lima's disintegrating shantytowns. This grave, like those: without a single marking on it. No name, no date of death, no date of birth. Anyone, any mourning family, could claim this makeshift memorial. This was how people mourned, they came to a site and remembered. David fingered the dirt on which he sat. The ground was covered by nothing more than dirt and coin-sized rocks and a smattering of old leaves and sticklike weeds, sharp and awkward.

David looked at the dirt and he looked at the silhouettes of the people down below. Safety in numbers. Everyone in the park at this hour was paired off or traveling in large groups. David tried to tune out their noises, to quietly remember (to recall Jessica and himself as a pair; Jessica, rushing along the streets of this city, pulling David behind her), but the soft sounds around him ("Is that Seventy-second Street?" he heard a man ask his date; "Let's find the horses!" came from a group of girls; and from nowhere, horns, alarms, the small skid of tires) got in the way. Maybe, he thought, he had done all his remembering. He took a pen and tonight's party invitation from his pocket. The invitation like a postcard: on one side a picture of what this evening had held for him, the other side blank.

David turned the card over now, balanced it against his knee, uncapped his pen. Below, a policeman walked past, stirring up dust as he kicked the brush by the side of the trail. David held still, watched him until he walked away. The last time David had looked so hard at an official through a cloud of dust was almost five years ago, and he could still picture Jessica's face back then: Jessica, at the wheel of their rental car, trying to reason with the two cops on the road between Oropesa and Cuzco. "They want our car," she'd explained as she tried to speak with the policemen. We'll laugh about this someday, David had told himself then, trying to distract himself from the trauma at hand. But it had been no trauma at all, simply one more minor incident in Peruvian day-to-day history. Simply two inexperienced honeymooners testing out life off the beaten path. David put his pen to the card but didn't know what, if anything, to fill in.

A small boy wearing a cloak, like an emissary from some forgotten century, laughed as he ran across the path below. He stumbled and his mother immediately jumped to his side. She grabbed his hand and looked nervously over her shoulder, smiled apologetically to the rest of her family, two men and a teenaged girl who soon caught up with her. One of the men took the boy's other hand ("Past his bedtime," David heard) as they all walked on down the steep slope of the path. David conjured the hills of his own childhood. Big green lawns, his family's and the neighbors'. He remembered a time (recently, too recently) when he hadn't even known that South American shantytowns or unmarked graves or this kind of urban, nighttime dust existed. Back in New England, after the heavy rainstorms, the sky would often remain a pale gray for days, so gray that as the lawns soaked up the moisture and grew increasingly green, a fantastic shade of yellow-green against the gray, the grass appeared to glow against the sky.

David was surrounded by those night sounds and the heavy darkness and the dim color-depleted light from the street lamps below, and by his small lime shrine, frail and unadorned. David could imagine a day later this same week when he'd be sitting in a New York City bar he'd never been to before, wearing new clothes maybe—it was time to restock, to find a new uniform—drinking a very decent cocktail and tuning out the cell phone conversations of the well-coiffed stranger on the stool next to him and waiting for the night, or the week, or the month to begin. David put the invitation card back in his pocket and the pen on the ground next to the limes and the gin. He stood up and he dug his heels into the rough dirt as he descended the slope back toward the city—a city of three hundred square miles that was choked-up and relentlessly exuberant and—David was excited by this—largely unexplored. When his footing was sure enough, he looked up over New York, its entire expanse, and smiled. There was a beauty to the three-dimensional land-scape of the city, a jammed sprawl shaped by the pattern of its residents' day to day lives. There was a beauty to this. *My God*, David looked at the ground again and continued down the slope, what was he waiting for?

SEPTEMBER 1996

Oh! Fall can be beautiful, even in New York, even without the oaks and maples and deadly goldenrod that Jessica took for granted growing up. It's mid-September, not even cold yet, but a tinge of color marks the sparse line of trees down the street, enough of a hint of autumn to remind Jessica that there was a time when the mere change of season excited her. And now? *What happened to all that,* she wonders, walking quickly, turning the corner, heaving open the heavy glass door to the coffee shop only two blocks from her apartment. This morning she is proud simply to be showered and out of bed. David is in Sun Valley; she has nothing to do all day. She has nothing, truly, to be awake for. But here she is.

Oh, um, a decaf? She says to the boy behind the counter. *Large. To go.*

Yesterday, in the teachers' lounge, Jessica and a few others hovered over the coffee machine. "Caffeine's a depressant, you know," said Bob Walbert, always looking to impress. No, that's alcohol, Jessica had thought. But now, she figures, why not cut out the caffeine? She worries about how much unnecessary material she pumps into her body on a regular basis. She worries about the effects of it. All those tests and all that prodding at the hands of the so-called fertility experts could make a woman question her every move. Perhaps she can fool herself into thinking that all it will take to make things better is a decrease in her caffeine levels.

Anything else? The boy hands her the cup of coffee and cites the price.

That's it, she says, fumbling in her pocket for the cash. She doesn't want to take her whole wad out. She has more than three hundred dollars with her, doesn't want the other patrons to see it. The whole wad was sitting on her dresser as she ran out for this coffee and she'd simply grabbed the entire thing. She shouldn't have taken so much. Surreptitiously she peels off a bill and hands it to him. She quickly pockets the change.

Yesterday she'd gone to the bank and withdrawn enough cash to last her until David returned from his work trip. Enough cash to last her through drinks with Sally and Marion tonight (and dinner, Sally would likely want to go out for a ridiculously overpriced meal beforehand) and perhaps brunch tomorrow and maybe some shopping, a trip for all the grocery basics they were running out of. Tonight's activities alone might easily top a hundred dollars. Jessica cringed at the thought.

There's a rapist in the neighborhood. Thieves and criminals have a reputation for staking out victims at ATMs. She'd wanted to be sure she wouldn't need to run to the ATM in the dark on the way to dinner, or in the deserted early Sunday morning hours on her way to the supermarket.

There is a rapist in the neighborhood. You can see this fact on the faces of all the women. At night, on the sidewalks, on their way home, the women on the street wear their faces as hard masks. They look straight ahead or to the ground while they walk, not wanting to see what might be hiding in the shadows, not wanting to tempt it to make a move. These women walk quickly to their destinations. They cup their keys in their palms. The bills in Jessica's pocket feel like freedom, like her own defense, her own proactive stance against danger.

At her apartment door she stops and reaches into her coat pocket for her keys. But they're not there. She's about to check the pockets of her jeans, but stops, knowing they're empty. *Shit,* she'd been distracted by the wad of money, by the weight of it in her pocket, and had forgotten to grab her keys on the way out. *Shit,* this is a hassle. She leans against the brick wall of the building. She can picture those keys, next to the phone in the living room, practically within her grasp.

She can call Will and Annette, they have a set of spares. But damn, she'd rather not. They live uptown and she doesn't feel like facing them and their smug, perfect life. They've barely even called Jessica and David recently. David seems bothered by this, but it sits just fine with Jessica. She doesn't begrudge David his desire for acceptance by his brother. Jessica is an only child and figures that the sibling bond thing is something with which David has more experience.

Seeing Will and Annette would turn this minor mishap into an ordeal. *How could she forget the keys!* She tucks her hair behind her ears, feels the stress in her shoulders. *How could she be so stupid!* David is gone for a long weekend and she locks herself out. What a profoundly idiotic move. She can call Sally. Sally will surely offer to put her up for the weekend, lend her an outfit for tonight, keep her occupied. But Jessica doesn't want to put anyone out, this isn't her style. She can call a locksmith, that's what people do, she figures. She can pay whatever the ridiculous cost to have her own locks busted into and replaced.

She could check into a hotel for a night, treat herself to a bit of luxury and deal with the locks tomorrow. Then again, three hundred dollars doesn't get a girl much luxury in New York these days, and her credit cards are all inside the apartment. Jessica thinks about the other places where, during the past few months, she has pictured herself. The other places she's wanted to be at this time when her life has started to look suddenly *set,* startlingly unyielding, like a trap that she has unwittingly laid for herself, like some sort of purposeful mistake. The times she's looked at all the *things* hanging on their walls and stacked on their shelves, things to be proud of, the things she thought she'd needed, and pushed away the thought: This isn't the life I was meant for, this isn't all there is.

She'd thought about Europe. She liked the idea of an ocean between herself and this life she's led, full of catches and caveats and expectations, stifling with all its trappings. She'd imagined all the anonymous cities of Europe, Frankfurt or Vienna or Milan, full of histories and high-rises and new vocabularies. And she'd thought about the forgotten Plains states in this country, or those unknown towns in West Virginia or the Florida panhandle, places where she imagined a girl might just *be*. Where the pressures you felt were simply your own. Where you could start with nothing and earn your living and truly inhabit it, call it your own. Was she fooling herself? She didn't know. And now, outside her apartment, she imagines a small house off the coast of Portland, Maine, and she imagines the ways you might get there and still have most of your three hundred dollars left to spare. She figures you could probably get from here to Portland, Oregon, even, and still have money left for rent, if you planned it right.

She'd thought about sharing her fantasies with David, about taking some time away alone. When it became increasingly clear that there would be no child of their own, truly, she felt everything she'd built crumble, like a stack of logs missing the foundation piece that would hold them in place, the piece they had been waiting for, which she'd been sure would support the rest of the stack and keep it strong. But these thoughts would sound silly spoken aloud. And she could hear David's arguments. Because what was wrong with her life here? What kind of fool would want to trade this in simply for the sake of trying anything else? *We'll take a vacation*, she could hear David say, *I work for a travel magazine, it'll be tax-deductible*. What kind of fool would leave all this? *This* is what she had worked so hard to build.

She can hear David's arguments. She can hear him listing all of the things they *have*: financial security, an apartment they own, a home, a kid on the way—*really, it will be ours no matter what the procedure*, he'd plead—steady employment, art galleries merely a dozen blocks away, health insurance and their health, *and all those friends!* She can hear the simple love in his voice drawing her back, overriding, even in her own mind, the fact that maybe this isn't enough. She knows how easily he will convince her that she is being irrational, that she simply needs *more* caffeine in her life, or less wine, or a weekly dose of therapy, or a few extra weekends in the country this year, or an extra week of skiing in February. Because how would she explain it?

Deep down, she thinks David understands. He can feel it, she knows he can. The ways he incessantly talks his way through every situation, with his cute little jokes as if they will make everything okay. The ways, with his snide, sly, asides he can convince himself that everything is great, that every trauma is merely a passing glitch that will solve itself, that in the end he will be as happy as he's been told this life should make him. The way he finishes her sentences for her, giving them perfect endings, the conclusions that her tongue stumbles over.

How would she explain it? Maybe the only way is *not to.*

She tries the doorknob, which is unyielding. Inside is everything she owns, none of which she feels the need for right now. She takes a deep breath and holds it. Then she turns and begins to walk. She wonders how far a girl can get on three hundred dollars and not even her driver's license. *It's a challenge!* she thinks, smiling at the thought, wondering if she'll even make it to the other side of the city. Yes, she will make it to the other side of the city, she knows this. *Put that on the list!* she thinks. But how far will she go? When will she come back? She can imagine leaving, she's pictured it a hundred times (Milan, Minnesota, Maine), she's doing it right now. Isn't she? And she can imagine coming back. Yes, she can imagine coming back, but can't picture who she will be when that time comes. She walks on a congested side street now, her steady gait almost keeping up with the car traffic. She is not turning back. She apologizes silently to David, telling herself that if she goes through with this, if this is more than a ten-block fantasy, if she is really going to find her way, someday he will forgive her. Someday he, too, will find the life he's meant for, someday he will appreciate the ways that her being gone has freed him, too. And, feeling the heft of each steady step, she continues walking directly away from their home and she does not look back.

About the Author

ALLISON LYNN has written for *People, InStyle,* and *The New York Times Book Review,* among other publications. She received her MFA from New York University and lives in New York City. *Now You See It* received the William Faulkner medal for best novel-in-progress, and also the Chapter One Award from the Bronx Writers' Center.

NOW YOU SEE IT

1. What is the significance of the opening scene of the novel in which David, then six years old, veers slightly from the main path and finds himself utterly lost as he is walking back to the house from the beach?

2. In a frenzy of baby-making, the first year when they were attempting to conceive, David and Jessica had sex in every room of their apartment, sometimes all in the same night. But two years of trying to get pregnant, and three failed in-vitro procedures have taken a heavy toll on their sexual urges. What does the erosion of desire a mere four years into marriage say about their relationship? Have they simply hit "a demon of a rough spot," as David speculates? Is it caused solely by their failure to conceive? Or is the author suggesting a more serious flaw in their marriage?

3. What is the significance of the title, *Now You See It?* What is the author saying about the illusory or transitory nature of what we think we know—about the lives we lead, the people we love, and ourselves? Do you agree or disagree? Why? What other themes does the novel explore?

4. When David returned home from his business trip to find Jessica missing with her keys left at home, no missing luggage, no missing valuables, and nothing in the apartment seemingly awry, what was your initial reaction to her disappearance? Did you suspect foul play—or think that she had voluntarily taken off? Why?

5. How do you feel about David? Do his reactions to his wife's vanishing seem appropriate? Why or why not? Is there such a thing as an appropriate reaction to a loved one's mysterious disappearance? David questions his own responses, and asks himself how Jessica would act in this situation. *"But he knew Jessica wouldn't be in this situation. He wouldn't allow himself to be taken from her."* What are we to make of this statement? Does David suspect that Jessica had a choice in the matter?

6. *Now You See It* weaves back and forth in time. Why do you think Allison Lynn chose to employ flashbacks? How does she use the flashbacks to thematically connect Jessica's disappearance with the story of the American businessman/hiker Derek Mark Jhensen reported missing in Peru? In what ways does the story of the missing Jhensen add depth and richness to the novel?

7. What does David's fixation on tracking down Jhensen, even if it means separating from his bride on their honeymoon, tell us about David and his feelings about being married? *"Do you know what it feels like to be left behind? It's my worst fear, David,"* she confronts him when he finally arrives home nearly six weeks later. Why do you think Jessica told David it was okay for him to stay behind in Peru while she returned home alone when clearly it was not okay with her? Do you think David would have returned home had Jessica spoken her mind earlier? Would he have resented her if he had to give up his story?

8. As the novel unfolds, David slowly begins to entertain the possibility that Jessica has simply walked out of their life. He remembers the last dinner party before she disappeared. *"I feel like I've had it,"* Jessica had said. He pictures her standing at the top of the Tipón ruins in Peru during their honeymoon, her toes inches from the ledge. *"A girl could just step right off if she wanted,"* she'd said. Do you think Jessica had given David enough clues for a caring husband to have picked up signals of her unhappiness with the life she was living? Or is he reinterpreting her words now with the perspective of hindsight?

9. How do you think the author expects the reader to react to the "hissy fit" David's sister-in-law, Annette, throws at David at the conclusion of the birthday party for her two-year-old daughter? *"Try having an emotion some time, why don't you? Be human,"* she screams at him. Do you think the accusations she hurls at him are justified? Why or why not?

10. Six months into Jessica's disappearance, her mother becomes certain her daughter is dead, just at the time when David becomes convinced his wife is alive but does not want to be found. As Elaine seeks the closure of a memorial service for Jessica, David makes plans to take off for Peru to chase down a Jhensen spotting. What does Elaine hope to accomplish with a memorial service? What does she hope to learn from David and the other people who knew Jessica? What is David really seeking when he takes off for Peru?

11. Out of his struggles to come to terms with Jessica's disappearance, David reaches a fairly charitable interpretation of her actions. Talk about the kind of person who could walk away from her life and all the people who care about her without a word. What do you make of the closing pages of the novel in which we get to observe Jessica's disappearance from her point of view? Was that wrap-up necessary to the novel? Why or why not? Did it change your perceptions of Jessica's actions?

12. A literary suspense novel that has already won two awards in manuscript form, *Now You See It* has been compared to such novels as *The Invisible Circus* by Jennifer Egan, and *Single Wife* by Nina Solomon, which also examine the possibility of ever really knowing another person, as well as the fiction of such contemporary voices as David Schickler, Erika Krouse, Thisbe Nissen, and Laura Zigman, all of whom, like Allison Lynn, delve beneath the surface of seemingly familiar lives to reveal a deeper truth. What books or movies does *Now You See It* remind you of? Why?